Meet ~~cute~~
Dare

THE DEMPSEY SISTERS

D. E. Haggerty

Also by D.E. Haggerty

Meet Disaster
Meet Not
Meet Hate
My Forever Love
Forever For You
Just For Forever
Stay For Forever
Only Forever
Bragg's Truth
Bragg's Love
Perfect Bragg
Bragg's Match
Bragg's Christmas
How to Date a Rockstar
How to Love a Rockstar
How to Fall For a Rockstar
How to Be a Rockstar's Girlfriend
How to Catch a Rockstar
Before It Was Love
After the Vows

While We Waited
A Hero for Hailey
A Protector for Phoebe
A Soldier for Suzie
A Fox for Faith
A Christmas for Chrissie
A Valentine for Valerie
A Love for Lexi
About Face
At Arm's Length
Hands Off
Knee Deep
Molly's Misadventures

Chapter 1

Cassandra – a woman who can rescue herself thank you very much

"No."

"But—"

"But nothing. No."

"You should—"

Come ons are seriously my least favorite thing about bartending at the *White Stag*. Except the name, of course. How cliché can you get?

Don't get me wrong. I love a good flirtation as much as the next woman. But there's a difference between flirting and leering. And this guy passed the line to leering when he lunged over the bar and grabbed for my ass. He's lucky his hand is still attached to his arm.

Plus, I'm working here. My sisters may not take my job as a bartender seriously, but I do. I ignore creepy dude to walk to the other side of the bar.

"What can I get you?" I ask the patron patiently waiting his turn.

Before he can answer, Mr. I Get Whatever I Want Whenever I Want pushes him out of the way.

"I was talking to you."

"And I told you. We're done talking."

"We're done talking when I say we are."

I roll my eyes to the ceiling. Why do men think whatever they say goes? A woman who's this demanding is labeled a bitch and promptly ignored. But a man demanding whatever he wants? No problem. Totally fine.

"Excuse me. Is this guy bothering you?"

I open my mouth to tell the man to mind his own damn business, but the words get caught in my throat when I catch sight of him. Yowzah! Mr. Hottie has entered the building.

Lush brown hair, square jaw hidden by a sexy beard my hands want to dig into, smoldering hazel eyes. Yes, yes, yes! If *he* asks me what I'm doing after I get off work, I'll answer. Especially since he's tall with broad shoulders. I do love a pair of broad shoulders I can hang onto. And tall is a basic requirement since I'm five-eight.

"Ahem." He clears his throat. "Do you want me to handle this guy for you?"

Oops. I might have gotten lost in those hazel eyes for a minute.

"I got this," I tell him before focusing my attention on Mr. Handsy. "You need to step away from the bar before I have you removed from the premises."

"You can't have me—"

The rest of his words are cut off when one of his colleagues clutches his shoulder and steers him toward their table. I eye the group. With their suits and ties, they're obviously businessmen enjoying a drink after a day of work. Except for Handsy, they're drinking beer and watching the basketball game on the television. They've got him.

I wipe my hands on my jeans. Time to get back to work.

"What can I get you?" I ask Mr. Hottie.

"You sure you're okay?"

"I'm fine," I grit out. I don't like anyone questioning my ability to perform my job even if the questioner is a fine specimen of manhood.

He studies me for a long moment before nodding. "I'll have a beer. Whatever IPA you have on tap."

After I hand him his drink, a group of women arrive and push their way to the front of the line demanding daiquiris and margaritas. While I make their drinks, I keep an eye on Mr. Hottie. He's sitting at a high table in the corner by himself nursing his beer.

I wonder what his story is. I haven't seen him in here before. With a face and body like his, I wouldn't forget.

Once the group of women have their drinks, I decide it's time for my break. I pick up a case of empty bottles and carry them to the storage room. After I set the case down in its proper place, I lean against the wall for a breather.

I'm feeling restless and jumpy. I don't know what my problem is. I love my life here in Colorado. I may have fought moving here from St. Louis last year – what thirty-three-year-old wants to relocate across the country with her brother and two of her sisters? – but I was wrong.

Colorado rocks. I've made a ton of friends. I've got a good job as the night manager here at the *White Stag*. The nature is beautiful. And there are no ex-lovers to bump into. What's not to love? Except I'm feeling edgy.

I check my watch. I need to get back to work. The mystery of why Cassandra is feeling edgy will remain unanswered for today.

I fix my ponytail and straighten my t-shirt before opening the door to the hallway.

"Hello, beautiful."

Seriously? Someone can't get a clue if they were giving them away.

I cross my arms over my chest and his gaze drops to my cleavage. Creeper. I don't drop my arms, though. Nope. I refuse to change who I am for a man. Especially this one.

"What do you want?"

Mr. Handsy steps closer and draws a finger up my arm. "Like I said, I want to know what you're doing tonight after you get off work."

I grab his finger to stop him before he reaches my shoulder.

"What the hell is going on here?"

I glance behind me to discover Mr. Hottie standing there.

"I got this," I tell him.

He motions his hand forward. "Get on with it."

"I don't need your permission to handle Mr. Handsy."

"Didn't say you did," he grumbles before crossing his arms over his chest causing his biceps to bulge and I nearly forget why we're standing here talking.

Mr. Handsy tries to yank his finger from my grasp. Ah, yes. Now I remember what I was doing.

"It is not okay to touch a woman without her permission," I tell him as I bend his finger backwards until he squeaks and wrenches his hand away.

"You bitch! You broke my finger."

I chuckle. "Don't be a crybaby. It's not broken. Although, I could have broken it if I wanted to."

"Who do you think you are? I'm going to sue you!"

"Okay." I shrug. "I guess I'll be phoning the police to file a report on you then."

"You, you, you," he sputters. "How dare you?"

"Did you or did you not touch me without permission?"

"The permission was implicit."

"Implicit?" I snort. "There was nothing about my behavior to suggest I gave you permission to touch me. In fact, I have about fifty witnesses who heard me tell you no twice."

I reach for the phone in my back pocket.

"No." He slaps at my arm, but I retreat a step before he can touch me.

"No? All of a sudden you understand what the word no means? Huh. Interesting."

"Come on, Freddy," his colleague calls from the end of the hallway. "We're going."

Freddy glares at me for a few seconds before marching off.

"Have fun at the strip joint," I holler after him.

"Am I allowed to ask if you're alright or are you going to bite my head off if I do?" Mr. Hottie asks.

"I don't bite." I waggle my eyebrows. "Unless I'm asked to."

He smirks. "Good to know."

"What's your name?" Because I can't continue to refer to him as Mr. Hottie forever.

He pauses for a second. "Archer."

I extend my hand. "Cassandra."

As we shake hands, I can't help but notice how large his are. They're also calloused as if he works with them. I do love a man who knows how to use his hands.

"You handled Freddy well," he says as his thumb rubs circles into my hand.

My skin tingles from his ministrations, and I want to climb him like a pole. Ding. Ding. Ding. I believe we've uncovered the reason why I'm feeling restless and jumpy.

"Thank you." I clear my throat. "I should probably get back to work."

"Do you work until closing?"

"Why?" I sass. "Are you going to escort me to my car if I do?"

"And what if I do?"

I'll probably shove him into my vehicle and kidnap him to my apartment to have my wicked way with him all night long.

"It might be dangerous. You never know what'll happen in the middle of the night."

"For you, I'm willing to risk it." He winks.

"I'm working until close."

"I'll see you then." He lifts my hand and kisses it.

His lips feel soft and warm against my skin. I want to feel those lips touching other parts of my body. My naked body. I tremble and Archer's eyes flare. Good to know we're on the same page.

"Cassandra!"

Dammit. "Duty calls."

I hurry away before I change my mind and say to hell with work and leave this minute with Archer. Later, I promise myself.

Chapter 2

Archer – a man who knows a good thing when he finds her

ARCHER

I sniff my pillow and freeze. My pillows don't smell like vanilla. I sniff again and something tickles my nose. I swipe at it and realize this isn't my pillow. It isn't a pillow at all. It's someone's hair.

Cassandra. Memories of last night hit me – the way she melts when I nibble her ear and how she tastes of the sweetest honey – and I feel myself harden. What a night. Cassandra knows exactly what she wants and doesn't hesitate to ask for it. I loved every freaking minute.

I don't usually pick women up from a bar, but I took one look at the gorgeous bartender at the *White Stag* and I wanted her. Blonde hair, high cheekbones, cute nose, slightly pointed chin. My hands itched to touch her. I could barely hold myself back until closing time.

The little minx teased me the entire night as I waited for her to finish her shift. Gazing at me from beneath her eyelashes while biting her lip. Or staring right at me while licking her lips. The woman is a siren and last night I was the sailor being lured to her rocks.

"Go back to sleep," she grumbles.

I brush her hair away from her neck and kiss her there. "But I'm wide awake."

She wiggles her ass against me. "Yeah, you are."

I wrap my arms around her waist and haul her closer. She slaps at my hands. "No. I need my beauty sleep. You may wake me at noon."

I chuckle as I kiss her hair before rolling away. She snuggles into her pillow and a few seconds later she's snoring.

I scan the floor for my jeans before I remember they're in the hallway near the front door. Once I'm dressed and have taken care of business, I go in search of the kitchen and some coffee.

With a cup in my hand, I wander around the apartment. I'm surprised to discover the kitchen has brand-new stainless steel appliances and marble countertops. In the living room, there are floor to ceiling windows with views of the Rockies in the distance.

This apartment isn't what I expected of Cassandra. She's such a free spirit. A cookie-cutter place doesn't seem to fit her. But I'm not one to judge. I've had enough of people judging me for the choices I've made in my life.

I check the time. It's still several hours before Sleeping Beauty will wake. I settle on the sofa to drink my coffee and answer some work emails.

I'm finishing up her breakfast when she stumbles into the kitchen a few minutes before noon.

"Huh. You're still here," she grumbles.

I hand her a cup of coffee. She grunts her thanks before gulping half of it down in one go.

"Ah," she says as she cradles the mug to her chest.

"Feeling better?"

"Yes, thank you." She sniffs and her nose wrinkles. It's adorable. "What am I smelling?"

I open the oven and remove the plate of eggs, bacon, and pancakes.

"Did you order breakfast? I didn't know you could have breakfast delivered to your door here."

"I didn't order in." I nod to the place I set for her at the island. "Sit."

She plants her fists on her hips and her breasts jut out. "What if I'm not hungry?"

She's dressed in a thin tank top with no bra showing off her perfect breasts and a pair of tight leggings displaying her shapely legs. I have plenty of ideas of what we can do if she doesn't want to eat.

I step closer until I'm crowding her against the kitchen counter. Her breath hitches and her green eyes flare. I trail my nose along her neck until I reach her ear where I bite on the lobe.

"I can think of several other things I'd rather be doing," I growl into her ear.

She shivers and arches into me. "What kinds of things?"

Her stomach growls, and I retreat before indicating the seat. "You need to eat first."

She bites her bottom lip and bats her eyelashes at me. "I know something I want to eat."

My cock twitches. He's on board with her plan. I'm not. For some reason, I feel the need to take care of this woman. I'm not questioning it. When my gut speaks, I listen.

"Food first. Other stuff later."

"I'm not—" Her words are cut off when her stomach growls again.

I herd her to the spot at the island before grabbing the plate I prepared for her. When I set the food down in front of her, her eyes widen.

"You made this?" I nod. "I didn't realize I had the ingredients for pancakes."

"You had butter and flour and eggs."

She freezes with her hand holding a fork of eggs in the air. "You made pancakes from scratch?"

"It's not difficult."

"Considering my idea of cooking is dialing a restaurant for take-out, I'll decide what's difficult or not."

I chuckle and nudge her fork. "Eat."

She shovels the eggs into her mouth. Her eyes widen as she chews. "Wow. These are good."

I bow. "Thank you."

"Are you a chef?"

"No." Being stuck working at the same restaurant day in and out is about as appealing to me as sticking my foot in a bear trap. I need the freedom to move on when my gut says it's time.

"What do you do for work?"

I fetch myself a cup of coffee to avoid the question, but she doesn't let it go. I doubt the woman ever lets anything go.

"You know what I do for work," she reminds me.

I sigh. "It's boring," I hedge.

"Boring isn't an answer. Unless you're afraid to tell me because you're some kind of gangster."

I tweak her nose. "You have quite the imagination. I'm not a gangster. I'm a financial advisor."

"A financial advisor for gangsters?"

"What gave you such a crazy idea?"

"Why else wouldn't you want to tell me what your job is?"

Because I'm not used to anyone knowing what I do. Because I prefer to keep myself to myself. I don't reveal any of those responses to Cassandra, though. My replies would lead to more questions. Questions I'm not prepared to answer. And this woman doesn't appear to be the type to keep quiet when she's curious.

"Because my job is boring."

"It would be less boring if you worked for gangsters."

I can't help myself from grinning. "Why do you sound excited by the idea?"

She shrugs. "I like excitement. So sue me."

"Being involved in crime is exciting?"

"Meh. Crime is such a nasty word. I prefer misdeeds."

I laugh. "You're a troublemaker."

"Not so much lately."

"Why not lately?"

"Because I promised my sister I'd behave when we moved to Colorado," she pouts.

"Why'd you promise her if you didn't want to?"

"She gave me a guilt trip and I fell into her trap."

"A guilt trip about what?"

"Never you mind."

I frown at her refusal to answer my question. Wait a second. Why am I frowning? I don't usually spend the morning after sex quizzing my one-night stand about her life. But I'm fascinated with this woman and want to know more. Before I have a chance to push her, she waves her fork at me.

"Why aren't you eating?"

"Not all of us are Sleeping Beauty."

"I worked until 3 a.m. Sleeping until noon doesn't make me lazy," she snarls.

I've obviously touched a nerve. I raise my hands. "I didn't say it did. I ate already."

"You've made yourself right at home, haven't you?"

"Have I overstayed my welcome?"

Probably. I've never eaten breakfast – let alone breakfast at noon – with a one-night stand before. I know how to avoid an awkward morning after. I've become an expert at it considering I never stay in one place too long. Serious relationships and moving every couple of months don't exactly go together.

But for some reason I can't figure out, I can't walk away from Cassandra. She gave me the perfect opportunity to slip out when she fell back asleep this morning, but I didn't take it.

Instead, I've been answering emails on my phone all morning while waiting for her to wake up.

Shit. I sound like a creeper. My heart races. My mother would be appalled.

"Nope. I did say you could wake me at noon, after all." Cassandra's response has my heart slowing back to normal.

"Good. Because I have a few ideas of what to do with the maple syrup once you're done eating."

"I have maple syrup?"

I laugh as I haul her out of her chair and throw her over my shoulder before grabbing the bottle.

"Let me show you."

Chapter 3

Old Man — someone who knows more about what the town gossips are up to than he lets on

I EXIT THE APARTMENT building I just finished helping my sister, Elizabeth, move into in the small town of Winter Falls. When her 'best friend' River showed up, she couldn't kick me out fast enough. Those two claim to be 'friends only' but the heat between them doesn't lie.

All of my siblings are falling in love these days. First, my big brother Beckett found Lilac and convinced her to give him a chance. Then, my baby sister, Gabrielle, fell for the goat farmer, Phoenix. If Elizabeth and River ever seal the deal, I'll be all alone.

I do have another sister. Olivia. But I gave up on her a long time ago. When our parents died, she went off the rails and she hasn't found her way back yet. I know Elizabeth begged her to come to Colorado with us, but Olivia was bound and determined to stay in Saint Louis. I'm surprised she didn't throw us a 'go away and don't come back' party.

I could use a distraction. My mind immediately conjures up Archer. What a wonderful distraction he was. I wouldn't mind taking him for another ride, but I don't double dip.

Maybe a walk will get me out of this melancholy mood. I leave my car in the parking lot of Elizabeth's apartment building and wander toward the hiking path behind her building. Winter Falls claims to be the first carbon neutral town in the world. I don't pretend to understand what that means, but I do know their love of the environment equates to plenty of hiking trails around the town.

I travel westward for about ten minutes before I happen upon anyone else. An elderly man stands in the middle of the path leaning on his cane blocking my way.

"Hello," I greet.

"You're going the wrong way," he responds.

"I'm sorry. Am I trespassing on your land? I didn't notice any signs." I glance behind me to make certain, but there's nothing visible back there but trees.

"You need to travel north past the falls," is his bizarre response.

Need? This is getting interesting. "Why?"

He glares at me for a good, long time before he finally answers. "There's someone there you want to meet."

"Who?"

"Stop dilly-dallying and get your butt moving."

I'm officially intrigued. I consider asking him more questions but the scowl on his face has me shrugging instead. "Okay."

I follow the old man's directions and begin marching north.

"If you manage the impossible, I'll be in your debt," he calls after me.

I merely wave in response because I haven't the first clue what he's talking about. Is he sending me on a quest? Or am I dreaming this? Frankly, I don't care. I'm always up for an adventure.

I hike for another twenty minutes without seeing anyone. Did I take a wrong turn somewhere? Is the old man crazy and cackling about sending the stupid outsider off into the woods to get killed by a bear? Shit. Bears. Are there bears in this forest? Maybe I should go back.

I round a curve and nearly stumble when a cute little cottage in the middle of a clearing comes into view. Is this where the old man meant to send me? And if he did? Why?

I sneak closer but skid to a halt when I hear someone chopping wood. I do not want to encounter a stranger when he's wielding an axe. No siree bob.

My body disagrees. My feet carry me toward the house until I can peek into the side yard where a man is chopping wood without a shirt on. The muscles in his broad shoulders flex as he brings the axe down on the wood.

Where's a bag of popcorn when a girl needs one? Because this is some prime entertainment right here. I watch as the man chops two more logs. He turns around to pick up another piece of wood and I gasp when his face comes into view. I recognize him. Archer.

"You!"

"Holy crap, Cassie. You scared me. What are you doing out here?"

Will he believe me if I claim an old man pointed me in his direction? Or will he think I'm crazy? For some reason, I don't want him to think I'm crazy. Weird. I'm usually proud of the title Crazy Cassie.

"Out for a hike."

"Do you live in Winter Falls?"

"You've been to my apartment. Was it in Winter Falls? Or do you think I can snap my fingers and my apartment magically appears wherever I want it to?" I snap my fingers but nothing happens. "Huh. My magic doesn't appear to work in front of mere mortals."

"Wisecracker," he mutters.

"I prefer wise ass."

"You want to come inside?" He motions toward the cottage, which appears even smaller now that I'm close to it.

"You live here?"

"For now."

"Are you squatting?"

"Don't get too excited. I'm not doing anything illegal."

I hunch my shoulders. "Too bad."

He chuckles as he wraps an arm around my shoulders and kisses my cheek. "Hi, princess."

I'm no princess, but if he wants to refer to me as one, he may have at it. To him, I will be a princess.

Once we're inside the house, I don't bother to hide my curiosity as I study the place.

"This is tiny."

"That must be why they call it a tiny house."

I pinch his side. "I'm the smart ass in this relationship."

Shit. I didn't mean to say relationship. We're not in a relationship. We had a one-night stand and ate a lovely breakfast together before I sent him on his way. None of which spells relationship.

"My apologies. I didn't intend to step on your toes," he says, and I realize he didn't notice my misstep.

"Apology accepted," I sass as I scoot further into the home.

Although further is relative. I can make it about five steps before I've entered the kitchen from the living room.

"How does a big guy like you live in such a small place?"

He waggles his eyebrows. "Are you saying I'm big?"

I shove him. "Not what I meant and you know it. You're six-foot tall. Don't you feel cramped in here?"

"Nope. I spend most of my time outdoors."

"What about when it's freezing outside?" Today is relatively mild for November in Colorado, but it's going to get colder.

He shrugs. "I move on."

"You move on?"

"Did you not notice the wheels under the house?"

Did he expect me to notice wheels when he was standing out there bearing his naked back with all its delicious muscles? I can prioritize and wheels did not make the priority list.

He chuckles and lifts a table to reveal a wheel well. "Wheels."

"You hitch your house up to your truck and off you go whenever you're bored?"

"Yep."

Sounds lovely. Of course, if I tried to live on the road, my sisters and brother would probably follow me the entire time. It'd be a caravan every time I moved. Although, Gabrielle won't go anywhere without Phoenix now and he has the farm. And Beckett is the CEO of his company.

I rub my chest. Everyone in my family is moving on and I'm stuck. I can't find a partner to settle down with when I don't deserve love.

"What about your job?" I ask to force my thoughts away from the doom and gloom of my lonely future. "Doesn't the mob want to know where you are at all times?"

"They're actually pretty cool about it. Of course, they probably have some tracking devices attached to my house and truck."

I nod. "Naturally, they need to keep tabs on you in case you decide to launder all of their money into an account in the Cayman Islands."

He wraps his arms around me and draws me near as he barks out a laugh. I enjoy the feel of his body vibrating against mine, although it would feel better if we were naked.

"You're one of a kind, princess," he says as he kisses my hair.

"I know."

He releases me, and I have to stop myself from pouting. "Do you want a tour?"

I throw my arms out to the side and twirl around. "I think I can see everything from here."

"There's a great view of the mountains from the loft."

I indicate the window in front of us. "There's a great view from where I'm standing." Which makes me wonder. "Do you own this land?"

"Nope. Owning land makes it hard to relocate."

Makes sense. "Why did you choose Winter Falls? Have you been here before?"

"Do you want to continue to hash out our pasts or do you want to learn how soft my bed is?"

Learn how soft his bed is. Obviously. But I need one thing to be crystal clear first. "You're not staying in Winter Falls?"

"I'm not planning on it."

In that case, I whip off my shirt. "Bet you can't catch me."

He can. Totally worth it.

Chapter 4

Sage – a police dispatcher who thinks gossiping around town is part of the job description

I STARE AT THE old-fashioned sign in the window for another second before I grasp the door handle and enter the bar. *Electric Vibes* in Winter Falls is unlike any bar I've ever been in before. Probably because I'm thirty-three and didn't grow up during the hippie generation. Because this bar screams HIPPIE.

Musical posters from folk singers? Check! Walls covered in peace signs and daisies? Double check! Colored lights on the walls and ceilings? Check! At least, with none of the chairs in the place matching, there's no need to worry about the cost of replacing them after a bar fight. Although, I can't imagine a bar fight happening in the peace-loving Winter Falls.

"It's about time," Lennon says when I enter the bar.

Lennon owns *Electric Vibes*. He also believes he's the reincarnation of John Lennon. Never mind he was born before Lennon was shot down in the street in New York City.

"About time?"

"Took you long enough."

"Have you been hitting the wacky tobacky too hard lately?"

"Nope. Hitting it just about right I'd say."

I love a crazy convo as much as the next person, but he's seriously confusing me. "What are you talking about?"

He indicates the window. "I put the help wanted sign out the last time you were in here with your sisters."

I know. I saw it. It's why I'm here.

"Do you still need help or not?"

"I need more than help. I need you."

I smirk and do a curtsy. "At your service."

"Come on, crazy girl." He motions toward the back hallway. "We've got things to discuss."

When he opens the door to his office, my eyebrows nearly fly off my forehead. I've seen some messy offices in my time, but this one wins 'messiest office of the century' hands down. I glance down at the floor – or, rather, what I can glimpse of the floor – and wonder if I need a hazmat suit.

"Do you want to hire me to organize your office?"

"Nope. I want you to take over my business."

I shake my head to clear it. I must be hearing things. Why would Lennon, a man I've met less than a handful of times, want me to take over his business?

"Do I need to repeat myself?"

"Maybe?"

"I want you, Cassandra Dempsey, to take over my business."

"But you don't know the first thing about me."

He snorts. "I know you graduated near the top of your class in college with a double major in English and education. I know you worked as an English teacher for one year before quitting to become a bartender. And I know you currently work at the *White Stag* in White Bridge. Enough for you?"

I cross my arms over my chest. "How do you know all those things about me?" I narrow my eyes on him. "Have you been spying on me?"

He chuckles. "This is Winter Falls."

He says the words Winter Falls like they're an explanation for everything. They kind of are. Winter Falls is a small town in Colorado about thirty minutes from White Bridge where I currently live. The residents are environmentally-conscious, hippie-orientated, and have a love of pagan festivals. All of which rocks.

What doesn't rock about the town is the lack of privacy. I don't think anyone who lives here understands what the word means. Which was freaking hilarious when the town decided to get all up in my sister Gabrielle's business when they matched her with Phoenix. It's less funny now that it's my privacy being invaded.

"What makes you think I want to take over your bar?" I ask because there's no sense discussing how he learned everything about me. I know a losing battle when I encounter one.

"Darling," is all he responds.

Another question he's unwilling to answer. Fine. I stare at him as I try to think of a question he will answer.

"Why are you retiring?"

"I want to enjoy my golden years. Staying up until three in the morning working in the bar and then getting up at nine to start all over again is too much for these old bones."

Makes sense. And, despite what my sisters think, I'm not stupid. I know a good opportunity when it hits me in the face.

"We'll need to go over the accounts and come up with a mutually acceptable price."

He grins and holds out his hand. "You're in?"

"I'll think about it." I probably won't be able to think about anything else until I make a decision.

"Good enough," he says as he grasps my hand and forces me to shake his.

"Don't get too excited, old man. We haven't even agreed to a price yet."

"But you can pay any price."

Yeah, yeah. My family has money. But I'm not touching it. I don't deserve it. If I buy this place, I'll come up with the money myself.

"I'd like to work at the bar in the meantime."

"Let me get you set up," he says and leads me out of the office.

"Did she say yes?" Sage asks when we return to the bar.

I glance over my shoulder toward the exit, but Lennon blocks me. Damn. This is not good. Sage is the leader of the gossip gal gang. Together with the other members of the gang – Feather, Petal, Cayenne, and Clove – she plays matchmaker to the residents of the town.

It was hilarious to watch the gossip gals maneuver Phoenix and Gabrielle until the two fell in love. But I don't want them getting any ideas about matching me. Love isn't for me. I don't deserve it.

"Can I get some service?" A blonde at the end of the bar yells.

Lennon starts toward the bar, but I stop him. "I got this. You talk to your friend." I nod toward Sage.

"What can I get you?" I ask the blonde.

"You?" She sneers. "You're next? This is unbelievable. Un-freaking-believable."

"I don't know what you're talking about. I'm merely the bartender here." I prefer the term mixologist, but I don't think this woman cares about my preferences at the moment.

"Don't be jealous," another woman says as she approaches carrying a crate of beer.

"Jealous. What would I be jealous about?" I ask her.

I'm confused, which is nothing new in Winter Falls. I often feel as if I'm joining a conversation after it's started when I'm here.

She sets the crate of beer on the bar. "Here you go." What she doesn't do is answer my question. Typical.

I point toward the beer. "What's this?"

"Lennon said you're low on the Naked Falls Brewing Winter Bok."

"You're from the brewery?"

"I'm Moon." Before I have a chance to introduce myself, she adds, "And you're Cassandra."

"Is the meet and greet over now? I want to order," the blonde snaps.

Moon gestures toward her. "And this is Love Hill. Don't worry. Her bark is bigger than her bite."

"I'm going to die of thirst in here," Love Hill says.

Moon rolls her eyes. "Don't be overdramatic."

"I'm not being dramatic," Love Hill insists.

"Please. You put the drama in dramatic."

"What can I get you?" I interrupt to ask.

Love Hill smirks. "A Ramos gin fizz."

If she thinks she's tricking me, she's in for a surprise. There's a reason I refer to myself as a mixologist after all. A Ramos gin fizz is notoriously difficult to make because it requires vigorous shaking during each step to create the perfect foam and consistency. Shake too much and the drink becomes too frothy.

I search the shelves for the necessary ingredients and gather them on the bar along with a shaker. I add the syrup, gin, heavy cream, lime and lemon juice, egg white, and orange flower water to the shaker.

"Are you from Winter Falls?" I ask Moon as I work.

"Born and raised."

"And you work at the brewery?"

"Hey!" Love Hill interrupts. "Shouldn't you pay attention to what you're doing?"

I roll my eyes. This drink needs to be mixed for at least five minutes. I can chit-chat and shake with my eyes closed.

"I'm good," I tell her. "The brewery?" I prompt Moon.

"I work there, and I work at the inn, too."

"Busy girl."

I stop to add ice to the mixture before giving it an additional shake to get it well chilled. I pour the drink into a cocktail glass, add a bit of club soda to the shaker, and swish it around to pick up the remaining egg and cream. I top the drink off with the egg mixture before placing it in front of Love Hill.

"There you go."

She purses her lips as she considers the glass. I lean on my elbows to watch as she takes a tentative sip. Her eyes widen before she guzzles half of the drink down at once. She stands and walks to a table near the door.

"You're welcome," I holler after her.

"Congratulations," Moon says, and I return my attention to her.

"For?"

"For winning your first encounter with the mean girl of Winter Falls."

I chuckle. "If you think that was an encounter, you ain't seen nothing yet."

"I have a feeling this is the beginning of a beautiful friendship."

Sounds good to me. I could use some new friends since my sisters are now too busy with their men to spend time with me. Although, there is Archer. I plan to spend as much time with him as possible until he departs for greener pastures.

I haven't spent more than one night with the same man in decades, but with Archer, I can since he isn't staying. There's no danger of me falling in love with him when he'll be gone in a few weeks.

The future is looking brighter than I expected.

Chapter 5

Ashlyn – a woman who thinks you're never too old to believe in imaginary friends

ARCHER

I clutch the stuffed bear in my hands as I stare at the door to my brother's house. I haven't seen Rowan in over a year, but when he told me his wife, Ashlyn, was pregnant, I couldn't stay away. I've been in the area for over a month now and haven't worked up the courage to visit yet. But Ashlyn had their baby a few days ago. I can't stay away any longer.

I lift my hand to knock, but the door opens before I can connect with the wood.

"I was starting to wonder if you were ever going to knock," Rowan greets. Before I have a chance to respond, he wraps an arm around my back and slaps me a few times. "Good to see you, brother."

"Yeah."

"Come inside and meet our little girl."

I hand him the stuffed bear before following him into the house. Ashlyn waves at me from her spot on the sofa. "I'd get up but big guy here won't let me."

"You're supposed to be resting," Rowan growls at her.

"I am resting. I've been sitting in this very spot for one hour and fifty-two minutes."

Rowan sighs. "You remember Ashlyn?"

I lean over to kiss her cheek. "How could I forget the girl who protested the cheerleading squad by streaking across the gym?"

"First of all, I didn't streak. I was wearing shoes. Second of all, you had already graduated and left Winter Falls when the 'alleged' event occurred. You shouldn't know about it."

I chuckle. "It's funny you think you can keep a secret in Winter Falls."

"And, finally, those girls should have begged me to be on the cheerleading squad."

Rowan cocks a brow. "Despite your inability to do a cartwheel?"

"I still don't understand what the big deal about cartwheels is."

The baby monitor on the coffee table sputters to life before a baby's wail screeches out of it.

"Are you ready to meet Patience?" Rowan asks.

Ashlyn starts to stand. "I'll get her."

Rowan glares at her and she holds up her palms in surrender as she sits back down. "I'm not an invalid," she mutters under her breath.

"No, you're my wonderful wife who gave me a daughter three days ago."

He leans over to kiss her, and I glance away. I never thought Rowan would find happiness with another partner after what his first wife did to him. She was a Class A bitch. But somehow Ashlyn caught his attention and now they're happily married with a baby.

I want what they have. I startle at the stray thought. I've never been one to imagine life with a wife and kids. What woman would want to hitch herself to me when I relocate every month or two? And constantly traveling is no way to raise a family.

Although, Cassandra seems like the kind of woman who wouldn't mind living a life on the road. What am I thinking? She's made it perfectly clear she's not in the market for a relationship.

Rowan returns with a tiny bundle in his hands. "You want to hold her?"

To my surprise, I find myself nodding. He places Patience in my arms.

"Hi, little girl." I kiss her forehead. "I'm your uncle."

As I rock her back and forth, I realize returning to Winter Falls was a good call. I don't know how long I'll stay but coming here to visit Rowan, Ashlyn, and their baby was the right thing to do.

"Enough," Rowan grunts before snatching Patience away.

"It's nothing personal," Ashlyn explains. "He doesn't let anyone hold her for too long."

"Have a seat," Rowan orders as he hands the baby to Ashlyn. "Do you want a coffee?"

Ashlyn raises her hand. "I want a coffee."

"I'll make you a decaf," he says, and she pouts.

Once Rowan returns with our coffees, he settles on the sofa next to his wife and daughter while I sit across from them. Silence falls. I'm fine with the quiet but Ashlyn appears ready to burst.

"Are you back to stay?" Rowan asks.

"Finally!" Ashlyn shouts. "I thought we were going to sit here and say nothing all afternoon."

"It was two minutes," Rowan says.

"It felt like two hours. Never mind. Time to discuss the elephant in the room. I hate ignoring Elsie. She gets agitated and throws water at me when I do."

"Elsie? Who's Elsie?" I scan the room but no one else is here.

Ashlyn rolls her eyes. "The elephant. Duh."

Rowan sighs. "Dream girl."

"What? Is there or is there not an elephant in the room?"

"There is no actual elephant. It's a metaphorical idiom."

"Now you hurt Elsie's feelings."

I chuckle. Ashlyn's as crazy as I remember her from high school. She was five or six grades behind me, but in a town the size of Winter Falls, everyone knows everyone.

Rowan grunts but guessing by the warmth in his eyes as he gazes down at Ashlyn, he doesn't mind his wife's shenanigans.

"I don't know if I'm here to stay," I say before Ashlyn gets some other bizarre idea.

Rowan leans forward. "You don't know?"

I nod.

"Are you saying you could be here to stay for good?"

"Maybe," I hedge.

"This is the best news."

"Hello." Ashlyn elbows him. "I gave you a daughter this week."

"On the floor of a construction zone."

"It was an accident."

"An accident? You forgetting to tell me you were in labor for a day was an accident?"

"How's your family?" I butt in to ask Ashlyn because this argument could go on for days.

Ashlyn has four sisters. Although I've stayed in touch with Rowan, I haven't followed the gossip about the West sisters.

"They're good. Aspen married her high school sweetheart, Lyric, a few months ago. Ellery has a baby girl and is engaged to Cole. He's the out-of-towner who's managing the project to build the community center. Lilac is engaged to Beckett. Also, an out-of-towner who lives in White Bridge. And you probably already know Juniper is engaged to the movie star Maverick Langston."

Wow. The West sisters have been busy.

"I don't know what I'm more surprised about. Juniper marrying a superstar or Lilac falling in love."

"Lilac was in the same grade as you in school, wasn't she?"

"Yep, but I haven't seen her in a while. What's she doing now?"

Ashlyn rubs her hands together. "Get this. She fell in love with her boss."

"Things are never dull in Winter Falls."

"Yep. You should probably stay in town permanently, so you don't miss a thing."

"Smooth move, dream girl," Rowan grunts.

"What? Am I supposed to be subtle about convincing him to stay in town? You didn't warn me in advance."

He grins. "You? Be subtle? I know better than to ask for miracles."

I wave a hand toward Patience who's now sleeping in Ashlyn's lap. "I think you got your miracle already."

And, make no doubt about it, Patience's birth is a miracle. Rowan thought he couldn't have children, which fucked with his head. I don't how Ashlyn did it, but she pushed her way past Rowan's reservations and now they're happily married.

I stand. "I should probably get going."

"Already?" Ashlyn pouts. "I can try to be subtle. Promise. There's no need for you to permanently return to Winter Falls. We'll keep you updated. Although, it'd be more fun if you were here. See? Subtle."

I chuckle as I lean down to kiss her goodbye. "Behave, sister-in-law."

She sits up straight and beams up at me. "I always behave." She winks.

I ruffle her hair. "Sure, you do."

"I'll follow you out," Rowan says as he motions toward the door.

We stand on the porch, and I scan the streets to make certain no one's spying on us. I'm not ready for the gossips of Winter Falls to invade my sanctuary.

Rowan claps me on the back. "Will you join us for Christmas next week?"

The idea of spending a day with all five of the West sisters and their partners makes me want to run away as fast as I can. Crowds are bad enough. But a crowd of people who haven't seen you in years and think they have the right to know every single thing you've been doing in the meantime? I dread the thought.

I shrug and he sighs. He knows my shrug is a no.

"Will you at least promise to not leave town without letting me know?"

"Yeah."

It's an easy enough promise to make since I don't plan on leaving anytime soon. I might not be ready to get involved in the daily life of Winter Falls, but I'm not ready to flee town yet. My gut is telling me to stay for a while.

"Good. I've missed you, brother."

Chapter 6

Attachment – something that wouldn't happen if Cassandra would stick to her rules

"CAN YOU PICK UP some eggs on your way to my place?" Archer asks.

His words should shock me. Hell, they should send me fleeing as fast as my car can drive me away from Winter Falls. A man expecting me to pick up some groceries for him on my way to his place is not the norm in Cassandra's world. Except, when it comes to Archer, nothing is normal.

"Anything else?" I ask as I switch on my turn signal to make a U-turn as I'm now driving in the wrong direction.

"If you pick up some corn tortillas, I'll make you Huevos Rancheros for breakfast."

He's assuming I'm staying overnight. Awesome.

"I like how you think. See you soon."

"Drive safe, princess."

My body warms at his nickname for me. Princess. I wish I was a princess. I'm not. I'm a thirty-three-year-old woman who doesn't deserve this kind man. But I'm not stupid. I'm going to enjoy him while I can.

When I arrive at the parking area as near to Archer's tiny house as I can get forty-five minutes later, he's waiting there for me.

"What's up?" I ask.

"Didn't want you carrying the groceries," he grumbles as he opens the trunk and picks up the bag.

"It's some eggs and tortillas. I think I would have managed."

He grunts in response. Over the past two months, I've learned Archer doesn't talk much. Fine with me. I can talk enough for the two of us.

He grasps my hand to lead me through the woods to where his tiny house is located. Holding hands with a man is another big no-no in Cassandra's rules of life, but I don't pull away. Instead, I enjoy the feel of his calloused hand in mine.

I need to watch myself with him before I get emotionally attached, but there's no need to worry since he's leaving soon. He never stays in one place for more than six months and he's already been here for three. I'll be sad when he's gone, but it's for the best. I don't deserve love.

He opens the door to his tiny cottage on wheels and the smell of rosemary hits me. "Yum. What are you cooking?"

"Baked pumpkin gratin with rosemary and goat's cheese."

My stomach growls at the description.

"It should be ready in about thirty minutes," he says as he puts away the groceries. "Do you mind if I deal with an email in the meantime?"

Do I mind? This is his house. He can do whatever he wants. "Have at it."

"Thanks." He kisses my hair before settling at the kitchen table with his laptop.

I plop down on the sofa with my tablet. Lennon sent me the profit and loss statements for the past seven years of *Electric Vibes* the other day, but I haven't had a chance to review them yet. As I'm scanning the documents, it doesn't take me long to realize I'm in over my head.

I've been managing bars for several years now, but managing is completely different than owning a business. I close the documents and open Google. I need to research business classes. I could ask Elizabeth or Gabrielle for their help – both of my sisters own their own businesses – but I'm not ready to tell them about *Electric Vibes* yet.

They'll figure out I'm working there soon enough since they're both living in Winter Falls. But I'm keeping Lennon's offer a secret until I decide whether or not I want to buy the place. Otherwise, my sisters will dive in with their opinions and railroad me into doing what they want. I already know what they want. They want me to live in Winter Falls.

While I find the town eccentric and the gossip gals and their matchmaking hilarious, I'm not certain I actually want to live here. I was all for it until I realized how little privacy I'd have if I lived here. Privacy doesn't exist in this small town, but I guard my privacy with my life.

"What are you watching?" Archer asks as he sits next to me.

"Nothing," I murmur and quickly switch my tablet off before he can see what I'm researching. "Is dinner ready yet? I'm starving."

"Almost."

I spring to my feet. "I'll set the table."

While I set the table, Archer makes a salad to go along with the pumpkin casserole. I stumble when I realize how familiar this feels with me helping out while he cooks. Although I usually work in the evenings, I've spent nearly every off day with him in his house for the past six weeks. Shit. I'm getting attached.

This is why I stick to one-night stands. To stop myself from getting attached. Dang it. I need to pull back from Archer before I develop feelings for him.

But when we sit across from each other at his tiny table with the food he prepared in front of us, I realize I won't do it. I won't pull back from him. I'm going to enjoy the time I have with him while I have the chance.

"How did working at *Electric Vibes* go last night?" Archer asks as we dig into our food.

Yesterday was my first evening shift at the hippie bar. Until now, I've only worked there during the day as I can't give up my evening shifts at the *White Stag* until I decide whether to accept Lennon's offer.

"Typical Winter Falls."

"Really? Tell me more."

Archer always wants to know the latest gossip in Winter Falls. For someone who's a wanderer, he sure enjoys his local scandals.

"Mean girl Love Hill showed up and threw a glass of beer at Eden."

His brow furrows. "Eden?"

"She owns the local plant shop, *Eden's Garden*."

"Gotcha. What did she do to piss off Love Hill?"

"Apparently, Eden stole her man."

"Her man? Love Hill has a man?"

I roll my eyes. "I don't know what man would put up with that woman. She's a maneater. I fear for the life of any man she sinks her claws into. She probably has a trophy room at home containing the hearts of any man foolish enough to date her."

Archer barks out a laugh. "I hope the hearts are in trophy cases."

"Nope." I wag my fork at him. "They're not. She's got them rigged up to buckets to collect the blood. Drip. Drip. Drip. Once she's collected enough, she adds it to her daily smoothie."

"Is she a vampire?"

"Either she's a vampire or she has a plastic surgeon on speed dial because the woman doesn't have a single wrinkle or laugh line. Of course," I pause to consider. "I can't recall her ever smiling. Which could explain the lack of laugh lines."

"Women in their thirties don't usually have wrinkles."

"How do you know how old Love Hill is?"

"You told me."

"Oh." I guess I must have.

"Do you want to watch a movie?" he asks as we finish up our meal.

I wave a hand toward the blank walls in the living room. "On what? You don't own a television."

I made the mistake of asking him why the first time I was here. Never again. For someone who doesn't talk much, he didn't have a hard time lecturing me about how televisions are ruining the next generation.

"Smartass. We can watch on my laptop."

"Okay. Pick out a movie and I'll clean up."

This is our usual routine. He cooks. I clean. Oh no. We have a routine. The situation is more serious than I thought. Are we – gulp – in a relationship? I should go. I can come back when I've got my head screwed on right.

But do I go anywhere? Of course not. No one ever accused me of being smart when it comes to men.

We settle on the sofa with Archer's laptop. He wraps an arm around my shoulder, and I cuddle into him. This is exactly what I mean. Not smart.

My phone beeps with a message while the opening credits are still rolling. I dig it out and read the message from Gabrielle.

"I need to go." I force myself away from him and stand.

"Is everything okay?"

"Elizabeth is having a crisis. I'm on deck to bring the alcohol to cheer her up."

I sit on the floor to put on my boots. "I'll be back for my car in the morning."

"You're not leaving your car here," he grumbles.

"What? Why not? Are you ashamed of me visiting you?"

"Why would I be ashamed of you?" He appears genuinely confused.

I finish with my boots and stand to confront him. "Why else don't you want my car parked next to your truck?"

He motions outside. "Because the sun is setting, and I don't want you trekking through the woods alone in the dark."

All my bluster flees at his explanation. "Oh."

He tweaks my nose. "Yeah. Oh."

He grabs his jacket and shrugs into it. What is he doing? He must notice the confusion on my face because he explains. "I know you can walk back to your car by yourself, but there's nothing wrong with me escorting you like a gentleman."

I waggle my eyebrows. "You sure weren't acting like a gentleman when you tied my hands to your headboard last week."

His eyes flare causing the green to swallow the brown. Stupid sister and her stupid crisis. I had plans for the night.

He opens the door and motions me outside, "Come on, trouble."

I can practically feel my heart begin to tether itself to him as he accompanies me to my car. *Knock it off, heart.* We don't deserve love, remember?

Chapter 7

"ARE YOU SURE YOU don't want to come to the bar for New Year's Eve? It'll be fun, I promise. I can—"

I cut myself off when I realize I'm begging. Cassandra's life rules are quite clear in this aspect. No begging a man for what you want.

"I'm sorry, princess," Archer mutters.

"Whatever. I'll see you when I see you."

I hang up before he can answer. The last thing I need is to listen to him make excuses. If he doesn't want to spend time with me, I won't force him to. I'm not some needy woman.

"You ready?" Lennon asks as he enters the storage room.

I shove my phone in my back pocket. I feel it buzz with a message, but I ignore it.

"All ready."

"Your family is coming."

"I'm aware." Elizabeth and Gabrielle will be here with River and Phoenix. I told them I'd meet them here.

"There's no keeping secrets in Winter Falls."

"I know."

"You make up your mind yet?"

I don't need to ask him to clarify. He poses the same question every night before I begin my shift. Am I going to buy the bar? I don't know. I'm ready for the next step in my career and buying a bar is the logical choice. But is *this* bar the one for me?

"Maybe?"

He leans against the door. "This'll give you something to think about. The town approved you."

"The town approved me? Do I need the town's approval to own a business?" I'm officially confused.

"All the property on Main Street is owned by the town itself. You need the town council's approval to operate a business on Main Street."

I cross my arms over my chest and glare at him. "Why didn't you tell me this before?"

"I'm old, not stupid. I knew you wouldn't give the bar a chance if you knew."

He's not wrong. I love Winter Falls and how zany the people are here. But apparently zany equals nosy as hell and I wrote the book on privacy restrictions.

"When do you need an answer?"

"As soon as possible. The California Zephyr books out months in advance." I giggle at the idea of the hippie traveling on a train cross-country and he sobers. "Seriously, Cassie. Soon. You're my first choice as successor, but I don't have long."

I grasp his forearm. "Are you okay? Are you sick?"

He pats my hand. "No. Just tired."

I consider him. "You wouldn't lie to me, would you?"

He winks. "Never."

"Lennon," one of the extra bartenders hired for tonight, Soleil, bustles into the room. "The ball keeps falling on the dance floor."

After they rush off, I pick up a case of Heineken before making my way to the bar to re-stock. By the time I spot my sisters in the crowd a while later, the bar is packed.

"Why are you working tonight?" Elizabeth asks when she bellies up to the bar.

"One word. Tips," I lie.

Her eyes narrow. She knows I'm a liar since I technically don't need the cash. My parents inherited an obscene amount of money when we were young. Since then, no one in the Dempsey family has needed to work. We all do, though. Except Olivia. I have no idea if she works. She doesn't exactly keep in touch.

"What do you want?" I ask before she interrogates me about why I'm working at *Electric Vibes*.

"Can I get a pitcher of margaritas and a pitcher of beer?"

"Margaritas?" I scoff. "I've got something better for you."

"I'm fine with …" I show her my back before she can finish her complaint. I quickly mix up a pitcher of Jack Frosties for her. Considering the alcohol content in these drinks, she won't be back anytime soon.

"What the hell is this?"

"Jack Frosties. You're welcome."

"What's in it?"

I wave and walk off to help another customer. She'll learn soon enough the drink is made of vodka, prosecco, Blue Curacao, and lemonade, although I may have added a bit more vodka than strictly necessary.

Elizabeth needs the liquid courage. She's been going back and forth about giving River a chance for the past week. It's driving me batty. She finally made a decision to go for it today, but I'm not convinced she'll stick to her guns. Thus, liquid courage.

The next hour flies by as everyone orders drinks before the game can begin. Apparently, the residents play this wishing game every New Year's Eve. It works like this. You put your wish for the new year in a jar. Lennon reads the wishes out loud, and everyone guesses whose wish it is. Whoever guesses the most wishes correctly gets to lower the ball at midnight.

I didn't put a wish in the jar. I work hard for what I want. I don't wish it to come true.

"Bets are closing," Sage hollers from her spot next to the stage.

"What are they betting about?" I ask Soleil.

"This is Winter Falls. They'll bet on absolutely anything, but the big bet at this moment is your sister and River Alston."

This I know. The gossip gals have their sights set on matching River and Elizabeth. It's not a bad bet since Elizabeth is in love with River.

Lennon taps the microphone. "Next wish." He reads the card, and his eyes widen as a smile spreads across his face. "I wish for River to be my boyfriend."

I chuckle. My sister Elizabeth is such a dork sometimes.

River's response to the wish is immediate. He kisses my sister before hauling her out of her chair and throwing her over his shoulder.

"Go, River!" I holler and wolf whistle at them.

Once they're outside, I open the window behind the bar to eavesdrop.

"Do you want to return to the bar to yell at your sister or do you want me to escort you home, strip you bare, and worship every inch of you?" River asks Elizabeth.

"I vote for worshipping!" I yell out of the window.

Elizabeth must agree with me because they run off down Main Street. Phew. I hope this is the end of the Elizabeth and River rollercoaster because I am ready to get off. Friends. Lovers. Enemies. Lovers. Friends. Enemies. Who can keep up?

The rest of the night passes in a blur as I mix drinks. By the time two a.m. hits, my feet are killing me, my t-shirt is soaked with sweat and something sticky, and my hair is plastered to my face.

After I lock the front door behind Soleil, Lennon, and the rest of the employees, I nearly collapse against it. Tonight was crazy busy. At this moment, I wish I lived in Winter Falls. A thirty-minute drive back to White Bridge is going to be hell. I should make myself a coffee for the drive, but I don't have the energy.

I walk through the bar switching off lights as I go until I reach the back door. I exit and lock the door behind me. When I turn around, a large figure lumbers toward me. I scream and retreat until my back hits the wall.

"Don't eat me, Mr. Bear," I beg with my eyes closed and my hands covering my face.

"Mr. Bear?"

My eyes fly open at the laughter in Archer's voice.

"Freaking hell. You scared me."

"I kind of got that when you screamed."

"Shaddup." I slap his shoulder. "I must be hallucinating due to exhaustion."

He frowns. "I'll drive you home."

"I—" My response is cut off when a yawn hits me. "Sorry."

"Come on." He grasps my hand and draws me across the parking lot toward my car.

"What are you doing here anyway?" I ask once we're driving out of Winter Falls.

"If you would have answered any of my messages, you would know I planned to pick you up at the end of your shift."

"Sorry. It's been crazy busy."

I'm not exactly lying. It has been busy. But could I have found two seconds to reply to him? Probably. Okay, fine. Most definitely.

"You missed a great night."

"Yeah?"

"The gossip gals are crazy. They got down on the floor to pretend they were dancing on the ceiling, but then they couldn't get up again. Forest tried to do a strip tease on the stage, but Lyric handcuffed him before he could get his pants off."

Archer bursts into laughter. His obvious enjoyment of the antics of Winter Falls has me thinking.

"Why didn't you want to come to the bar tonight?"

"I'm an introvert. Crowds aren't my thing."

I study him for a moment, but the inside of the car is dark and his outline is hard to make out. In the end, I shrug. "Okay."

"Princess." Archer pokes my side and I swat at him. "Sleeping."

He lifts me into his arms. I inhale the scent of firewood. Archer. I cuddle into him knowing I'm safe and secure.

If I were the kind of woman to make New Year's wishes, I'd wish Archer and I could have a real relationship. One where he didn't split after six months and I deserved love.

Chapter 8

*When life offers you an opportunity, you accept it ~ Archer's rules
for getting what he wants in life*

ARCHER

I spot the crowd in front of the new spa on Main Street in Winter Falls and scowl. I have no desire to mingle with the nosy residents of this town. After today, they'll never leave me alone in peace again.

But I promised Ashlyn I'd come to the opening of *Glitter N Bliss*. She considers the owner, Elizabeth, to be her sister for reasons too convoluted for me to understand. When I said wasn't going, she pushed and needled until I gave in. My poor brother doesn't stand a chance with her.

I feel as if everyone in the place is staring at me as I nod and smile at people while wandering through the business. I need to find Ashlyn and say hi and then I'm out of here. I get jostled by someone from behind and decide I'm done with this. I'll risk Ashlyn's wrath.

I march toward the exit, but before I can make it there, a very angry Cassie stops me.

"What the hell are you doing here?"

Crap. I didn't expect her to be here. Her sister, Elizabeth, is the owner of the spa, but I was counting on Cassandra's dislike of waking before noon to save me from this confrontation.

"Cassandra?"

"The one and only. Do I need to repeat my question? Should I speak slower?"

"What are you doing here?"

I throw her question back at her in the lamest attempt in the world to buy myself time to come up with a story. I didn't expect to come clean about who I am this morning, but I guess today's the day. This is going to be a clusterfuck of epic proportions.

She crosses her arms over her chest and throws daggers at me from her eyes. Lucky for me, the daggers aren't real because I'd be a goner otherwise.

"I asked first."

If I have to have this conversation today, I'm not doing it here where the entire town of Winter Falls is listening. Knowing this town, the betting sheets are being drawn up as we speak.

I shackle her wrist and tug her out of the spa and down the street. Out of the corner of my eye, I notice Sage and her cronies following us. The gossip gals were a pain in the ass when I was a kid, and, based on the stories Rowan has told me, they've only gotten worse. Lucky for me, Lyric stops them.

I draw Cassandra into the alley between *Naked Falls Brewing* and *Bertie's Recording Studio.* When we're halfway down the alley, she tears herself away from me and retreats a few steps.

"What's going on? Why are you in town?"

I shove my hands in my pockets and shrug as I try to come up with a way to tell her the truth, which won't cause her head to explode.

"Okay. Fine. I'll return to the party and ask them."

I can't let her go. She'll burn my tiny house to the ground if she learns who I am from the town and not me. And, make no mistake about it, the residents of Winter Falls are done keeping my presence here a secret. I'm surprised I got away with it for as long as I did.

I know they're aware of me camping outside of town. The pies and casseroles left on my doorstep aren't exactly stealthy, although the box of condoms did come in handy.

I grasp her shoulder before she gets too far. "You don't want to do that."

She rears back. "I don't, do I? You don't know what I want to do or don't do. You don't have the first clue about me."

I use my hold on her shoulder to haul her near. "Wrong. I know lots of things about you. I know you melt in my arms when I nibble on your ear." She shivers and I continue, "I know you taste of the sweetest honey."

She leans into me for a few seconds before shaking herself and pushing me away. "Stop it. I'm not going to let you have your wicked way with me in an alley."

At the thought of having my wicked way with her, I smirk. Wrong move. A muscle ticks in her jaw as her nostrils flare. She resembles a princess riding out to defend her kingdom. I don't tell her what I'm thinking, though. I prefer my balls where they are.

"How do you know everyone in town?" she grits out.

I can't continue to delay. I should have told her the truth by now anyway. But I wanted to stay in our bubble for a little while longer.

"Rowan's my brother."

Her jaw drops open. "Rowan as in Ashlyn's husband?"

I nod.

"But his brother's name is Cedar."

"Cedar Archer to be specific."

She pokes my chest with her finger. "You lied to me."

I capture her hand and caress her wrist as I explain, "I never said Rowan wasn't my brother."

She yanks away from me. "You never said he was!" she screeches.

"You didn't tell me you knew everyone in Winter Falls." As defenses go, this one is pretty lame.

"Don't turn this on me," she snarls. "You know I've been working at *Electric Vibes*. Of course, I know everyone. Hell, I've told you all the rumors in town. You're the one who lied and didn't tell me you grew up in Winter Falls." She leans close to hiss in my face. "In fact, you claimed you'd be gone by now."

Did I? I know I told her I live in one place for a maximum of six months before moving on, but I thought I avoided specific questions about staying in Winter Falls. I haven't been back in over a decade and my brother just had a baby. I don't know how long I'm staying.

I scratch my beard and lie, "I planned to."

She snorts. "Of course, you did. You're a wanderer. You can't stay in one place for very long or it would kill you."

I scowl. "It won't kill me."

She raises her eyebrows. "Oh yeah? I dare you."

"What are we? Kindergartners?"

"Never mind. You can't handle the dare. It's okay." She pats my chest. It's condescending and has me growling.

"I can handle a dare. There's a difference between being able to handle something and not doing it because it's childish."

"I understand. You're scared to lose. It doesn't make you less of a man to back out before you have the chance to lose," she taunts.

"You can't trick me into accepting your dare."

She widens her eyes. "Me? Trick you? I would never."

"I'm not going to accept this dare to prove you wrong."

She snorts. "That would be silly, wouldn't it?"

Curiosity gets the better of me and I ask, "What's the dare?"

"I dare you to stay in Winter Falls for six months."

Perfect. I want more time with Cassandra, but she doesn't do relationships. The only reason I've lasted this long is because she thought I would be gone in a few months.

"Too easy."

"I'm not finished yet." I motion for her to continue. "You have to come into town and interact with the residents at least once a week."

"After today, they're not going to allow me to hide out anymore," I grumble. "And what are you going to do?" Two can play at this game and playing with Cassie is one of my favorite things in the world.

"What do you mean? Dares aren't reciprocal."

"This one will be."

"What do you want me to do?"

I tap my chin and pretend to consider the question. I don't need to consider it. I know exactly what I'm going to dare her.

"I dare you to keep a pet for six months."

"No problem," she immediately agrees.

Not so fast, princess. "The pet can't be a cat or any type of rodent."

"What type of animals are left?" She asks as if she doesn't know.

"A dog. You need to keep a dog as a pet for six months."

"What if I'm allergic to dogs?"

She's not allergic to dogs. She's allergic to commitment.

"I understand if you can't handle the dare," I goad her.

"Fine. You're on." She holds out her hand. "What do I win when you flee town before the six months are up?"

She has no idea what she's signed up for. Six months in this town is nothing.

"I'll pay for those business classes you've been researching."

She narrows her eyes on me. She thinks I don't know how worried she is about acquiring *Electric Vibes.* How she doesn't think she can handle it. This woman can handle whatever the world throws at her. But it's cute how she thinks she can hide from me.

I bop her nose. "I told you. I know you."

"Fine." We shake hands.

Her green eyes sparkle. She thinks she's already won. She has no idea. This dare is the perfect opportunity. It gives me six months to work on convincing her how great we are as a couple.

Chapter 9

JUNIPER LAUGHS AT MY car when I pick her up at the wildlife refuge outside of Winter Falls. Juniper is the sister of my soon-to-be sister-in-law Lilac. She's also the world's biggest animal lover, which is why I asked her to join me on today's adventure.

"Why are you laughing?"

There's nothing funny about my car. Unless you think an electric car is ridiculous. But it's not like I have a choice since my brother is the CEO of an environmental engineering company.

"You're picking up a puppy in this car?"

I growl at the reminder of the stupid dare I made with Archer. No, not Archer. Cedar. I can't believe he lied to me about who he is. If I had known he was Rowan's brother, I would have never spent as many nights in bed with him as I did.

What am I saying? I should have stuck to my one-night-only rule period. This is what happens when I break my rules. I end up adopting a dog and having feelings for a man. A man who can't be trusted.

"I never said I was getting a puppy," I tell her as I drive toward the animal shelter in White Bridge.

"Don't you want a cute little bundle of fur to cuddle?"

I roll my eyes. "Animal freak."

"Ashlyn is super jealous I'm accompanying you today by the way." She rubs her hands together. "I love making my baby sister jealous."

I thought I had it tough growing up with three sisters, but Juniper has four. The oldest is Aspen and then there's Ellery, Lilac, Juniper, and Ashlyn. Ashlyn is married to Rowan, Cedar's brother. Dang it. Why does my every thought end with Cedar? I push him and his deceit out of my mind.

"You don't exactly have to work hard at making Ashlyn jealous. You're engaged to a movie star."

"And she's married to the man of her dreams who also happens to be a former NFL star."

I feign gagging. "You can keep your love and marriage and babies. I know fairytales aren't real."

"Really? I heard you and a certain someone have a thing going on."

"Had. It's over." My stomach clenches in protest, but I ignore it. I'm not built for relationships.

"Maybe if we weren't on the way to the shelter to adopt a dog because you and Cedar made some weird dare/bet thing, I'd believe you."

"I don't know what you're referring to." I can act prim and proper when the situation demands it.

"Ha!" She barks out a laugh. "You're hilarious, but I'll drop the subject."

My hands loosen on the steering wheel. "Thank you."

"Did you put in your bet about Elizabeth and River yet?"

I guess 'dropping the subject' doesn't mean not discussing love. "Why? They're together now."

This time it's going to stick, too. River declared his love for my sister in front of half the town. If he tries to run away again, the gossip gals will chase after him with pitchforks until he changes his mind. I'll be joining them.

"The bets are open on when River will pop the question."

"Is there something in the water in Winter Falls? Every time I turn around, someone else is falling in love."

"You make love sound like a bad thing."

"Because it is."

I'm lying. Love isn't bad. Love is glorious. And, despite my grumpy words, I am happy for my sister. The same as I was happy for my other sister, Gabrielle, when she found love. But love isn't for me. I don't deserve it after what I did.

"What kind of dog do you think I should get?" I ask in a blatant attempt to change the topic of conversation.

"Kind of dog? You mean breed? Well, I think…"

She launches into a lecture about dog breeding and how bad it is for the dogs because … I have no idea why. I stopped listening two sentences into the lecture. My mind wanders to

Cedar as it's wont to do. I wonder if he'll manage to stay in town.

"It's here," Juniper points to the left, and I realize my mind drifted off for most of the drive. Good thing this car has a fancy schmancy collision avoidance system.

Juniper winds her arm through mine as we enter the animal shelter. "I love this place."

"Naturally."

"But I'm not allowed to adopt another dog."

I don't get a chance to ask her why before the woman at the desk greets us. "Can I help you?"

"I'm here to adopt a dog." There's a sentence I never expected to speak in my life.

A smile breaks out on the woman's face. "Wonderful. I'm Melanie. I'll be happy to help you expand your family today."

She leads us through a door into the kennels. "Walk around and see if any dog tickles your fancy. If you find one, we can bring them out for a cuddle."

Crap. This is really happening. "Thank you."

Juniper drags me toward the kennels. "What do you think of this big guy?" She motions toward a dog about the size of a horse.

"I live in an apartment," I remind her.

"Good point." She marches on.

"What about this cutie pie?" She's gone from huge to tiny.

I shrug. "He's okay, I guess."

The words are barely out of my mouth before Melanie's there popping open the kennel and retrieving the dog. She sets the furball on the ground in front of me and he immediately latches onto my leg and starts humping me.

I shake my leg, but he holds strong. "Get him off! Get him off!"

"Don't be such a baby. It's natural," Juniper says.

"Natural? A dog humping my leg is natural? What does he think is going to happen? We're going to make human-dog hybrids?"

"It's a girl. Pretty sure she knows no puppies are coming."

"Oh my god! It's a girl? I'm being humped by a girl dog?"

She disentangles the dog from my leg. "Be a good girl, baby," she coos at it.

"Be careful," I warn as I back away. "She'll French kiss you if she gets the chance."

She returns the dog to the kennel. "I think little horn dog only has eyes for you."

"This is a bad idea," I grumble as we continue our search. "Maybe I should let Cedar win this bet. The world won't end if I don't complete the dare. What do...?"

I trail off when I realize I'm talking to air. I search for Juniper and find her kneeling in front of a kennel petting a dog through the bars.

"Who's a good boy?" she murmurs.

"He's too big for me," I tell her.

"Good. Because he's mine."

"I thought you weren't going to adopt a dog today?"

She scrunches his face between her hands. "Have you seen this face? How can you say no to this face?"

Melanie's not stupid. She hurries to let the dog out of the cage. Apparently, the dog isn't stupid either because as soon as he's free, he bounds to Juniper and jumps on her to lick her face.

"Hi, baby boy. Are you excited to go home with your mommy?"

I leave her to her love fest and continue down the hallway between the kennels. This place is beyond sad. Many of the dogs don't bother to look up as I pass by. They've given up on finding their furever home. Poor things.

Stop it, Cassandra. I can't be feeling sorry for these animals, or I'll end up sponsoring the entire shelter. It wouldn't be the first time. It's easy to give away money when you have a bunch of it you didn't earn and don't deserve.

A dog scratches at the cage and I kneel to say hi. He's about the size of a corgi, but he's missing an ear and one of his rear legs. Poor baby.

"She's been here for five months," Melanie says as she squats next to me. "No one wants a three-legged dog."

"Why not?"

She gestures to the rest of the kennels. "Why choose a dog with three legs when there are plenty of four legged dogs?"

"What happened to her?"

"We think she was run over by a car."

"She was living on the street?"

"We believe so. She isn't chipped and she wasn't wearing a collar when she was brought in."

I scratch her behind her remaining ear, and she leans into my hand. She's desperate for a bit of affection.

"I'll take her."

"Are you certain?" I glare at Melanie. "A dog with medical issues won't be cheap."

"You can't put a price on love," Juniper says as she joins us.

I chuckle when I notice her dog now has a collar and is on a leash. She didn't waste any time.

"I'm certain," I tell Melanie. "I want her."

She grins. "Excellent." She opens the kennel, and the dog comes barreling out toward me. Her missing leg doesn't slow her down one bit. She sticks her snout under my hand and begs for pets.

"Demanding little diva, aren't you?" She barks in response as if she can understand me. "It's settled. I hereby name you Diva." She barks and runs circles around me as we make our way back to the reception area to complete the adoption process.

"This is why I laughed when I first saw your car," Juniper explains as I stare at Diva jumping up and down on my leather back seats.

"We need to stop at the pet store anyway. I'll get one of those backseat thingies for dogs."

"Backseat thingies?" She giggles.

"Whatever. Let's go." I switch on the car and drive toward the nearest pet store.

"Oops. I think it's too late for your backseat thingy."

"What do you mean?" I glance into the backseat to discover Diva peeing all over it.

"Crap."

"Not crap. Pee."

This is all Cedar's fault. I should send him the bill to clean the piss out of the leather seats. Dare me, will he? I'll teach him.

Chapter 10

"SHE'S HERE! SHE'S HERE!" Elizabeth exclaims as I enter Beckett and Lilac's house on Friday night.

I pretend to not understand why she's excited. "Why wouldn't I be here?"

"Ha! As if you don't know."

I do. Elizabeth and Gabrielle have been pushing me about who I've been dating since November. No matter how many times I explained to them I don't date – I love 'em and leave 'em – they persisted.

Of course, me letting it slip how I'd been with the same man more than once didn't help with the situation. And after getting caught having a knockdown fight with Cedar, I have no chance of stopping the barrage of questions now.

River arrives and wraps an arm around Elizabeth. "Let her be, Bessie. You didn't enjoy it when she teased you when we were having issues."

"But did she stop? Nope. She kept banging on and on about it."

"Banging?" He grins.

She elbows him. "You know what I mean."

When he whirls her around and sticks his tongue down her throat, I'm outta here. I have no interest in watching my sister make out with her man. Yuck! I enter the living room where Gabrielle and River and Lilac and Beckett are waiting for my arrival.

"What's that?" Lilac asks while gesturing toward Diva.

"I think you mean who."

"No. Who refers to a person," Lilac corrects. "When referring to a dog—"

I hold up my hand before she can continue. Lilac is Ms. Encyclopedia. I should have known better than to correct her.

"I don't care if it's a who or a what," Beckett grumbles. "She better not make a mess on my carpet."

"She won't," I insist despite having picked up quite a few Diva messes in the past few days.

The shelter claimed she was potty trained when I adopted her. They lied. Unless 'potty trained' means taking a dump in my hiking boots.

"I can't believe you got a dog." Gabrielle drops to her knees to pet Diva who shies away from her. "I won't hurt you baby." She holds out her hand and Diva sniffs at it before lifting her snout in the air.

"Figures you would get a snooty dog," she grumbles as Phoenix helps her to stand.

"She probably smells Pan on you," Phoenix explains.

"The devil goat," I mutter.

"Nice of you to join us," Lilac says when Elizabeth and River return. She's not being sarcastic. Lilac doesn't 'do' sarcastic, which is a shame since sarcasm is my favorite thing in the world.

Elizabeth's hair is a mess, and her cheeks are flushed. Meanwhile, River has lipstick smeared all over his lips.

"The temperature in the entryway must be too warm since someone appears overheated," I tease, and Elizabeth's cheeks darken further. She's a redhead with light skin so getting her to blush is always fun.

"And where's your man this evening?" she asks.

I glare at her, and she smiles. She knows I don't want Beckett to find out about Cedar. Big brother can be a little overprotective. Never mind I'm thirty-three and have been living on my own for over a decade.

When our parents died, Beckett was barely nineteen, but he took on the monumental task of raising his four younger sisters without a blink of an eye. I will be forever grateful to him for ensuring we didn't end up split apart in various foster homes, but he needs to treat us as adults now.

"Cassandra doesn't have a man," Beckett says.

"Yeah, she does." Elizabeth doesn't hold back from selling me out.

"I will get you for this," I mutter to her.

"Payback's a bitch."

Exaggerate much?

"It's not my fault you packed your vibrator in a faulty box." Everyone knows you move your sex toys yourself.

"That's no excuse for playing catch with it."

Beckett groans. "I don't want to hear this shit."

"Sex is perfectly natural," Lilac says.

Beckett ignores her to ask me, "What's this about you having a man?"

"I don't have a man."

He snorts. "You can't lie to me. Do I need to repeat the question?"

"What's for dinner, Lilac?" Gabrielle asks, and I could kiss her for interrupting.

"Eggplant rollatini."

Beckett glares at his fiancée. "Why are you answering Gabrielle?"

"Why wouldn't I answer Gabrielle? She asked a question. It's polite to answer."

"She's trying to distract you from whatever's going on with Cassandra."

Lilac frowns, but she's not stupid. She knows exactly what Gabrielle was doing.

"Don't you have anything to say for yourself?" Beckett prods when Lilac doesn't respond.

"I should check on dinner." She tries to flee, but he grasps her hand to stop her.

"What's going on?" he asks the room. "And don't lie and say nothing. When my fiancée gets involved, I know it's something."

"I'm not involved," Lilac immediately says.

"You're not trying to distract me?"

She purses her lips but she doesn't speak. She hates to lie. In fact, she won't unless you ask her to in advance.

"It's fine, Lilac. I don't want you to be in trouble." I let her off the hook.

Beckett's going to find out about the whole Archer Cedar debacle at some point. It might as well be now when I can control his response.

"I'm not in trouble. I'm never in trouble. I'm a model citizen, a model employee, a model fiancée," Lilac claims.

Beckett chuckles. "Now, I know the lot of you are hiding something."

Elizabeth raises her hand. "Can I tell, please?"

I roll my eyes at her. She's way too excited about this.

"Cassandra has a boyfriend," she blurts out.

"Bessie," River chides from beside her.

"What? She does."

I don't, but I keep my mouth shut. I don't have boyfriends. Boyfriends can lead to feelings and emotions and eventually to love, and I don't do love.

"Aren't you supposed to be united with your sisters against the world?" River asks.

"Sisters above misters only applies to the outside world. Within the family, it's a free for all. You have two brothers. You should know this."

"He knows," Phoenix says. Which is appropriate since he's River's little brother.

The other brother is Lyric, the Chief of Police in Winter Falls. He's married to Aspen who is Lilac's oldest sister. We're just one big happy complicated and confusing family. And everyone's in love. Gag.

"Can we cut the bullshit now?" Beckett growls. "Who is this man? Why haven't I met him? Where is he?"

I cross my arms over my chest and stare at him. Since he's four inches taller than me, he's not intimidated. Dang it.

He sighs. "At least tell me he's not in prison for carjacking."

I huff. One time. One time I hooked up with a guy from a bar. How was I to know the car he was driving was stolen? Does Beckett expect me to ask a guy for his license and registration before hooking up?

"Or absent without leave from the Army," he continues.

Also, not my fault. He was a sexy guy in a uniform. How was I to know he didn't have permission to leave the base? Although, I figured it out pretty quick when the military police knocked on the hotel room door.

"Or in the country illegally."

I roll my eyes. "His tourist visa was expired. Big deal."

It was a big deal when ICE showed up. Those people don't mess around.

"Do I need to get the bail money ready?"

I throw daggers out of my eyes at him. "You have never bailed me out."

Elizabeth raises her hand. "I have."

River pushes her hand away from his face. "Maybe not smack me in the face next time, klutzy girl."

"It's not my fault your face walked into my hand."

Elizabeth is full of shit. She's a total klutz. I can't believe people let her near them with scissors, but they do. Based on how busy her spa is, multitudes of people let her cut their hair.

"It's Cedar," Lilac says.

"So much for sisters before misters," I mutter.

"You'd avoid answering the question all night. I'm hungry and the casserole's ready."

"Cedar? Who's Cedar? The name sounds familiar, but I can't place him."

"He's Rowan's brother."

"Why don't you give Beckett his resume while you're at it?" I ask Lilac.

"Okay. Cedar is—"

I hold up my hand. "I was being sarcastic."

"Oh," she says but her eyes are sparkling. She knew what I was doing.

"Why does everyone know about Cedar except me?" Beckett asks.

"If you had been on time for the grand opening of *Glitter N Bliss,* you would have known," Elizabeth says.

"I told you I'm sorry. And I bought you those roses."

Lilac sighs. "You should know better than to buy cut flowers."

"Oh my god! Enough!" I throw my arms in the air. "Cedar and I are friends."

Elizabeth snorts. "Friends with benefits."

I ignore her. "He's not my suitor, he's not my boyfriend, he's not my man. We played around some, but it's over now. Since he's a big fat liar."

Beckett's nostrils flare. "Played around some? He played with you?"

"Yes. And I played with him. It was mutually beneficial."

"I'm going to kill him."

"I'm a grown ass woman. You can't threaten to kill a man because we had sex."

"Chill it with the s-e-x talk," Elizabeth whispers. "You're making things worse."

"No. I will not chill it. It's about time big brother realizes his sisters are adults and do adult things such as have sex. Hell, Gabrielle's trying to get pregnant."

Gabrielle drops her chin until her blonde hair forms a curtain over her face. Phoenix circles his arms around her waist and draws her near. Crap. I'll apologize for embarrassing her later. Maybe. It's not as if Beckett doesn't know she's trying to have a baby.

Diva buts her head against my leg. She's trembling and her eyes practically swallow her face. I pick her up and cuddle her.

"Nothing's wrong, baby." Although she did give me the perfect excuse to leave. "I'm going. I don't want Diva upset."

"But…"

I walk away before I can hear the rest of whatever Beckett is going to say. I'm not interested.

Did I screw up with Cedar? Yes, I did. But not because we had sex. I never regret having sex. Except for the time

ICE broke down the hotel room door. Being handcuffed while naked is zero fun when your hotel room is being searched by government officials.

What I regret is getting involved with Cedar in the first place. I should have walked away after the first night. I shouldn't have followed some weird old man's order to travel north. And I definitely should have kept on moving when I noticed Cedar chopping wood outside his house.

I blame the stupid sexy shoulder muscles for hypnotizing me.

Chapter 11

Never back down from a fight with an overprotective brother ~ Cedar's rules for surviving life

CEDAR

I hear someone tromping through the woods toward my house and sigh. I knew the residents of Winter Falls wouldn't leave me alone now that I've made an 'official' appearance in town. They know I enjoy my peace and quiet but apparently, they no longer care if they disturb me.

I slip my feet into my boots and don my jacket before going outside. I don't usually allow people in my house. Cassie being the exception. Damn, I miss the crazy girl. She hasn't responded to my calls or texts since she learned I'm Rowan's brother. The woman holds a mean grudge.

I stand on my porch and wait for the intruder to arrive. I frown when an unfamiliar man marches into the clearing in front of my house. Who is he and what is he doing here?

One thing's for certain. He can't be from around here. No one who grew up in Winter Falls would tromp through the woods as loudly as he did. We learn from an early age how to visit nature without disturbing it.

"Who are you?"

"I'm the man who's going to kick your ass."

Kick my ass? Definitely not from Winter Falls. Violence is not tolerated in this town. I'm surprised the high school is allowed to have a football team.

"Do you own this land?" I checked before I parked my house here and, according to the county records, the town still owns this land. But maybe there was a mistake in the deeds.

"I don't own the land."

"I'm confused. Why do you want to beat me up if this isn't your land?"

His hands fist and his nostrils flare. "Because Cassandra is my sister."

"You're Beckett?"

He appears confused. "Cassandra told you about me?"

"You're her brother. Of course, she told me about you. Why? Is it a secret she's your sister? Is she the product of an extramarital affair?"

That would explain why she's skittish about relationships.

"Don't be an idiot. She's one-hundred percent my sister."

"Then, why wouldn't she tell me about you?"

"Are you two done yet?" Rowan hollers as he approaches from the path from the south.

"Bringing in back-up? Guess you're afraid you can't handle me on your own," Beckett taunts.

"When did I have the chance to phone Rowan? You literally showed up on my doorstep two minutes ago. I have no idea why he's here."

"Lilac messaged me," Rowan says. "She ordered me to quote 'make sure my brother doesn't harm her fiancé too much'."

At Rowan's explanation, Beckett spins around to confront him. "You stay out of this."

Rowan raises his hands and backs away a few steps. "I'm here strictly as an observer." He checks his watch. "Speaking of which, can we hurry this along? Ashlyn's home alone with the baby."

"You don't trust your wife with your baby?" Beckett asks.

Rowan blows out a puff of air. "I trust her with our baby. I don't trust her not to throw a rave while I'm away."

"She'd throw a rave with a baby in the house?"

"It's Ashlyn. She'd have a concert in the living room while the baby's sleeping on her chest."

I chuckle. "Maybe buying her a recording studio wasn't the best idea you've had."

Rowan renovated the old building next to the brewery to create *Bertie's Recording Studio* for Ashlyn. In addition to recording the audiobooks she narrates there, she rents out the studios to all kinds of musical performers.

"My dream girl can have whatever she wants."

I want what they have. The thought nearly knocks me on my ass. I've never wanted a woman to call my own before. Meeting Cassandra has changed everything.

"Are you done with the brotherly bonding now?" Beckett's question forces my thoughts away from Cassandra and back to the situation at hand.

Rowan motions toward Beckett. "Go ahead."

"Go ahead? You want him to beat me up for no reason?"

"My beat down is not without reason," Beckett claims.

I cross my arms over my chest. "What's this supposed reason?"

"You used my sister."

"I didn't use Cassandra. We're friends."

"Friends with benefits," he sneers. "Every man knows friends with benefits is a convenient way to have sex without commitment while waiting for the 'one' to show up."

He's wrong. I'm not waiting for the 'one' to show up. In fact, I've always thought marriage and kids weren't for me since I can't settle down in one place. But since Cassie burst into my life, everything's turned upside down.

I step down from my porch into the clearing. "I don't want to fight you."

"Aha! You admit you used my sister."

"I'm not admitting to shit, but I can recognize crazy when I see it and you're not willing to listen to reason at the moment."

"I'm not crazy. I'm pissed. I raised Cassandra and her sisters after our parents died. I'm responsible for her."

"She's thirty-three years old. You're not responsible for her any longer."

He snorts. "You obviously don't have children. You remain responsible for them until you die. There are no off days."

"Tell me about it," Rowan mumbles. "I haven't had a full night's sleep in what feels like years. And then there's the spit-up and poopy diapers. I don't know what Ashlyn's milk contains but those diapers are rancid. I have never seen anything similar to it in my life and I used to play pro ball with a bunch of pranksters."

"They graduate from poopy diapers to teething to repeating every word you say. Just when you think you have it all figured out, boom! Puberty hits."

"I'm fucked. Ashlyn had to give me a daughter. Considering how gorgeous her mother is, Patience is bound to be a beauty. I'm going to spend her teenage years chasing boys away." Rowan buries his face in his hands.

I bark out a laugh. "Aren't you glad Ashlyn was on a mission to give you a child now?"

And make no doubt about it. The woman was on a mission. The second Rowan admitted he loved her, she threw away his condoms and her pills and it was on like bang-a-con.

"It's worth it, brother. Every second of noxious diapers is worth it." Judging by the stars in his eyes, he believes his words.

I wonder if he's right. Is settling down with a woman worth giving up my wandering ways? My gut hasn't urged me to get moving since I parked my tiny home in this clearing. Not even a bit of gurgling and it's been months already.

"You should settle down in one place. Give yourself a chance to have a woman," Rowan says and Beckett growls.

I shake my head at my big brother. "You had to mention I'm a wanderer."

"A wanderer? Is that what we're calling a hobo these days?"

"Hobo? How old are you, old man?"

"However you name it, it's all the same. You can't stay in one place, which means you're using Cassandra."

And we're back to square one again.

"I am not using Cassandra. Do you want me to speak louder so you can hear me, old man?"

I don't know why I'm goading him. Maybe I am feeling a bit guilty about my relationship with Cassandra. Not about having sex with her. I did nothing wrong there.

But I did lie to her. I thought omitting the truth was a white lie. I was wrong. Too bad I didn't figure out how wrong I was until the grand opening of her sister's spa.

I should have told her the truth earlier, but I knew she'd ghost me if I did. The woman is terrified of commitment. And it's not only the sex I was afraid of losing. We're friends. I enjoy her company. She's funny if a bit on the crazy side.

"I'm done talking. It's time to fight." Beckett raises his fists.

"Winter Falls doesn't believe in violence."

I know I can take him. We're the same height but I've got twenty pounds of muscle on him. Not to mention I've spent some time in seedy areas where being able to defend myself was a necessity. But I don't want to fight him.

"We're not in Winter Falls now."

"Technically, we are. This land is owned by the town."

Beckett cocks an eyebrow in question at Rowan who nods. "It's true. The town owns hundreds of acres of nature surrounding the town."

"Why?"

"How else can they build a wind farm and biomass power plant to provide the town with electricity?"

"Makes sense. But it doesn't matter. No one from town is here."

Rowan raises his hand. "Am I a ghost? I'm pretty sure I'm from town."

"Technically, I'm from Winter Falls, too," I add because I can't stop myself from goading him. I blame Cassandra for mentioning how overprotective her brother is and how he stifles her.

"Are you trying to piss me off?"

I shrug. A shrug is not an admission of guilt according to Cassie. Damn. Why can't I stop thinking about her?

"Can you get on with it?" Rowan asks. "Ashlyn. Baby. Rave."

I smile at him. I'm happy for him. And Ashlyn is perfect for him. When I said I didn't think I'd return to Winter Falls for their wedding, she bought plane tickets for Vegas and I met them there. No one knows I witnessed their wedding, though. Ashlyn's mom would lose her ever-loving mind if she found out I was there.

"No one will be fighting today," Cassandra declares as she stomps into the clearing.

"Thank goodness. Nice seeing you, bro. I gotta get home," Rowan says and hurries off before I can respond.

Chapter 12

Never allow yourself to have what you want if what you want could lead to emotions or feelings or other squishy stuff ~ Cassie's rules for surviving this thing called life

YOU NEED TO GO *to Cedar's house.*

Why?

When Lilac doesn't respond, I phone her. She doesn't pick up. Of course not. She probably doesn't want to lie about whatever's happening at Cedar's house.

Cedar's a big boy. He can take care of himself. But what if he's hurt? What if there's a fire? I clench my chest. I can't abandon him if he's in danger no matter how big of a liar he is.

I sprint to my car and break all the speeding laws as I race to Cedar's house. I notice Beckett's car parked next to Cedar's truck when I arrive. Uh oh. Beckett's presence can only mean one thing. Big Brother Protector has emerged from his winter slumber.

I run down the path until I enter the clearing where Cedar's tiny house is parked. Rowan, Cedar, and Beckett are all standing there staring each other down. Good news. No one is bleeding.

"Can you get on with it?" Rowan asks.

"No one will be fighting today," I declare.

"Thank goodness. Nice seeing you, bro. I gotta get home." Rowan winks at me as he hurries off.

I cross my arms over my chest and glare at Beckett.

"What?" He throws his arms in the air. "I didn't hit him."

"Because I arrived in time to stop you."

His eyes narrow. "How did you manage to arrive on time?"

"Lilac."

He sighs. "I love the woman to the moon and back, but she needs to stop interfering when it comes to me raising you girls."

"*You* raising us *girls*?" I screech.

"Have I not raised you and your sisters since Mom and Dad died?"

"Raised. Past tense. We're grown now. We don't need you." He flinches, and I backtrack. "We don't need you to protect us. We'll always need our big brother."

Except Olivia. The only thing she needs is a swift kick up the ass. My foot is ready and waiting.

"I need to protect you. Dad's not here to do it."

My stomach clenches at his words. I know Dad's not here. Mom either. There's been a hole in my heart since the moment I found out they were gone. And it will never be filled. Not by booze or drugs or one-night stands. Trust me. I've tried them all.

I grasp his hands. "I'm going to tell you what I wish I could tell Dad at this moment. You need to let me and my sisters make our own mistakes."

"I can't stand it when you get hurt. It hurts me, too."

I squeeze his hands. "And I love you for that. I do, but it doesn't change things. You need to let us be the adults you raised us to be."

He smirks. "I did do a fantastic job raising the lot of you heathens."

I shove his shoulder. "Don't get cocky. Did you forget about Olivia?"

His shoulders hunch. Fuck. Why did I mention the sister who should not be named? We all pretend she doesn't exist, although I know Beckett wires her money and Elizabeth sends her postcards for all the holidays. Elizabeth's a sucker for family.

Moving on. I motion between Beckett and Cedar. "Are we done with this now?"

"I'm done," Cedar says.

I glare at him. "I wasn't asking you."

"Duly noted."

"Well?" I raise my eyebrows at Beckett. "Done?"

"I guess."

"And not just for today. No matter what does or does not happen between me and Cedar, you will not be returning here to 'give him a lesson with your fists'."

"I would never say something as dorky as 'give him a lesson with my fists'."

True. My brother is a Class A grump but he's not a dork. He's also avoiding the question.

"You didn't answer."

"Sorry, Cassie. I can't promise to never defend you again. What if Cedar hits you?"

Cedar growls, but I hold up my hand. I got this.

"Then, his dumbass will be in jail with a split lip and a boot imprint on his ass."

"I would never hit her," Cedar adds because he apparently can't follow direction. Good to know.

"And I never thought Gabrielle would be emotionally abused," he replies.

Crap. He feels responsible for what happened to our baby sister. I wrap my arms around him and hug him up tight.

"It wasn't your fault."

"I should have known."

"We all should have known. We didn't. Gabrielle can be sneaky when she wants to be."

He releases me. "I thought you were the sneaky one. Those poor trellises on our house in Saint Louis never recovered."

"I never did like those clematises. They smell of almonds. Who wants a flower to smell of almonds?"

"Mom hated them, too."

"But Dad bought the bushes for her, and she couldn't get rid of them."

"He had no idea how much she hated them."

"She loved him. She didn't want to tell him."

He cups my cheek. "I want you to find the kind of love they had. None of this one-night-only bull crap. You're worth more than one night."

I lock my body to stop myself from flinching at his words. I am not worth more. But I'm also never ever telling him why I'm not. It's my secret to carry with me until my grave.

"I agree with Beckett," Cedar says.

"You're not part of this conversation."

"Really? Why is this conversation happening in my front yard if I'm not part of it?"

"This isn't your front yard. This isn't your anything. You don't own this land."

"No one should own land."

Beckett sighs. "You remind me of Lilac."

"How is Lilac by the way?"

"You know my fiancée?"

"Of course. We were in the same grade in school."

Beckett narrows his eyes on Cedar. "You didn't date her, did you?"

Cedar snorts. "Of course not."

"Why not? She's gorgeous and smart."

"I agree she's gorgeous. She's also too smart for me."

"Bullshit," I mutter. "Everyone is equal. No one's too smart for another person. Or too pretty. Or too rich. You should date whoever you want."

"Except Lilac. He shouldn't date my fiancée."

I roll my eyes at Beckett. "I guess you can be a dork after all."

"Drawing boundaries does not make me a dork."

"If Cedar had wanted Lilac, he could have dated her in high school."

"Let me make it clear," Cedar interrupts. "I never dated Lilac or any of the other West sisters."

"Really?" My nose wrinkles. "All of the West daughters are gorgeous. And funny and smart."

"Have you not met their mom?"

"Yeah. Ruby's cool."

"She also handed out condoms to any boys who dated her daughters."

I giggle. "She gave my sister a box at Patience's Sip N See Party. My sister's face turned the color of an overripe tomato. It was hilarious."

"It's not as hilarious when you're a pimple-faced fifteen-year-old who has Mrs. West for English class the next day."

"Isn't Ruby the principal?"

"She is now. When I was in school, she was the English teacher. An English teacher who didn't shy away from literature with explicit sex scenes." He shivers.

"I'll get a list from you later," I tell him before focusing on Beckett. "Are we good?"

He ruffles my hair. "Always." He leans down to kiss my cheek. "Be good."

I smirk. "But being good is boring."

"You're going to be the death of me," he mutters before pointing a finger at Cedar. "I've got my eye on you." Cedar salutes in response.

Beckett marches toward the car park and I start to follow him, but Cedar grasps my elbow to stop me.

"Can we talk?"

"Can we? Yes. Will we? No."

"We need to talk."

"I thought my not answering your texts or picking up your calls would clue you in. I don't want to talk."

The man is a filthy liar.

"I miss my friend."

I snort. "You miss your benefits."

"Miss giving you naked pleasure? Damn straight. I'd be an idiot not to, but I miss hanging out with you, too, princess."

My anger ignites at him for using the pet name he gave me. "Oh no, you don't! You don't get to call me princess. Not after you lied to me for months. Months!"

"If you'd let me explain—"

"Explain? Did you forget Rowan is your brother? Did you have some kind of accident and lose all your memories of growing up in Winter Falls? Maybe you were undercover for the DEA because they think Winter Falls is one gigantic meth lab. Do any of these scenarios apply?"

"No."

"Then, I guess there's nothing to explain. You're a filthy liar."

With my parting shot voiced, I'm out of here.

"Prin— Cassie! Wait."

I ignore him and march to the pathway and toward my car. I don't tolerate liars.

My heart clenches and I rub my chest. Maybe he has a reason for not telling me about his brother. Nope. I can't entertain any options. I'm already too attached to Cedar as it is. Attachments lead to love, which is a no go for me.

Chapter 13

"GOOD THING I EXTENDED the lease on this apartment," Elizabeth says as she sets a box down in my new place.

After the last time I nearly fell asleep driving home from an evening shift at *Electric Vibes,* I decided it was time to move to Winter Falls. After all, I can't depend on Cedar, the big fat liar pants, to drive me home anymore.

Plus, I've pretty much decided to buy the bar. There's no sense living out of town when I'm working in Winter Falls. Sure, I could try to protect my privacy by continuing to live in White Bridge, but it'd be a useless endeavor since the gossip gals don't hesitate to meddle in my life when I'm at the bar.

My new apartment isn't a new location since I'm taking over the lease at Elizabeth's former apartment. Or should I say Gabrielle's former apartment since she lived here first?

"I wonder how many more sisters I'm going to move into this apartment?" Gabrielle mimics the complaint I made when we were moving Elizabeth in.

"Technically, she's not moving a sister in. She's moving herself in," Elizabeth points out.

"Except we're doing all the work. She hasn't lifted a finger."

"Hey!" I interrupt them. "I'm supervising."

"Do you even know what supervising means?" Elizabeth asks.

"Yeah. It's me ordering you to get your butt going." I motion toward the kitchen.

"I don't take orders from you, Cassie the crazy."

I growl as I march toward Elizabeth, but Gabrielle rushes to stand in between us. "No. Can't you two be in the same room without bickering for ten minutes?"

Elizabeth smirks. "I'll set my watch. Let's time how long Cassandra can keep her mouth shut. Usually, she only stops talking when she's got her mouth full."

"My mouth full?"

"You know because you're enjoying what you're eating…"
She cuts herself off when I burst into laughter.

Her face flames as she glares at me. "I didn't mean oral sex. You're misunderstanding me on purpose."

I am. I smirk and she grunts before twirling around and marching down the hallway. "I'll empty the boxes in the bedroom."

I know exactly what she's up to – the little snoop – but I give her a few minutes to enjoy herself before following. She's squirming underneath the bed when I enter the room. What is she expecting to find under there?

Beckett and River placed the bed there less than an hour ago. Does she think I slunk in here to hide all my sex toys under the mattress in the meantime? And doesn't she know sex toys should be easily accessible?

"If you're looking for my vibrator, you can stop what you're doing now."

"What?" She squeals before there's a thud.

"Elizabeth?"

No response. I kneel down and peek under my bed. "Elizabeth?" I repeat.

Again, she doesn't respond. Crap. She's out cold.

"River!"

"I'm kind of busy in here," he huffs.

I sprint down the hallway to the living room where he's carrying the sofa inside with Beckett's help. "You need to come quick. Elizabeth's hurt."

He drops the sofa and Beckett howls. "My foot!"

River ignores my brother and races to the bedroom. I'm hot on his heels.

"Why is she laying under the bed?" he asks as he drops to his knees. "Bessie?"

When she doesn't answer, he crawls under the bed. "Her head is bleeding. What happened?"

How to explain? "I'm not certain." It's not a lie since, technically speaking, I don't know why she was under the bed.

"We need to get her out of here."

"You shouldn't move someone with a head injury."

"Are you fucking kidding me right now?"

"Fine. Whatever. What do you want me to do?"

"Pull her out by her legs while I keep her head and neck steady."

I lift her feet. "Ready?" At his grunt, I drag Elizabeth out from under the bed.

"Damnit. I'm never going to get my deposit back," I grumble when I notice she's dripping blood all over the carpet.

"What happened?" Gabrielle asks when she enters the room and notices me on the floor with Elizabeth.

"Klutzy girl strikes again."

"Is she okay?"

Elizabeth moans as she regains awareness. "Where am I?"

"I think we should take her to the hospital to get checked out. She hit her head and lost consciousness for a while."

"Good idea," River agrees.

Gabrielle presses a towel in my hand and I place it on Elizabeth's forehead.

"I'm bleeding." Elizabeth licks her lips and gags. "Blood. Gross."

"I'm surprised you're not used to it."

She sticks her tongue out at me but the action causes her to cringe. "Ow. My head hurts."

"Which is why we're going to the hospital. Or we will be going once River crawls out from under the bed."

"About that." River clears his throat. "I'm kind of stuck."

"Get Beckett and Phoenix," I order Gabrielle and she hurries off.

She returns seconds later with Beckett hobbling behind her. Lilac trails after them.

"What happened to you?" I ask him.

"River dropped your couch on my foot. I think it's broken."

"I didn't do it on purpose," River shouts from under the bed.

"Why is River underneath the bed?"

"He's stuck."

"How did …" He cuts himself off. "Never mind. I don't want to know."

"Do your arms work?" I ask and he nods. "Can you lift the bed?"

"Yeah, asshat," River yells. "My woman is bleeding and needs to get to the hospital. Maybe a little less talking and a little more action."

Beckett limps to the bed and lifts the frame, except nothing happens. He grunts and tries again. His face turns red and sweat pops out on his forehead. "A little help."

Lilac grasps the other end of the bed. "Not you. Where's Phoenix?"

Lilac blows out a breath of air. "Are you saying a woman is not as capable as a man in performing manual tasks?"

"I don't want you to hurt yourself."

"Because I'm of the weaker sex and I should stay home and knit all day?"

"Don't be silly. You don't know how to knit."

"Hello!" River hollers. "Maybe you could have an argument about women's rights when I'm not stuck under the bed while Elizabeth is hurt."

"I'm fine," Elizabeth says. "I don't need a doctor."

"I'll be the judge of your condition."

"How are you going to judge anything when you're stuck under the bed?"

Phoenix enters the room, takes one look around, and marches to the bed to lift it up. River scurries out and rushes to Elizabeth.

"Bessie, can you hear me, Bessie?" He lifts up the towel and his face blanches when he notices the amount of blood.

She swats her hand at him. "Of course, I can hear you. You're in my face."

"We're going to the hospital."

"I don't need the hospital."

Beckett grunts. "I do."

I glance over at him. He's now sitting on the bed with his shoe off. His foot is swollen and bruising is already visible.

I stand and clap my hands. "Let's go. River and Elizabeth you're with me."

River lifts Elizabeth up into his arms and cradles her near as he walks to the door.

"Lilac, I assume you'll drive Beckett?"

"If the little woman is allowed to drive," she grumbles before helping her fiancé to his feet.

The front door opens before we reach it.

"Yoo-hoo!" Sage greets as she strolls into my apartment with the rest of the gossip gals trailing after her. Without an invitation, mind you. Note to self – always lock my doors when I'm home.

"There's no time for your infernal matchmaking."

When Gabrielle moved to Winter Falls, the gossip gals showed up on moving day with a list of possible matches. Then, when Elizabeth took over the apartment, they actually had profiles of her potential matches added to her welcome basket. They think it's my turn now. They couldn't be more wrong.

I am destined to die alone. Well, not completely alone. I have my Diva now. I miss the little rascal, but I left her with Juniper for the day because I didn't want her getting hurt with everyone rushing around carrying boxes and furniture. Considering we're on our way to the hospital, I made the correct decision.

"Besides, I don't need you to match me."

Feather smiles from behind Sage. "We know. You're with Cedar."

"I am not with Cedar. He's a liar."

"Is he?" Clove asks. "Did he lie to you?"

"Duh. He told me his name is Archer."

"His name is Archer," Petal says.

I roll my eyes. "You know what I mean. He didn't tell me his brother is Rowan and he neglected to mention how he grew up in Winter Falls."

"An omission of the truth is a lie," Lilac adds.

Crap. If Lilac the literal is agreeing with me, I may need to re-evaluate my thinking. Nope. I'm not doing it. Cedar is a liar. Plain and simple. I can agree with Lilac this one time without the world going up in flames.

Beckett groans. "Can we have this conversation another time? I don't know how long I can stand for."

"What happened?" Sage asks.

"Did your lovemaking become too vigorous?" Petal asks.

"You're done," River announces before pushing his way past the woman and out the door. "I'll be waiting in the car for you to drive us to the hospital," he calls to me.

"The hospital!" Sage springs into action. "I'll phone the emergency room and tell them we have two casualties on the way. Cayenne, you phone Dr. Blue and have him meet us there. Clove, you contact Ever and Radiance and let them know their daughter-in-law is injured. Petal, you can pick them up since they'll probably need a ride to the hospital."

She claps her hands. "Let's go, people. Let's go!"

By the time we arrive at the hospital in White Bridge, we've become a convoy of five cars. I feel bad for the hospital staff. I don't think they're used to people arriving at the emergency room with an entourage.

Once they rush Elizabeth off for an MRI scan and Beckett to get an x-ray on his foot, I collapse in a seat in the waiting room. I thought the worst part about moving day would be cleaning. The hospital is the last place I expected to end up.

Gabrielle sits next to me, and we settle in to wait. "Don't think you're off the hot seat."

"It's not my fault Elizabeth and Beckett were injured."

She elbows me. "I'm not talking about them and you know it."

I do know it. I've been withholding information from my family about why I'm working full-time at *Electric Vibes*. But they're not stupid. They know I've been keeping secrets. But I'm not ready to reveal my big plans for buying the bar.

If I do, Beckett will butt in and throw his knowledge and money around. I don't need his help. I don't want his help. And I don't deserve any family money. Nope. I'm doing this on my own.

I smile when big brother enters the waiting room. Excellent timing. He's in a wheelchair and his foot is in a cast.

"We'll chat later," I lie to Gabrielle before hurrying off. I can hear her sigh all the way across the busy emergency room.

Chapter 14

It's all well and good to be patient, but sometimes you have to force your way in when dealing with the world's most stubborn woman ~ Cedar's rules for getting what he wants in life

CEDAR

Ashlyn opens the door and jumps right in, "I have a beef with you."

I lean over and kiss her cheek. "Hi, Ashlyn. It's lovely to see you. I'm fine, thank you for asking. How are you?"

"I'm annoyed you lied to my sister from a different mister." I had to ask, didn't I?

"Can you at least let my brother in the house before you attack him?" Rowan yells from inside their house.

Ashlyn shackles my wrist and drags me into the house. Or, rather, I allow her to drag me inside. She may be tall at five-eight, but she recently gave birth to my niece, and I've been ordered by my brother to treat her with kid gloves.

"I didn't realize you and Cassandra are friends."

Ashlyn rolls her eyes. "Her brother is in love with my sister and we both live in Winter Falls. Of course, we're friends."

"Cassandra doesn't live in Winter Falls."

"She does now."

"What?" When did this happen? And why didn't she tell me? Maybe because she's not speaking to me because she's still mad at me.

Rowan slaps me on the back. "This is why you need to come into town more often."

"I don't need to know all the gossip."

"You don't want to know Cassandra is living in town?"

I don't respond since, despite what Cassie thinks, I prefer not to lie.

Ashlyn grins. "This is going to be more fun than Project Lothario."

Unfortunately, I know exactly what Project Lothario is. I may be a bit of a hermit who prefers to avoid humans more than he prefers to avoid gossip, but it's impossible not to know how the gossip gals dubbed their quest to match River and Elizabeth Project Lothario.

"The gossip gals better not set their sights on me and Cassandra."

"Why not? What's wrong with Cassandra? You've been playing hide the dragon with her for months."

"Hide the dragon?" I sputter.

Rowan hands me a beer. "Don't encourage her." As if it's my fault he married a crazy woman.

I sip on my beer as I figure out a way to formulate my question.

"There's no need to ask. I'll tell you everything," Ashlyn says and dives in. She explains how Cassandra moved into

Elizabeth's old apartment as she's now working full-time at *Electric Vibes*. Apparently, the move didn't go as planned since she ended up in the emergency room.

I stand. "Is Cassandra okay? Did she get hurt? Why didn't anyone contact me?"

Ashlyn waves away my concern. "She's fine. Elizabeth has a concussion and Beckett broke his foot, but Cassandra wasn't injured."

"What the hell happened? How did Elizabeth get a concussion?"

"You'll have to ask Cassandra." She winks.

"Let me guess. You joined the gossip gals."

She sticks out her bottom lip and pouts. "No, they won't let me. They have a strict age requirement. It's ageism, but Lyric won't let me file a complaint with the police. He said it's a 'civil matter'. As if anything the gossip gals do is civil."

Rowan blows out a breath. "Aren't you busy enough with your audiobook narrating, managing the recording studio, and taking care of our baby?"

"I'm wonder woman. I can do it all."

The baby monitor crackles.

"Patience is probably hungry." Ashlyn grunts as she stands. "Told you I'm Wonder Woman."

"I should probably get going," I say as soon as she's out of hearing range.

Rowan smirks. "Say hi to Cassandra from me."

I don't bother to deny it. He's my big brother. He knows when I'm lying. And I would be lying. I haven't seen Cassie since she stopped Beckett from fighting with me. I know she's still mad, but I don't care. I'm done waiting for her to get over it.

"She's living in Lilac's old apartment," he hollers as I walk out the door.

I check the time. It's nearly five. Cassie won't be at home. She'll be at work.

When I enter *Electric Vibes,* the place is deserted except for Cassandra and Lennon stocking bottles of liquor behind the bar.

"How can I…" Cassie cuts herself off when she realizes it's me. "What do you want?"

I stuff my hands in my pockets. "Can we talk?"

"Is your name still Cedar?"

I sigh. "Yes."

"I'm busy."

Lennon grunts. "You're on break. Use my office."

Cassie throws her towel on the bar and marches toward the hallway. Before I can follow her, Lennon stops me.

"You better treat her right, Cedar."

I hold up my hands. "I never meant to lie to her."

He grunts. "I know what you were doing. Time to come clean."

How could he possibly know?

"I won't hurt her again."

He chuckles. "Yeah, you will. You're human. You'll mess up again."

How reassuring. I nod to him before following Cassie down the hallway to the office. A three-legged dog meets me at the door.

"Who's this?" I kneel down and hold out my hand for the dog to sniff.

"It's my dog. Who else would it be?"

I didn't expect Cassie to follow through on the dare and actually adopt a dog. I should have known better. She doesn't back down from any challenge.

"What's her name?"

"Diva."

"Hi, Diva," I murmur as I scratch behind her ear. She only has the one. "What happened to her?"

"Are you making fun of my dog?"

I glance up at her to find her scowling down at me. "I would never make fun of an animal."

She crosses her arms over her chest. "I can't believe how many people have made nasty remarks about her. It's not her fault a stupid car ran my Diva over."

At the sound of her name, the dog yips and makes her way to Cassandra who picks her up and cuddles her. For someone who never wanted a pet before, she's awful comfortable with the dog in her arms.

"People here in Winter Falls have made fun of her?"

The residents of Winter Falls may be nosy as all get out and forget the word privacy exists in the dictionary, but they are never mean. Bullying is considered a felony here. You learn awful quick in elementary school not to tease your fellow students if you don't want to stay after school and help the janitor.

"No one in town."

"Good. Then, you won't have any problems anymore since you're living in Winter Falls now."

She glares at me. "How do you know?"

I shrug. "Winter Falls."

She sighs. "I don't know if I'll ever adjust to how meddlesome everyone in town is."

"You get used to it."

She raises her eyebrows. "You do? You hid on some land outside of town for months because you're used to it?"

I run a hand through my hair. "Speaking of hiding. I came to apologize."

"You think you can apologize and things will go back to the way they were?"

I wish. "We're friends."

She growls. "Friends don't lie to one another."

I didn't lie. I omitted the truth. There's a difference, but I don't bother trying to explain the distinction to Cassandra. She obviously doesn't agree.

"Can I explain why I didn't tell you I'm Rowan's brother?"

"I don't want to hear it," she growls.

Damn she's stubborn. She's also gorgeous as hell with her green eyes flaming in anger and her luscious pink lips pursed together. I want to reach out and haul her into my arms. Comfort her for all the pain I've caused her, but I know better. She'd probably slap me. I stuff my hands in my pockets instead.

"Friends should listen when one of them is trying to apologize."

"You think you can say 'I'm sorry' and I'll forget all about how you deceived me for months?" She snorts. "Fat chance."

"Can you try and understand things from my viewpoint?"

"No." She checks the clock. "I need to get back to work. The after-work rush will arrive soon, and we're not done stocking the shelves."

"I'll see you later."

"Not if I see you first," she mutters.

I nearly collide with Lennon when I exit the office. He frowns at me. I can't blame him. I'm disappointed in me, too.

I never thought not acknowledging Rowan as my brother would lead to the end of a friendship with a woman with whom I want more than friendship. Friends with benefits is fun, but I want more. I nearly trip on my own two feet when I realize how serious I am about Cassandra.

I haven't been serious about a woman since high school. I need to figure out a way to make my princess forgive me. There has to be a way.

Chapter 15

Always let someone sweat before forgiving him ~ Cassie's rules for living a fun life

I SINK DOWN INTO the chair with Diva in my arms once Cedar leaves. I had to pick her up and hold her before I did something incredibly stupid such as grab hold of Cedar and never let him go. He's a liar. And I won't forget it.

"You disappoint me."

At Lennon's words, I jump in my chair. I didn't realize he was in the office. I get to my feet and place Diva in her dog bed.

"I'm sorry. I should be helping you stock the shelves."

"I don't give a damn about the stock."

My brow wrinkles. "Then, what are you talking about?"

"You and Cedar."

"There is no me and Cedar."

"Why the hell not?"

I narrow my eyes at him. "Are you on the matchmaking committee?"

"Do I resemble an old lady to you?"

I don't dare answer his question. Not when there's a chance one of the real gossip gals is in the bar. I swear they have listening devices planted all over town. How else do they know everyone's secrets?

Usually, I admire sneaky women and jump into join the fun. But how can I join in when I'm the one being targeted?

"You're off tonight."

"What? It's Thursday. It's one of the busiest nights of the week."

"And I managed fine before without you."

"Except you can't pick up a tourist and go home with her if I'm not here."

"If she's worth it, she'll wait until closing."

Notice he didn't deny he's a horndog. He can't. I've watched him pick up too many tourists with a crook of his finger.

"Now, get your ass out of here and go apologize to Cedar."

"Apologize to Cedar? He's the one who owes me an apology."

Although, he did say he was sorry. But saying the words is not enough in my book. I need to know the reason he lied. And it better be a good one.

"And you need to apologize for being bitchy."

I stumble and have to catch the edge of the desk before I face plant on the floor. People in Winter Falls don't call each other names. And I hate being called the b-word. Accuse me of being a hussy? Fine. A bitch? Them's fighting words.

"I'm not a bitch."

"Didn't say you were. I said you were acting bitchy and need to apologize."

Is this really happening? Can someone explain to me why I wanted to live in Winter Falls again? This conversation would have never happened in White Bridge. The owner of the *White Stag* could not have cared less about my private life. Seriously. When I gave him my notice, I tried to explain why I was quitting, but he stopped me and told me those exact words.

"Go before I decide to change my bet."

"Change your bet? What does your bet have to…" I cut myself off. I've learned it's better not to ask questions when people in Winter Falls start talking about bets. Bets are serious business in this town.

I hook Diva up to her leash and wave as I make my way to the exit.

By the time I arrive at Cedar's house thirty minutes later, I'm working up a good mad. How dare Lennon say I'm bitchy? How dare he insist I apologize to Cedar?

"This is some bullshit," I tell Diva as we trudge through the forest to Cedar's place.

"What's bullshit?"

I scream. I'm not alone in the forest. What's out here? Do I want to know? I pick Diva up and race through the forest.

"Stop!"

Not happening. I'm not listening to some scary werewolf telling me to stop. I'm not an idiot. I quicken my pace. It's dark out here. Why didn't I bring a flashlight? I have one in my car.

It wouldn't have been difficult to grab it before I ventured out into the woods. And now I'm going to be eaten by a werewolf.

"Aaaaggh!" I scream as I run as fast as my legs will carry me to the clearing where Cedar's house is parked. "Cedar! Cedar! Come out here and kill the werewolf for me!"

Something grasps my shoulder and twirls me around. I slam my eyes shut and cling to my dog.

"Please don't eat Diva. She's innocent."

"I'm not going to eat your dog."

"I'm sorry. I don't know what werewolves eat."

He chuckles. "Werewolves?"

I open one eye to peek at the speaker. It's Cedar. I slap his shoulder.

"Why didn't you tell me you aren't a werewolf?"

"Because werewolves don't exist."

"Are you certain?" I gesture toward the sky. "It's a full moon. They could be out there at this very moment getting ready to eat us."

"Wolves don't eat humans."

"But werewolves do."

He leads me toward his house. "Let's get you and Diva inside before the imaginary werewolves attack."

While I unlace my boots and shrug out of my coat, Cedar places a bowl of water and food on the ground for Diva.

"What are you feeding her?"

"Dog food. What else?"

"Why do you have dog food?"

"What are you doing here?" he asks instead of answering my question. "I thought after our talk at *Electric Vibes* I wouldn't see you for a while."

"Lennon made me come," I mumble.

"I'm sorry. What did you say?"

I throw my arms in the air. "Lennon made me come. Are you happy now?"

He chuckles. "Happy to have you in my home? Yes. Happy you had to be blackmailed by Lennon to visit me? No."

"He didn't blackmail me."

I collapse on the sofa and Diva whines and claws at my feet until I pick her up and set her in my lap. The dog has certainly earned her name Diva.

"Are you hungry? I made chili."

I feign indifference but my stomach growls and gives me away. "I could eat."

To Cedar's credit, he doesn't remark on my noisy stomach. He prepares me a bowl and sets it on the coffee table in front of me before lifting Diva from my arms and setting her on his lap so I can eat.

"Outside of Winter Falls, I go by the name Archer."

I motion for him to continue since my mouth is full of spicy goodness.

"Cedar isn't exactly a common name. Combine my unusual name with my resemblance to Rowan and everyone figures out awful quick I'm the brother of a Super Bowl hero."

I chew as I consider his words. "Aren't you proud of him?"

He cringes. Huh. What's the story there? I want to ask, but if I do, I'm opening myself up to him asking all kinds of questions about me. Questions I have zero plans to answer. Ever.

"What I'm trying to say is I didn't mislead you about who I am on purpose. It's natural for me to hide my relation to Rowan."

This is getting serious. My appetite disappears and I place the bowl of chili on the table. "But we were friends for months. You had plenty of time to explain who you were."

"I should have."

I wait but when he doesn't continue, I prod him. "But…"

"But I didn't think it mattered?"

"Didn't think it mattered?" My voice is dangerously close to shrieking. I hate shrieking.

"I didn't expect to stay here as long as I have."

I narrow my eyes as I study him. "You thought you'd be gone before I figured it out."

He glances away. "I guess. I don't know. This is all new territory for me. I've never wanted to stay anywhere for as long as I've been here."

"I'm not buying it."

"Excuse me?"

"I'm not buying it. There's something more."

His grunt tells me I'm right. I cross my arms over my chest and stare at him. I can wait him out all night long.

He sighs. "Would you have believed I wasn't staying in the area if I told you Rowan's my brother?"

I snort. "No."

"And there you have my why."

"You're not making any sense."

He grasps my hands and draws me near. I inhale his firewood scent and nearly forget all about this conversation. I'd rather have him pull me in his arms before melding his lips to mine and—

He pinches my chin until my eyes meet his. "I knew you wouldn't want another night with me if you thought I was staying in the area. And I would have done anything to have one more night with you."

I rear back. "How did you know I don't double dip? We barely knew each other then."

"It wasn't hard to figure out."

"But it's been months. You could have told me in the meantime."

"And look what happened when you found out. You ditched me."

"I ditched you because you lied."

"And I explained why. Can you forgive me? I've missed you. I miss our friendship."

"I don't know," I lie.

I've already forgiven him. He didn't tell me about his connection to Winter Falls because he wanted another night with me. It's hard to be mad when a man admits to how much he wants you.

I should probably tell him I forgive him, but I don't. I don't need him figuring out how attached I am to him. And make no mistake about it, telling a man you forgive him means you care.

But I can't care. Not when I don't deserve love.

Chapter 16

All the fighting is worth it if make up sex is the result ~ Cedar's rules for living his best life

CEDAR

Relief rushes through me. She's forgiven me. She hasn't said the words. Not my Cassandra. She's still afraid to share her feelings with me. Fair enough. I haven't exactly shared mine with her either.

I hold out my hand. "Friends?"

As we shake hands, her gaze zeros in on my lips. I growl.

"If you want to stick to friends only, you need to stop staring at my lips like you're ready to devour me."

She bites her bottom lip and my cock twitches. He wants more than friendship with this woman. As do I, but I'm trying to take things slow.

"Who said anything about sticking to just friends?"

Good enough for me. I use my hold on her hand to haul her to me. I lift her up to place her on my lap, but Diva barks and stops me.

"Crap. I forgot about your dog." I go to pick her up, but Diva snarls at me before jumping from my lap and strutting off to her dog bed.

"Why do you have a dog bed?"

"For Diva."

I keep my answer evasive. She doesn't need to know I rushed to the pet store in White Bridge after I met Diva tonight to pick up all the dog supplies I could think of.

She narrows her eyes on me. "Awful presumptuous of you."

"I prefer the word hopeful."

I wait for her to make the next move. It has to be her. She has to choose to be with me despite knowing I may stay in Winter Falls for longer than the terms of our dare.

She remains still, and I fist my hands before I reach out and drag her into my arms and meld my lips to hers.

"Your eyes are more green than brown now. What are you thinking about?"

I don't hesitate to answer. "Kissing you. Dragging you onto my lap."

Her breath hitches. "And then?"

She wants dirty talk? I can give her dirty talk.

"I'll slip my hands under your shirt to find your breasts."

"Go on," she urges.

"I'll knead them until you're begging me to pinch your nipples the way you love."

Her face flushes and her eyes fall closed. "What next?"

I lean close to whisper in her ear. "I'll rip your shirt off of you and bare your breasts to me."

"And?" she asks between pants for breath.

"I'll bite and nip at the soft skin until you're rubbing up and down my cock to find some relief."

She shifts until her body is pressed against mine. It's close enough to a first move for me. I grasp her around her waist and maneuver her onto my lap until she's straddling me. She grinds down against my hard length and I squeeze her hips to stop her. It's been too long since I've buried myself in her warmth. If she rubs up against me, I'll come before I can get my pants off.

"Why did you stop me?" She pouts.

"I need to slow down before I embarrass myself."

She gazes down at my cock before biting her lip and sneaking a hand in between us.

I shackle her wrist. "Naughty girl."

"You enjoy it when I'm naughty."

Hell, yeah, I do.

I stand with her in my arms. "This party is relocating to my bedroom."

Diva is snoring in her doggy bed when we pass her, but I check to make sure she has food and water in case she wakes. I don't want the little furball interrupting our activities.

I throw Cassandra onto my bed before shutting the door behind me. She giggles as she bounces. When she grabs for the hem of her shirt, I cover her body with mine.

"I remove your clothes."

"Then, get on with it."

"In a rush?"

She rolls her eyes. "Of course, I am. I haven't had sex in weeks."

I usually can go months without sex. My hand does perfectly fine when the urge hits. But not having Cassie in my bed for the past weeks has been torture. Absolute torture.

I bite her bottom lip. "I missed you, too."

She grunts. This woman will never admit to any weakness. Especially not one involving me. I've got my work cut out for me. Good thing I enjoy a challenge.

"Are we going to have sex or are we going to talk all night?" There's no doubt what her choice is when she wraps her legs around my waist and grinds her center against me.

My cock weeps. He wants in her now. He'll have to wait. I have some exploring to do first. It's been too long since my hands felt her smooth skin.

I get to my knees and grasp the bottom of her t-shirt before whipping it off of her. I use the material to tie her hands to my bed. She juts her chest out and rubs her thighs together. My girl loves to be restrained.

I trace the edge of her bra with my index finger and goose-bumps break out over her skin.

"Please."

I feign ignorance. "Please what?"

She glares at me. "You know what I want."

My finger freezes. "Maybe I forgot."

Her legs around my waist tighten and she bucks. "You know exactly what I want. Stop teasing me."

"But teasing you is so much fun."

I don't give her a chance to respond before I yank her bra cup down and suck on her nipple. She groans as her nipple hardens. I nip at it before moving to her other breast. I knead and play with the soft flesh as I bite and nibble on her nipples until she's writhing beneath me.

"I'm going to come."

I sit up and unwind her legs from my waist. "Oh no, you don't. Not without me."

She opens her mouth to complain again but I slam mine against hers. She sighs and I use the opportunity to thrust my tongue into her mouth. Cassie doesn't sit back and let me have control. Not my princess. Her tongue duels for supremacy. I moan and she sucks on my tongue until I grind my cock into her center.

I need to stop before I come in my jeans. The only place I'm coming tonight is in the wet warmth of my princess.

I pull away and she mewls in protest. Her lips are swollen from my kisses, her cheeks are pink from arousal, and her bra is twisted around her waist. She looks like a wanton woman. She's *my* wanton woman.

I unsnap and unzip her jeans before pushing them along with her panties down her legs. She helps me to kick them off. I keep her socks on. I don't have time to deal with those. Next round, I promise myself.

I grab a condom from my dresser before shoving my jeans to my knees and donning it.

"Spread," I demand.

She widens her legs and I crawl forward until my hips are nestled in between her thighs right where I want to be. Where I always want to be.

I slot my cock at her opening. "You ready?"

"Been ready," she grumbles.

"Hold on tight," I say and slam into her. Her walls flutter around me and she arches her back with a moan.

I get to my knees and throw her legs over my shoulders.

"This is going to be quick," I grunt out as I thrust into her.

"Quick?" She gasps as I grind against her clit. "You've been teasing me for hours."

I haven't but I will later on tonight because she's staying in my bed until I've had my fill of her.

I massage her breasts as I thrust into her over and over again. It's not long before I feel her walls tightening.

"Not yet."

"I can't stop this time."

"Fuck." I quicken my pace until the bed is banging against the wall. When I feel the telltale tingling in my spine, I slide my hand between us to find her clit.

"Come now," I demand with a pinch.

She explodes with a scream. "Yes! Cedar!"

I don't have time to appreciate how much I enjoy the sound of her shouting my real name while I'm inside her. I'm too busy coming myself.

"Fuck. Princess."

I continue to thrust in and out of her until our climaxes subside. Spent, I collapse next to her before untying her hands.

She smiles over at me as I rub her wrists. "Friends with benefits is way better than just friends."

We'll be more than friends if I have anything to say about it. But I know better than to clue her in on my plans.

Diva scratches at the door before barking. I debate ignoring her, but she whines and I give in. I stand and rid myself of the condom before donning my jeans.

I open the door and Diva dashes into the room. She claws at the bed next to Cassandra who picks her up and places her on the mattress.

"You don't mind, do you?" She bats her eyelashes at me. She knows full well and good I don't want the dog in the bed.

I grunt in response. I can hardly say the little dog will be in the way when I wake in the middle of the night with a taste for her pussy. Diva looks at me and I swear she smirks.

I had to dare Cassandra to get a dog, didn't I?

Chapter 17

"I CAN'T BELIEVE YOU'RE going into town without being forced," I tell Cedar as we walk toward Main Street where the Imbolc festival is happening.

"I'm kind of being forced. Or did you forget our dare?"

I motion toward Diva. "How could I forget?"

He throws his arm over my shoulders. "But aren't you glad you have her now?"

"What is Imbolc anyway?" I ask because I'm not talking about how the dare ended up with me falling in love with a dog. He's probably figured it out by now anyway.

"Didn't you come to the festival last year?"

"Nope. My first pagan festival was Litha. It was pretty cool. I was crowned empress of Winter Falls for the day."

"Of course, you were." He chuckles. "Imbolc celebrates the start of Spring."

My nose wrinkles as I indicate the snow on the street. "I think Mother Nature didn't get the memo."

"Don't worry. This is Colorado. Tomorrow we'll have sunny skies and a balmy fifty degrees."

"Cassandra Claire Dempsey!" A voice booms as we turn onto Main Street.

I recognize the voice as Forest's. He's the owner of *Unleashed* who thinks the phrase let it all hang out should be taken literally. In other words, he's a nudist. Or a half nudist I guess since he does prefer to wear a shirt.

"What's up, Forest?" I ask when we stop in front of his pet store.

"How could you get a dog and not tell me?" He pouts.

"I wasn't aware of any legal obligation to inform you of my pet choices."

He huffs. "It's common courtesy."

I pick Diva up. "Forest, meet my Diva. Diva, this is Forest."

Forest doesn't hesitate to snatch the dog out of my arms. "Hi, Diva. Do you want a treat?" He walks off with my dog talking to her the entire time.

"Did he just steal my dog?"

"Don't be silly, Cassandra of *Electric Vibes*. I'm getting her a treat and you some poop bags."

He returns with a canvas bag and presses it in my hands. "Don't get caught using those plastic poop bags in town. Lyric won't hesitate to arrest you."

"He can try."

"I can try what?" The man himself says as he joins us.

"To arrest me." I waggle my eyebrows.

"Is anyone dead or dying?"

"Nope."

"Then, I don't want to know. Have a blessed Imbolc."

I wait until the Chief of Police is out of earshot. "And there you have it, folks." I curtsey. "Lyric doesn't want to arrest me."

Cedar bends over to whisper in my ear. "But you enjoy it when I handcuff you."

I feel my face and other parts of me warm at the idea of being handcuffed to his bed. Hopefully naked.

"Cedar! Cassandra! Over here!" Petal hollers before I have a chance to say to hell with this festival.

Cedar grasps my hand and leads me across the street to *Sensual Scents,* the candle business owned by Petal. Although, I don't know how she has time for a store considering she spends most of her time on her gossip gal duties, aka being a busybody.

"Here." She hands me a bag.

I look inside to discover several black, taper candles. Knowing Petal these are not any ordinary candles. Nope. The woman specializes in sex candles of all types – massage candles, wax play candles. You name it, she makes it.

I shut the bag. "Sorry, Petal, but no wax play for me."

"I thought you were the adventurous Dempsey girl?"

"I am. But I don't do anything with flames or fire." I can't contain the shiver at the thought of fire. One close call is enough for me.

"I'll order another beginner bondage set for you."

"I don't need a beginner set." I wink.

Cedar clears his throat and I glance up at him. His cheeks are red.

"Are you embarrassed, Cedar Archer Hansley?"

"I'm not embarrassed, but I don't understand the appeal in letting one of the gossip gals know what you enjoy in the bedroom."

"What's she going to do with this information? Inform the FBI? They may be interested when the name Cassandra Dempsey is mentioned, but I'm pretty sure they're not interested in what happens in my bedroom."

"Why would the FBI be interested in you?"

I wave away his concern. "It was a misunderstanding."

You spend one afternoon – two hours tops – researching how to build a bomb and – boom! – they're all over you. I explained the prank I was planning but those special agents do not have a sense of humor. They must surgically remove their laughter genes when they're recruited.

I don't explain any of this to Cedar, however. The prank is a good one. No need for him to know about it in advance.

"Come on." He grasps my hand and leads me away from Petal's store.

Feather rushes up to us before we can make it very far. "Yeah!" She squeals.

"What are we squealing about?"

"The two of you becoming lovers."

I wag my finger at her. "Nuh-uh. No matchmaking us. We're friends is all."

She waggles her eyebrows. "Friends with benefits."

"Friends first and foremost," I claim although the benefits part is pretty spectacular. In fact, I don't want to know how it feels to give up the benefits. A few weeks without Cedar in my life was enough. Crap. I'm too attached to this man. I should probably get some space from him.

Cedar squeezes my hand as if he can read my mind and knows I want to flee. Not *want to* flee. *Need to* flee.

"Whenever we read a friends with benefits book in book club, the couple end up in love by the end of the story," Feather points out.

I gesture toward the town. "Spoiler alert. This is not a book. This is real life."

I glance up at Cedar for support, but his lips are pursed. My brow wrinkles. What does he have to be unhappy about? He knows we're friends with benefits. He knows I'm not interested in a relationship.

He doesn't know why – no one does – and I'm not about to tell him. It's my shame. No one needs to know about it. Ever.

Sage rushes over to us. "Excellent. Project Hermit is coming along nicely."

"I'm going to repeat myself one more time nice and slow so everyone can understand. I, Cassandra Claire Dempsey, am not interested in your matchmaking schemes. Do. You. Understand?"

At least not those involving me as the victim. Other match-making schemes not concerning me? I'm ready to assist at a moment's notice.

Sage pats my hand. "Of course, dear."

I've had enough of this. I love the gossip gals to bits. They're crazy and I do enjoy crazy. But not when their crazy is directed at me.

"Come on, let's go home."

"You can't go home!" Feather declares. "You haven't tried my new ice cream flavor yet."

Baa!

A goat butts into my leg and I screech.

"Get your devil goat away from me," I yell at Gabrielle.

She rolls her eyes. "She's not the devil."

Diva growls at Pan the goat who tilts her head and stares at the dog. She must decide Diva isn't harmful as she steps closer. Diva does not come to the same conclusion as she barks and growls and paws at the ground. Pan retreats and Diva gives chase.

The goat rushes off into the crowd with my dog hot on her heels.

"Great. Your dog is going to eat my goat," Gabrielle mutters as she rushes after them.

"Have you seen the size of Diva?" I shout as I follow her. "Pan would be enough food for her for a month."

"Not funny," she growls. "Not funny."

I elbow her. "It's a little funny."

We chase the animals until we reach *Bake Me Happy*. The bakery Cedar's brother owns. Pan is standing outside the door bleating at it while Diva is on the other side staring at the goat. I swear she's smirking.

Gabrielle attaches a leash to Pan while I enter the bakery to retrieve my dog who can apparently open doors now.

"This is the cutest dog ever!" Bryan declares.

Bryan works at the bakery with Rowan. He's also the most over the top person who lives in Winter Falls, which is saying at lot. This is Winter Falls after all.

He picks Diva up and cuddles her close. "I bet you would look adorable in a pink sweater."

Diva yips as if she agrees with Bryan.

I hold out my arms. "Give her back before she's completely spoiled."

Cedar snorts behind me. "Her name is Diva. She's already spoiled."

I snatch my dog from Bryan and rub my nose against her snout. "I don't spoil you, do I little girl?"

He laughs as he throws an arm over my shoulders. "I don't suppose you have any of those blondie brownies?"

Bryan sighs as he looks Cedar up and down. "You can't possibly eat brownies and look the way you do."

Rowan steps through the kitchen to the bakery. "I look better than him and I'm a baker."

Bryan moans. "I've had this dream before, but you were both naked and covered in chocolate ganache."

While Cedar chuckles, Rowan growls. Bryan pats his arm. "Don't worry. Your manhood is well represented if you know what I mean."

"I don't want to know."

"I do!" Ashlyn shouts as she enters the bakery with Patience strapped to her chest.

"It starts with us in the bakery—"

Rowan shoves a hand in Bryan's face to cut him off.

Bryan winks at Ashlyn. "I'll tell you later."

"Don't forget about me," I chime in. A dream about Cedar naked and covered in chocolate? Yes, please!

"What's everyone doing hiding out in *Bake Me Happy?*" Ashlyn asks. I don't have a chance to answer before she notices Diva. "Holy hearing aids! Your dog is the cutest thing in the world. Can I hold her?"

I nod toward the baby on her chest. "I think your ride is limited to one baby or dog at a time."

"I'll trade you."

She unwraps the thingamabob keeping Patience glued to her, but before she has the chance to hand me the baby, Rowan sweeps in and steals her away.

"Not my fault. I still have full rights to cuddle your puppy."

I giggle as I hand her Diva. "This town is crazy."

"And totally up your alley, right?" She winks.

I don't deny it. Winter Falls is totally up my alley. I glance over at Cedar from beneath my eyelashes. He's totally up my alley, too. Too bad I can't keep him.

I'm going to be devastated when he leaves. If he leaves. If he doesn't, then I'm going to have to find my lady balls and end things with him. I'm way too attached as it is.

Chapter 18

*Always make sure your family believes you're afraid of clowns.
Trust me on this ~ Cassie's rules for living in close proximity to
her sisters*

I FROWN WHEN I stick my key in the lock and my apartment
door creaks open. I know I locked up when I left for my shift
at the bar. I may live in the tiny town of Winter Falls now, but
I grew up in Saint Louis. I know better than to leave my door
unsecured.

I fist my keys and tiptoe into my apartment. I scan the living
room as I go. Phew. The television is still here. I guess I wasn't
robbed. I notice a light coming from underneath my bathroom
door. Welp. There's only one thing to do.

I snatch the baseball bat from behind the front door – a
souvenir from the bar I worked at in Saint Louis – toe off my
shoes, and creep through the hallway until I'm standing outside
the bathroom. I raise the bat and prepare myself to swing, but
then someone mutters shit balls and I relax.

The door squeaks open, and I step in front of it.

"Police!"

Elizabeth screams and runs away straight toward the wall. She slams into it, her legs give out, and she falls to the floor. I stand over her body sprawled in my hallway.

"Hey, sis."

"Holy crap! You scared the piss out of me. Literally. I think I peed my pants."

I cock my eyebrow. "Think?"

I know she peed her pants. She always does when she's frightened. Ask me how I know. I have stories.

"Whatever." She holds out a hand. "Help me up."

I haul her to her feet.

"What's up?"

"What do you mean?" Elizabeth feigns confusion. "I'm in the middle of pulling off an epic prank."

"Putting a cardboard shark in my bathtub is hardly epic."

"Good thing there's not a cardboard shark in your bathtub."

"Clown in the toilet?" I guess again.

She grunts, which means yes. Convincing my sisters I'm afraid of clowns was the smartest move I could ever make. All of their pranks now involve clowns. They think they're scaring me. They're wrong.

"Beer?" I don't wait for an answer before propping the bat against the wall and making my way to the kitchen.

"Well?" I ask as I hand her the bottle. "What's wrong?"

"Nothing's wrong. I'm getting my revenge."

I chuckle. Elizabeth sucks at revenge. Unmaking my bed. Really?

"Revenge for what?"

"You gave me a concussion."

I tap my chest. "*I* gave you a concussion?"

"Yes. It's your fault."

"It's my fault you're a klutz?"

"I'm not a klutz."

"And I suppose it was my fault you were snooping under my bed."

"Duh." She rolls her eyes. "You were the one who played with my vibrator."

"If playing catch is how you play with your vibrator, we need to have a talk."

Her cheeks darken. "I know how to use a vibrator."

"Do tell."

Her blush darkens until her face is the color of a fire engine. Having a sister who's a redhead is the best thing ever. She can't hide when she's embarrassed, which, of course, means I embarrass her every chance I get.

She clears her throat. "Stop it. I didn't come here to discuss my sex life."

"You didn't? Why did you come over?"

"I told you. To get my revenge."

Time to end this. This back and forth could go on all night. Don't get me wrong. I love to bicker with my sister. But I'm tired. I've been on my feet slinging drinks for ten hours. My feet ache, and I smell of the beer I spilled down my shirt hours ago. I just had to accept a dare to carry five beers, four cocktails, and two orange juices at the same time. I'm lucky the beer got me. Orange juice is sticky.

"You only pull pranks when your personal life is a mess."

Her nose wrinkles. "You can't possibly know that."

I cock an eyebrow. "I can't? I've known you for thirty years."

"I hate how smart you are."

"And I hate how pretty you are."

She snorts. "Someone needs to make an appointment at the eye doctor."

How Elizabeth doesn't realize how pretty she is, is beyond me. Her auburn hair is long and curly. And she has alabaster skin. She refers to her hair as a mop and hates the freckles dotting her skin. She even tried to bleach them when we were teenagers. It might have been my idea. It's my obligation as an older sister to tease my younger siblings and I am more than dedicated to the task.

I plop down on my sofa, and she sits next to me. We sip on our beers in silence. My eyes are falling closed when she finally speaks.

"I'm not pregnant."

I tap her beer bottle with mine. "I would hope not."

She sticks her tongue out at me. "I'm being serious."

"So am I. Drinking while pregnant is bad, but you wouldn't believe the number of pregnant women I've seen in bars ordering a drink."

Her nose wrinkles. "You're kidding."

"Nope. You need to pass a test to get a driver's license but there's no test before you can have children."

Her eyes well. Shit. This *not pregnant* thing is serious. I struggle to think of something comforting to say, but I'm not the comforting sister. Need revenge on the boy who cheated on you? I'm your girl. Need someone to listen while you cry? Better call Gabrielle.

Speaking of our baby sister, "Do you want me to phone Gabrielle?"

I reach for the phone in my pocket, but Elizabeth slaps my wrist. "What's your damage?"

"You can't call her! It's the middle of the night."

"As if there's a time limit on a crisis."

"She's trying to get pregnant. She doesn't want to listen to my sob story."

"Have you met our baby sister? She's going to be pissed you came to me instead of her."

"Pissed? Gabrielle doesn't get mad."

"Did you forget Christmas?"

Gabrielle insisted on holding Christmas at the farmhouse she lives in with Phoenix. She decided she was going to put on the best Christmas ever. She went a little overboard and ended up having a meltdown. It was hilarious. I won twenty bucks for predicting she'd throw the turkey at Phoenix.

"She wasn't mad. She was overwhelmed."

"Are you going to tell me what happened or are we going to analyze our baby sister's personality all night?"

"I was late."

When she doesn't continue, I push her. "And?"

"And I thought I was pregnant. I'm never late. I got super excited about having a baby."

"You've always wanted children."

"Yeah." She smiles and I hold in my cringe. Kids are not for me.

"But you're not pregnant?"

She plays with the label on her beer. "I got my period today."

"I'm sorry." I squeeze her hand. "What did River say?"

"He doesn't know."

"He doesn't know? You're a freaking mess and the man you're living with doesn't know?"

"He was at Rowan's watching the game."

I stand. "Go home. Now."

"You're kicking me out?"

I herd her toward the door. "I'm not kicking you out. I'm ordering you to go home."

"Semantics."

"You need to discuss this with River. He needs to know."

"But he didn't want children until a month ago. What if he thinks I'm trying to trap him?"

I bark out a laugh. "Trap him? He moved you into his house without your knowledge. The man is good and whipped."

She bites her bottom lip. "You don't think he'll be mad?"

"If you don't go tell him what's going on with you, he's going to be mad."

"Okay. Okay. I'm going already."

I open the door and shove her out of it.

"I'm sorry," she hollers before entering the elevator.

I make sure my door is locked before switching off the lights. I rip off my t-shirt and bra and throw them on the floor of the living room as I make my way toward my bedroom. My jeans hit my bedroom floor.

I sigh as I lift my comforter. "Ah, finally."

I crawl into bed, but when I push my legs under the covers, they get stuck. What the hell? I kick at the blankets. But no matter what I do I can't push my legs further under the covers. I must be more tired than I thought if getting into bed is defeating me.

I roll out of bed and switch on the light. I fist my hands at my hips and glare at my bed. It appears perfectly normal, but there must be something wrong. I flip off the comforter to discover someone short sheeted my bed. I burst into laughter. Elizabeth got me.

Chapter 19

I SIGH AS I feel the arm banded around my waist tighten. I wiggle my ass into Cedar's hardness, and he groans, "Princess."

"The things I plan to do to you are definitely not princess-like." I have a whole list of ideas to choose from. None of which scream royal.

"Oh yeah?" His palm scrapes against my skin as it moves from my waist to my breast. He glides the tip of his finger around my nipple, and I moan as I jut my chest forward in invitation.

His other hand sneaks down until he cups me. I've never been so happy to have been too tired to put my panties back on before I fell asleep in my life.

I reach my arm around to thread my fingers through his hair and twist my neck until my mouth meets his. I open for him and he thrusts inside. I immediately capture his tongue and suck on it. I'm rewarded with a pinch of my nipple. *Yes.*

His cock rubs between my ass cheeks and I writhe against him. I'm wet and needy and this party is only getting started. Awesome.

Yip!

I ignore Diva.

Yip!

I yank my lips from Cedar's to yell at my dog. "Not now, needy girl!"

Yip!

Cedar sighs before releasing me and rolling out of bed.

"Where are you going?" I pout.

"To look after your dog."

"She'll calm down eventually."

He chuckles. "Last time she yipped at the door for an hour, but you wouldn't let me open it."

"You were going down on me. Of course, I didn't let you stop. And it wasn't an hour."

His eyes twinkle. "Are you daring me to go down on you for an hour?"

I bite down on my bottom lip and bat my eyelashes. "Maybe?"

"Challenge accepted."

Yip!

"Ignore her," I demand as I spread my legs. His eyes widen as he stares at my center. I snake my hand down my stomach and he growls.

Yip!

This time Diva's yips are accompanied by her scratching on the door. I sigh and close my legs.

Cedar pulls on a pair of sweats before opening the door. My little diva rushes into the room and prances to my side of the bed. I cover myself with a sheet because someone thinks any dangling bits – including boobs – are toys for her to play with before helping her onto the bed. She runs in circles before finding a spot to settle down near my stomach. I scratch her ear.

"Where are you going?" I yell after Cedar when he ducks out of the bedroom. He doesn't respond. "It better be coffee!"

I open my eyes when I smell the delicious scent of coffee wafting toward me. I sit up and Cedar waves a cup underneath my nose.

"I thought this would wake you."

"Coffee now. Teasing later." I snatch the mug from his hands and down most of the scalding liquid.

"How the hell do you guzzle coffee without burning your mouth? Is your esophagus made of asbestos?"

I start to shrug but stop when I notice he's holding a package. A wrapped package.

"What's that?"

"It's a present."

My nose wrinkles and I inch away from him. "A present for what? It's not my birthday today."

He rolls his eyes. "You know what day it is today."

I do, which is why I'm confused.

He offers me the wrapped gift but I'm done inching away. I need out of here. Pronto. I scramble toward the other side of the bed. My boobs jiggle. Damn it. I'm naked and my clothes are on the other side of the room.

"Cassandra," Cedar grumbles.

"What?" I ask as I eye my clothes. Can I grab them and Diva before Cedar gives me the gift? Probably not. He is wicked fast.

I stare at the door as I consider whether I can run through the woods naked. I mean, I can. It's more a question of whether I want to considering all the wild life. Will a skunk attack me if I'm naked? Don't laugh. I'm a city girl. I don't know these things.

"Are you seriously considering running through the woods naked to avoid accepting a gift?"

I glare at him. "How do you know what I'm thinking?"

"Because I know you."

"Oh yeah? What am I thinking now?"

"You're thinking about kicking me in the gonads and ensuring I never have children."

Damn it. How does he know me this well? Am I transparent? Ugh! I knew – knew! – I needed to pull back from this relationship. No, not relationship. Friendship. We are not in a relationship. We're friends. Nothing more. Friends with benefits but still… Friends.

Cedar's done waiting for me. He prowls toward me until he's close enough to grasp my wrist. He hauls me to my feet and shoves the gift into my hands. I try to drop it, but he won't let me.

"What is wrong with you? It's a present, not a nuclear bomb."

"Can they make nuclear bombs this small?"

He cups my chin. "Open your present."

I look down at the wrapped gift in my hands. "We agreed on friends with benefits. Friends don't give each other Valentine's Day presents."

He frowns. "Friends with benefits?"

I poke him in the chest. It feels good, so I do it again. "Don't you dare say you forgot about our arrangement."

He crosses his arms over his chest, and I need all my willpower to keep my eyes focused on his face. His chest should grace the cover of fitness magazines the world over. It's hard but the skin is soft and…. I shut those thoughts down before I tackle him to the floor. It wouldn't be the first time.

"Open it." When I stand there frozen, he leans forward to growl in my face. "I dare you."

Damn it! He knows I can't resist a dare. It's like crack to me. I hear the word 'dare' and my ears perk up and I'm ready to do just about anything.

I rip the wrapping paper off of the box and fling it on the bed. Diva wakes up and pounces on it.

"Don't worry, Diva. I have a present for you, too."

What the hell? He's spoiling my dog as well? Although Cedar spoiling my dog is not a new thing. She's got him wrapped around her little back paw.

He taps the box in my hands. "Did you forget our dare?"

I open the box to discover a gray hooded scarf shawl inside. I can't resist touching the material. It's soft and I know it's warm.

"It's from Aran."

"Aran in Ireland?"

Now that he mentions it, I recognize the cable Aran stitch.

"Yeah. I was in Ireland a while ago and picked this up."

"Hold on. You bought a woman's scarf when you were in Ireland? Did you buy this for some other girlfriend?"

"Girlfriend?" He smirks.

I smack him. "I didn't mean I'm your girlfriend. In fact, this gift is completely inappropriate."

"Inappropriate?"

I ignore him as I'm on a roll now.

"You should save this for when you find a woman you care for to give it to."

"Care for? Do you think I don't care for you?"

"I mean care for as more than a friend."

He cocks his eyebrow. "I think we're more than friends."

Since I hate liars, I try not to be one. Which means it's time to get the hell out of here before I do something completely stupid and irresponsible such as tell him I care for him. Crap on a cracker. I care for him. When did this happen?

How did attached become care? I'm a freaking idiot. I should have never agreed to become friends with benefits with him. Not when I know I can never love him. Actually, I can love him. I'm probably halfway there already, but I don't deserve his love. I don't deserve love. Period.

I need to get the hell out of here.

"I can't accept this." I throw the gift on the bed, startling Diva awake.

"Why not?"

I ignore his question to gather my clothes from the floor. I throw on my sweater without a bra and my jeans without panties. Close enough to dressed for me. It won't be the first time I do the walk of shame without any underwear on.

I gather Diva in my arms and hurry out of the bedroom. My shoulders sag when Cedar doesn't chase me. Do I want him to chase me? No, I don't. I need to make a clean break.

"I'm letting you go, but this isn't over."

My heart warms at his words. *Shut up, heart. No warming allowed.* We don't deserve love, remember?

Chapter 20

If you want to keep secrets, don't move to a small town where being a busybody is celebrated ~ Cassie's rules for surviving this thing called life

"AHA!" ELIZABETH EXCLAIMS AS she enters *Electric Vibes* with Gabrielle.

I sigh. I should have known I couldn't get away with signing the lease for the bar and buying the business from Lennon without my family finding out.

I stand from the table where I was sitting with Daniel West, the town's attorney, to discuss the finalizing of the contracts to confront my sisters.

"Who told?"

"Who told?" Elizabeth shrieks. "Who cares who told?"

"I do."

"Who told is not the issue," she continues her rant. "The issue is you didn't tell us. Your sisters."

"And brother," Beckett adds as he hobbles inside with Lilac.

I point a finger at my brother's fiancée and the daughter of Daniel West. "You are dead to me."

She just moved to the top spot of my 'people to prank' list. Not only did she tattle to my family about my business dealings, but I'm too annoyed now to make fun of Beckett trying to move around on crutches. She's stolen all my fun!

Her brow wrinkles. "Dead to you? It's impossible for me to be dead to you when I am very much alive."

"You know what I meant," I snarl. Sometimes, I hate how literal Lilac is. She's entitled to her own brand of crazy, but I'm entitled to be annoyed to within an inch of my life about it. "Mr. West told you about today."

She rolls her eyes. "No, Dad didn't tell me."

"Hey, baby girl," Mr. West greets her and my stomach churns with jealousy.

I want what Lilac has. A dad who supports me. Who uses a term of endearment when he speaks to me. Who loves me no matter what.

But I can't have it because my parents are gone. And it's all my fault. I force those thoughts out of my mind. I can wallow in my guilt later. I've got a score to settle right now.

"How did you find out if Mr. West didn't tell you?" I demand of Lilac.

"Call me Daniel."

I nod at Lilac's father. "If Daniel didn't tell you, how did you find out?"

She doesn't hesitate to answer. "I'm on the committee, which approves all new business owners on Main Street."

Elizabeth crosses her arms over her chest and taps her foot. "Enough of this. Tell us why you kept this secret from us."

"Yeah," Gabrielle adds. Her cheeks darken – questioning anyone is way outside of her comfort zone – but she powers on. "Why did you keep this secret from us?"

"Who says it's a secret?"

"A secret is information you mean to—"

I thrust my hand in front of Lilac's face. "Everyone here knows the definition of a secret."

She cocks an eyebrow. "They do? Because you seem to be confused."

"Are you seriously being sarcastic with me now?"

Beckett wraps an arm around her waist and draws her near. He kisses her hair. "Proud of you, honey."

Lilac's nose wrinkles. "You're proud of me for being sarcastic? You do know I have a PhD and I'm the CTO of a company?"

He chuckles. "Since I'm the CEO of the same company, I am aware."

The door bangs open and Sage barges in. "Are we too late?"

She's followed by Feather, Clove, Cayenne, and Petal. Oh good. The gang's all here. And that, folks, is how you do sarcasm.

I throw my arms in the air. "Too late for what? What in the world are the gossip gals doing here?"

Elizabeth stomps to me and snaps her fingers in my face. "I don't care why they're here. The horsemen of the Apocalypse could ride into town and I wouldn't give the first flying fudge. I want to know why you hid your intentions about *Electric Vibes* from us." She pounds a fist on her chest. "Your family."

"Ten bucks says Elizabeth cries," Petal hollers.

I switch my attention to the gossip gals. "No one is betting on when my sister cries. Do you understand? No one."

"I knew it!" is Sage's bizarre response.

I can't stop myself from asking. "Knew what?"

"Knew you had a kind heart hidden under all the crazy prickly outer skin."

"Don't get your hopes up," I grumble at her before motioning toward the door. "Out. Anyone who does not have the last name of Dempsey or West needs to vacate the premises."

No one vacates the premises. Seriously. No one. In fact, the gossip gals gather together.

"Cedar was the correct choice for her."

"She's going to fix him."

"And then he can fix her."

"Or the other way around. I'm not picky."

"Fix us?" I explode. "We're not broken dolls. We're human beings."

Sage pats my hand. "Of course, dear."

I narrow my eyes on her. "Why do I feel as if you're patronizing me?"

She places a hand over her heart and feigns injury. "Me? Why I would never…"

My ass she would never, but I can be flexible. I try a different tactic.

"Can you please leave now? I need to discuss things with my family." Which is absolutely, positively the last freaking thing in the world I want to do but getting shot of the gossip gals is priority number one now.

"I'll go as soon as you give me some kind of indication of how things are going with Cedar."

I scowl. This is exactly why they need to leave. Things are going nowhere on the fast train with Cedar since I freaked out and stomped out of his house over a week ago. Lucky for me, there's no need to say any of this since Lilac takes over.

"No. I won't stop you from betting on Project Hermit—"

"Because you can't," Clove butts in to say.

Lilac's lip curls, but she motors on. "But I will stop you from trying to gain inside information in order to win the bet."

"But I still haven't been able to buy those all natural yoga pillows for *Earth Bliss*," Cayenne pouts.

"You'll have to buy those pillows for your yoga studio the old-fashioned way," Lilac says.

"The old-fashioned way?"

Lilac rolls her eyes. "Save the money from your profits."

"Sounds boring."

"Such is life," I say as I herd the women out of the bar.

If I thought I was off the hook with the gossip gals gone, I was wrong. I whirl around to find Elizabeth, Gabrielle, and Beckett standing in a line facing me down.

"Can I sign the contracts first so Daniel can get on with his day?"

"Don't mind me. I'm in no rush."

I frown at the town's legal counsel. He winks at me. Great. Another gossip. Is being a gossip a requirement to live in this town? As long as it's not about me, I'm all for it. In fact, I'll be happy to join in. Unfortunately, all the gossip seems to be about me and Cedar at the moment.

"It's time," Beckett growls.

Uh oh. When big brother – aka Mr. Overprotective – says 'it's time', it means he's not going to put up with any more 'pink bullshit', which is how he refers to our delaying tactics.

I'm tempted to kick his crutches out from under him. That'd show him. But I won't. I'm the crazy girl. Not the mean girl.

"I wanted to buy the bar on my own. I didn't want to use Mom and Dad's money."

Elizabeth crosses her arms over her chest. "Not wanting to use your trust fund is no excuse to keep buying the bar a secret from us. Your family."

I know we're a family. She doesn't need to remind me every other second. My memory's working perfectly fine.

"Really? Big brother wouldn't have charged in and seized control of the negotiations when he found out?"

"Beep! Wrong. He didn't seize control when I began my spa."

Damnit! I didn't know. "I assumed he barreled in and wrestled the reins from your control."

"Nope. Next bullshit excuse."

Crap. I don't have any more excuses. Time to dig in.

"I already told you. I wanted to do this all on my own."

"In other words, you didn't need us." Gabrielle's voice is almost too soft to hear.

Damn it. I didn't mean to hurt my sisters and brother. But I can't tell them it's my fault Mom and Dad aren't around. They'd never forgive me and despite how much I bicker with Elizabeth and how much I push against Beckett's rules and how much I tease Gabrielle, I need them. They're my family.

My eyes itch and I inhale a deep breath. I will not cry in front of them. I prefer not to cry at all. I try again.

"It's not as if I don't need you. But, in this instance, I wanted to prove I could do it on my own."

Apparently, I've managed to say the magical words as Gabrielle smiles and Elizabeth drops her arms.

"Why didn't you say so in the first place?" Elizabeth demands. "We understand wanting to prove things to the world."

"I don't get it," Beckett grumbles. "You could prove you could do it on your own and still have told us."

Lilac pats his arm. "I'll explain when we get home."

He waggles his eyebrows. "Naked?"

"Ew. Gross. I don't want to know about my brother's weird sexual kinks."

"There's nothing wrong or weird about having sexual kinks," Lilac says.

"Nothing at all," her dad agrees. Judging by the grin on his face he's thinking about his own kinks.

"Can we sign this contract now?" I ask.

Gabrielle smiles. "Yes." She waves her camera. "I'm all set."

I roll my eyes. "You're not going to seriously photograph me signing a contract?"

"Sure, I am."

I grumble as I return to the table where the documents are set out, but on the inside, I'm jumping for joy. I want my family to witness this monumental occasion in my life. But I would never ask them to. That's not me.

There's someone else I wish was here, but he can't be. I can't afford to care for Cedar any more than I already do. I don't deserve his love. No matter how much I may want it.

Chapter 21

Give your girl what she wants this St. Patrick's Day: a dare ~ Cedar's rules for winning his girl back

CEDAR

"I didn't expect to see you here today," Rowan says when I enter *Electric Vibes.*

The place is decked out for Saint Patrick's Day. Cassie's making changes already. Lennon wasn't much of a decorator. He blamed it on Winter Falls' rules about decorations, but, in truth, he was lazy.

"And miss the chance to kick your ass in a pub quiz?" I snort. "Never."

"Wait!" Ashlyn shouts. "Are we not on the same team? What the h-e-double hockey sticks? First, we lose Lilac to the Dempsey group, and now you? This is some big stinking baloney!"

I was only teasing Rowan but goading Ashlyn is too much fun to correct her misconception. "What's with the PG vocabulary?"

"I'm trying to curb my swearing since I don't want Patience to end up with a potty mouth."

"She's three months old. Surely, she isn't talking yet."

If Patience is anything like her mommy, we're in for some rough years. I pause when I realize I thought 'we'. I'm not supposed to stay in town after my six-month dare with Cassie is over. I'm supposed to restart my wanderer days. Except my gut is telling me to stay.

"My child is going to be a protégé," Ashlyn declares and interrupts my thoughts.

"We'll see you at our table." Rowan claps me on the back. Since he's five inches taller than me and a former NFL quarterback, I brace myself before I pitch forward.

Once he's no longer obstructing my view, I scan the area and my gaze falls on Cassie slinging drinks behind the bar. There's my reason to stay. I haven't spoken to her in the month since Valentine's Day. I've tried, but she's frozen me out.

I miss her. My hands itch to fist her blonde hair before melding my lips to hers. But I miss more than the hot nights between the sheets we shared. I miss talking to her. I miss teasing her. I miss how stubborn she can get when she knows she's wrong but won't admit it. I miss my friend.

I know better than to push our relationship too much – Cassie is skittish – but I have a plan. A dare to be exact. Because, if there's one thing I know about my princess, it's that she can't resist a dare.

I make my way to the bar. I notice the gossip gals in my periphery pushing the waiting customers away from the area. They're up to their old matchmaking tricks. It's impossible to live in this town and not know about Project Hermit.

Cassie spins around and her nose wrinkles when she realizes all her customers are now gone. Except me. She scowls at me.

"What do you want?"

"I'm thinking, since I'm in a bar and all, a drink."

"The management has the right to refuse service to anyone they want at any time."

I cock my eyebrow. "Are you kicking me out?"

Her scowl deepens. It's adorable.

"Are you afraid to be in the same room as me?"

"No," she grunts, and her cheeks darken. Good. I'm getting to her.

I lean close to whisper because I'm not an idiot. I know the gossip gals are listening to every word we speak.

"I dare you to come out from behind the bar and participate in the pub quiz."

"Foul! You can't dare me to do something if it affects my business."

Lennon rushes up. "I got this. You go have fun."

"Fun. Who said anything about having fun?"

I'm having fun, but I keep my mouth firmly shut since I prefer my balls where they are.

Lennon grasps her shoulders and shoves her away from the bar. "Live a little."

"Whatever," she mumbles.

I start to reach out for her hand but stop myself in time. I dig my hands in my pockets before the temptation to touch her overwhelms me. Her honeysuckle smell hits me, and I fist my hands in my pockets.

"What are the rules?"

"The rules?" What is she talking about?

"To this dare. And what do I win?"

Damn. She isn't talking about my hands on her naked body.

"No cheating."

She scowls. "I don't cheat."

She's a liar. She cheats all the time when we play games in bed. My cock twitches at the reminder. I ignore it. Now is not the time to pop a boner.

"You sit with the Dempsey sisters. I'll sit with the West sisters."

"But there are more West daughters than Dempsey daughters."

I shrug. "Then, we'll switch."

She narrows her eyes on me. "You're trying to trick me. Lilac sits with the Dempseys. I'm sitting with her."

Sitting with Lilac is a guaranteed ticket to win. The woman knows everything there is to know about everything. Except sports. She doesn't understand the appeal of them.

But I don't care about winning. The whole purpose of this dare is to get Cassie to talk to me again. I just want her to be my friend again. My cock calls me a liar. He's not wrong. But friends is the first step. A step I'm taking right here, right now.

I motion toward the two tables next to each other in the front of the room. "After you."

"You never said what I get when I win this ridiculous dare."

I lean down to whisper into her ear. "Whatever you want."

Goosebumps rise on her skin, and she bites her bottom lip before she shakes herself and marches off. I place my hand on her lower back to guide her. She shivers and I duck my chin to hide my smile. I love how responsive she is to me.

I rub my thumb in circles into her back and she sprints away. I don't bother to hide my smile this time. I never knew chasing a woman could be this fun.

The two remaining seats available at the Dempsey and West tables are back to back. I'm not surprised. I noticed the gossip gals working their magic while I was daring Cassie.

Cassie picks up the empty chair and tries to wedge it in between her sisters Gabrielle and Elizabeth. They both laugh at her and point to the empty spot. She slams the chair on the ground and plops down on it before crossing her arms in front of her while jutting out her bottom lip. Stubborn girl doesn't enjoy it when she doesn't get her way.

"If everyone could take their seats, it's time to get started," Forest says from the stage. He's wearing a green shirt with four-leaf clovers on it, a pair of boxers with 'kiss me I'm Irish' written on his crotch, and a pair of flip-flops. Good to know some things in life never change.

"Betting is now closed," Sage announces from her corner.

"The gossip gals better not be betting against me," Cassie grumbles.

You can bet the wagers today are all about Project Hermit. I'm going to disappoint a few people, though. I will not be taking Cassie home with me. Not yet.

"Love the boxers," a woman shouts from the crowd. "Is there a rule about where we can kiss you?"

"Darling, there are no rules."

"Ahem!" Lennon raps his fist on the bar.

"Clarification. There are no rules about where you can kiss me. There are, however, rules about the quiz. The first person to raise their hand will be called on for the answer. If the answer is correct, we'll continue on to the next question. If the answer is incorrect, the second person to have raised their hand will be asked to answer the question. And so on."

Ashlyn grabs the beer off our table.

"Hey!" Rowan yells. "I was drinking that."

She ignores him and plonks the pitcher down on the Dempsey sisters' table. Cassie reaches for it, but Ashlyn slaps her hand. "No. You have to drink a beer every time you get an answer correct."

"I'm not drinking a beer because I know the answers to all the questions," Lilac says.

Ashlyn wags her finger at her older sister. "You're the one who suggested this."

"I'm not waiting," Cassie declares before pouring herself a glass and drinking half the beer in one go.

"If the West and Dempsey families are ready, we can get started," Forest announces.

"Correction," Cassie hollers. "The Dempsey family was ready. The West family wasn't."

Ashlyn sits back down, and the quiz begins.

"What does the average person do thirteen times a day?"

Ashlyn's hand shoots into the air. "Orgasm."

I cock an eyebrow at Rowan who shrugs.

"Wrong! Next." Forest points to Lilac.

"Laugh."

Ashlyn giggles at her answer. "Finally. Something Lilac is below average in."

"I laugh," Lilac defends herself.

Ashlyn snorts. "Whatever."

"Next question. What is the cross between a donkey and a zebra known as?"

Everyone in the room looks at Juniper since the animal freak is the only person who will know the answer to this question.

"A zeedonk."

"Correct. The Wests and the Dempseys are now tied at one point each."

I lean back on my chair until I'm in Cassie's personal space. "What do I get when I win?" She glares at me. "What? It's a fair question."

She shoves me away and my chair skids across the floor. I grab onto the table to stop myself from face planting on the dance floor.

"Oops. Sorry." Her apology is ruined by the twinkle in her eye.

"It's okay. I know how hard it is to contain yourself when I'm near."

"Contain myself? Ha! More like refrain from gagging."

"As I recall, your gag reflex is almost nonexistent."

"Too bad you won't be recalling anything about my gag reflex anytime soon."

"Shush," Ashlyn hisses. "We're down to the last question."

"What is the collective noun for a group of unicorns?" Forest asks.

"Go ahead, Cassandra. Answer," Beckett pushes.

I can't stop myself from asking, "Why would Cassandra know the answer?"

A blush spreads across her cheeks and down her neck. I know from experience the color continues until the top of her breasts.

"Unicorns don't exist," she insists.

"You thought otherwise when you were five," Beckett says.

"Do you remember when we were packing up for the move here? We discovered some books in her closet about unicorns," Gabrielle adds.

"Holy cow! I remember. There was one about when unicorns poop." Elizabeth bursts into laughter.

"Do you want me to break your foot again, big brother?" Cassie snarls at Beckett.

I rub my hands together. "If you don't know the answer, I guess I'm going to win this dare."

With her eyes narrowed on me, she raises her hand. "A blessing."

"The Dempsey sisters win."

As soon as Forest announces the winner, Cassie pushes away from the table and marches away. I chase after her. I catch her in the hallway leading to her office. Someone was going to hide from me? Not happening.

I snatch her hand and whirl her around. "You won fair and square. What do you want?"

"I need to think about it."

I rub my thumb against her pulse and I feel it spike.

"You don't have any ideas?" I push.

Her breath hitches. "No."

I use my body to maneuver her until her back is against the wall and I'm looming over her.

"No idea at all?"

She stares up at me from beneath her lashes. "What if I want a kiss?"

I want nothing more in this world than to kiss her, but I am not going back to a friends with benefits arrangement. I want more. But I can't resist the opportunity to touch her with my lips, although the kiss won't be anywhere she expects it to be.

I kiss her forehead and her eyes fall closed. I step back before I decide to hell with my grand plans.

"I'll see you around, princess."

She cusses as I exit through the back door. She'll thank me later. I hope.

Chapter 22

From the text messages of Stubborn Princess and Cedar

CEDAR: WHAT'S A BABY unicorn called?

Stubborn Princess: Who is this?

Cedar: Too difficult? Here's an easy one. What's the name of the world's oldest unicorn?

Stubborn Princess: Seriously. Who is this? The unicorn trivia show? What do I win if I answer these questions correctly?

Cedar: The world, princess. The world.

Stubborn Princess is no longer available.

Cedar: *gif of unicorn backpedaling*

Cedar: Okay. I'll give you an easy question. What's a unicorn's horn called?

Stubborn Princess: *gif of a unicorn rolling its eyes*

Cedar: Aha! You had the unicorn gif already waiting for someone to talk unicorns with you. I knew it!

Stubborn Princess: Being able to search gifs in the blink of an eye doesn't make me a unicorn freak.

Cedar: Sure, it does. It's okay. I like you anyway.

Stubborn Princess: Are we in third grade now? Are you going to pull my pigtails during lunch break next?

Cedar: Princess, I will pull your pigtails whenever you want.

Stubborn Princess: Welp. That went downhill fast.

Cedar: *Gif of a unicorn sledding downhill*

Stubborn Princess: I think we know who the unicorn fan is now.

Cedar: Except I didn't know what the collective noun for a group of unicorns was.

Stubborn Princess: We can't all be superstars.

Cedar: *Selfie of him doing karaoke* I beg to differ.

Stubborn Princess: *Gif of princess bursting out laughing*

Stubborn Princess: Please tell me the hair wasn't a wig.

Cedar: It wasn't a wig.

Stubborn Princess: Are you pouting?

Cedar: *selfie of him sitting on his sofa with his bottom lip stuck out*

Stubborn Princess: I need to know more. Did you think you were sexy with this hair?

Cedar: Oh baby, I'm always sexy.

Stubborn Princess: Ha! Ha! Ha! Ha! Ha! Ha! Ha! Ha! Ha! Ha! Ha! Ha! Ha! Ha! Ha! Ha! Ha! Ha! Ha! Ha! Ha! Ha! Ha! Ha! Ha! Ha! Ha! Ha! Ha! Ha! Ha! Ha!

Cedar: Wow. Someone's seriously dedicated to the task of making fun of me.

Stubborn Princess: You make it easy.

Cedar: You're welcome.

Stubborn Princess: My boss is calling. I need to go.

Cedar: Hate to break it to you. But you are the boss.

Stubborn Princess: I meant Diva.

Chapter 23

Life without a bit of risk isn't worth living ~ Cassie's rules for leading an adventurous life

I GIGGLE AS I read Cedar's latest message. *What color is a unicorn's poop?* The man is obsessed with unicorns.

Mythical creatures don't poop I text back as I stroll through the rear entrance of *Electric Vibes*. I throw my purse in the office before walking toward the bar area.

"Surprise!"

I clutch my chest and lock my knees before I fall to the floor. Not happening. Elizabeth's the klutz in the family. Not me.

"What's going on?" I ask the crowd. And I do mean crowd. The bar, which isn't supposed to be open yet, is packed.

Elizabeth points to the banner stating *Happy Opening* and rolls her eyes. "Duh."

"*Electric Vibes* never closed. We don't need an opening party."

"Do you have any idea how hard it is to have a banner made that reads 'Happy Launch of the Same Business by a New Owner' with ecological products? Can't you say thank you? Do you have to be contrary all the time?"

I bat my eyelashes. "I'm contrary?"

Gabrielle stands between me and Elizabeth with her arms raised. "No bickering. Not today. You may resume your regularly scheduled bickering episode after the party."

I stick out my bottom lip. "But it's fun."

Elizabeth snorts. "Your definition of fun is whacked."

"Because you don't know how to have fun. You think a vibrator is for playing catch."

Her face glows bright red. "Can you not embarrass me all the time?"

"What kind of big sister would I be if I didn't embarrass you?"

River arrives and throws an arm around her shoulders. He whispers into her ear and guessing by how she melts into him, whatever he said was sweet and romantic. I want what they have.

I shake my head. No, I don't. I can't want it, because I don't deserve it.

Petal pushes her way to the front of the crowd. "I heard vibrator. What kind are you using? Do you want my top ten vibrator picks?"

The gossip gal is pushing seventy. Good for her. "Nope. I'm good. I learned early on in life different vibrators work better for different people."

Beckett growls. "Would everyone stop talking about vibrators? My sisters are virgins. They don't have sex."

I snort. "Wrong."

I point to River and Elizabeth. He has her pushed up against the wall in the hallway. His fingers are threaded through her hair and her hands are kneading his ass as he devours her mouth. They're about five seconds away from clothes coming off.

"Example number two." This time I point to Phoenix and Gabrielle who are glued to each other as they slow dance in the middle of the dance floor despite Pearl Jam blasting from the speakers.

"Nope. No. Just no. My sisters do not have sex."

Lilac sighs. "We've discussed this. Your sisters are adults, and they are free to live their lives as they wish."

I giggle. "Good luck with changing his mind."

Lilac drags Beckett away, and I'm left behind with Petal.

"You still haven't bought anything from my store," she accuses.

Damn straight I haven't. Petal owns a candle shop, *Sensual Scents*. Candles and I are not friends. Unless you don't light them, but what's the purpose of a candle if it isn't lit?

I scan the area for an escape since I know Petal has the ability to force me to buy her candles even though I don't want to. The woman has some magical powers. I notice a tall man making his way through the crowd toward me. *Cedar*.

His gaze is fixed on mine as he prowls through the crowd. And, make no doubt about it, he's definitely prowling and I think I'm his prey. I bristle. I'm no one's prey.

"Congratulations, princess." He bends over to kiss my cheek.

His woodsy smell hits me and I want to melt into him. It's been over a month since we've torn the sheets up together and I miss him. No, not him. It. I miss it. The sex. I don't miss Cedar. Except I've spent the past week since Saint Patrick's Day messaging with him every day. It's been fun, flirty, and completely platonic.

Uh oh. I'm in trouble. Flashing neon signs. Skywriter. Holy shit. Trouble.

A lump suddenly appears in my throat. "Thank you." I have to force the words out.

Petal squeals next to me and I jump. I forgot she was standing there. "Project Hermit is my absolute favorite."

"Having favorites is wrong," Sage declares as she joins us. "I love all my children the same."

"You didn't have any children," Cayenne points out.

Sage motions to all the people in the room. "I've changed everyone's diapers in this room."

I raise my hand. "Excuse me. You never changed my diaper."

"Except you."

"And you didn't change the diapers of my sisters or my brother either."

"And changing someone's diaper is not the same as actually being the parent of the child," Clove says.

Sage waves away her comment. "It takes a village."

This discussion could go on all night. The gossip gals enjoy bickering with each other almost as much as they enjoy gossiping. Almost.

I gasp and widen my eyes as I feign shock. "Oh my. I didn't know Eden and Miller hated each other."

"Where?" Sage shouts. "Where are they?"

I indicate the back corner where the flower store owner and brewery owner are obviously having an argument.

"This is not okay. They need to wait their turn. Gossip gals! Move out." Sage leads the women away.

"Eden is going to kill me," I mutter as they march in a single file through the room bulldozing anyone in their way.

Cedar laughs as he throws an arm around me. "She's a Winter Falls native. She'll be fine."

I snuggle into his warmth before I realize what I'm doing. Stop! Abort mission. Abort. Abort. I duck under his arm and rush away.

"I need to make sure the bar is stocked," I say with a glance over my shoulder.

Guessing by the amused expression on his face, he knows I'm running away. When I arrive at the bar, I lean against the coolers and inhale a few deep breaths. What is it about Cedar? He makes every nerve in my body crackle with awareness. Does he have to be cute and funny too?

My phone buzzes in my pocket. I remove it and read *What happens when you touch a pure white unicorn?*

I don't get a chance to type **peace** before he answers.

The same thing that happens when I slide into you.

Oh my. Is it hot in here? It feels hot in here.

"What are you reading?" Elizabeth asks from next to me.

I shove my phone into my pocket. "Nothing."

"Hmm… Avoidance. Plus, you're blushing. I bet it was dirty."

I snort. "Whatever. You shouldn't be behind the bar."

She leans close to whisper, "Don't worry. I know the owner."

I widen my eyes. "Oh yeah? Does the owner know the professional insurance policy doesn't cover risk when a non-employee is behind the bar?"

Her mouth drops open. "Who are you and what have you done with my crazy sister who thinks life isn't worth living without a bit of risk?"

"I never said a life without risk isn't worth living."

She barks out a laugh. "Ha! It's a direct quote from the time you decided to 'borrow' Beckett's truck before you had your driver's license and go mudding with it."

"Shush. Beckett doesn't know."

She rolls her eyes. "Please. He knows. He's not an idiot."

"I didn't say he was an idiot."

Gabrielle slow claps from the other side of the bar. "Wonderful performance. I always enjoy watching my sisters bicker at a party."

I say the only thing I can to distract her, "Where's Phoenix?"

She motions toward where Phoenix is standing with his brothers, River and Lyric, as well as Beckett and Cedar. My feet carry me to them before my brain can catch up.

I force my way to the middle of the group and poke Beckett with my finger. "You better not be doing some stupid initiation ritual. I will not stand for you bullying the man I'm with."

"We were discussing the Rockies game," River says but everyone ignores him.

Beckett crosses his arms over his chest. "Are you admitting you're involved with Cedar?"

"I don't discuss my love life with you."

"Love life?"

"Sex life. I meant sex."

Beckett blanches. "You don't have sex, remember?"

"Really? Because I seem to recall the time you—"

He shoves his palm in my face and forces me to back up. "Nope."

Cedar growls. "Hey! You don't shove your sister."

He pushes me behind him before confronting Beckett. "Are we going to have a problem?"

Beckett narrows his eyes on Cedar. "Are you telling me how to treat my sister? I raised her as my own."

I peek out from behind Cedar. "We know! Everyone you've ever met knows!"

"Are you—"

Cedar holds up his hand to stop Beckett. "I think we can agree a party to celebrate Cassie's new business is not the time or the place to discuss past hurts and insults."

"I don't agree," Feather says.

"Me either," Cayenne agrees.

Lyric sighs. "The gossip gals are the bane of my existence. You finish this, I'll handle them." He herds the gossip gal gang across the room out of hearing range.

"I'm sorry, Cassandra. We'll discuss this at a later time," Beckett immediately gives in. He may be a pain in the ass with his overprotective tendencies, but he does know when to admit when he's wrong.

"Okay," I agree, although I have no intention of ever discussing anything about our childhood with Beckett or any of my other siblings.

Cedar grasps my hand and leads me away through the back hallway to my office. He shuts the door behind us before pressing me against it and cradling my face in his hands.

"Are you okay?"

"Okay? Why wouldn't I be okay?"

"If you don't stop staring at my lips like they're your first coffee in the morning I won't be responsible for what I do."

"Who wants to be responsible?"

"I need to make sure you're okay before I proceed with the sexy portion of the evening."

Damn. Why does he have to be a good guy? Why can't he be some rough and tough motorcycle man I would never fall in love with? He's making it impossible to resist him with his concern and his stupid unicorn trivia.

Fuck it. I'm done. I'm done fighting the pull of Cedar. Will it hurt when I have to let him loose? Hell yeah. But I can't seem to stop myself from wanting him, from missing him, from – gulp – needing him.

"Take me home."

Chapter 24

Patience is not for a man who hasn't been with his woman for over a month ~ Cedar's excuse for not waiting to find a bed

CEDAR

"Take me home."

My cock immediately hardens and lengthens at her demand. But he needs to hold on. I'm not jumping back into bed with Cassandra until we have a few things straightened out.

"Are you sure?"

She lifts up on her toes. "Yes," she hisses against my mouth.

I resist the temptation to mold my lips to hers. "Because if I take you home and make love to you, it's not as your friend."

The fire in her eyes dims. "You don't want to be my friend?"

I tuck a strand of her silky hair behind her ear. "I want to be more than your friend. But I'm done with this friends with benefits bullshit. I want to be your lover. Your only lover."

Her throat bobs as she swallows. "Do we need to put a label on it?"

I caress her cheek. "I'm not labeling anything. I'm saying we're more than fuck buddies and we're exclusive. We'll figure the rest out from there."

A spark of hope ignites in her green eyes. It's as I've suspected all along. She's afraid to commit. I don't know why, but I'm going to find out.

"What do I get if I agree to this new arrangement?"

I lean close to whisper in her ear. "Lots and lots of orgasms. As many as you want. So many you pass out from pleasure."

"You drive a hard bargain," she says in a breathy voice.

"Princess, I've only begun to show you how hard I can drive."

Her smile is downright sultry when she asks, "What are we waiting for?"

That's a green light if I ever heard one. I step back before grasping her hand and yanking the door open. I drag her down the hallway to the rear entrance. I need to hurry before the gossip gals catch wind of our departure. I wouldn't put it past them to snap pictures and post them on the Winter Falls Facebook Group.

We dash across the parking lot to where her car is parked. It automatically unlocks when we're near and I open the passenger door and shove her inside.

"Are you in a hurry?" She teases.

I slam my hands down on the roof of the car and lean toward her. "I haven't been inside you for over a month and my cock is about to explode. Damn straight I'm in a hurry."

She rubs her thighs together. "Explanation accepted."

I fling her door shut and hurry around the front of the car to the driver's seat. Not an easy accomplishment with a cock hard enough to pound nails.

I frown when the touchscreen switches on, but I don't need to enter a PIN in order to start the car.

"You need to enable the PIN function for your own safety."

"Do you want to discuss the security of my vehicle, or do you want to get back to my place and strip my clothes off?"

My mouth waters at the image of removing her clothes. "I hereby table this discussion until a later moment."

"Duly noted."

I rocket out of the parking lot and down Main Street. I'm lucky Lyric is inside *Electric Vibes* because speeding in Winter Falls is a major offense. Feel free to dash around the town naked while walking your pet squirrels, but do not – under any circumstances – speed.

We arrive at the parking area of her apartment building in record time. Cassie undoes her seatbelt and reaches for the door handle, but I'm out of patience. I wrap an arm around her waist and haul her across the seat until she's in my lap.

She squeaks in surprise, and I smash my mouth down on hers. Her taste of honey hits my tongue and I devour. While I feast on her mouth, I reach down and hit the button to move the seat back. Once it's as far back as it can go, I readjust Cassie until she's straddling me.

I rip my mouth from hers. "If you don't want to have sex in this car in the immediate future, you need to tell me to stop now."

She leans close until her lips are brushing mine. "Don't stop."

I thread my hands through her hair and position her head just right before melding my lips to hers once again. While I explore every inch of her mouth, she clutches my shoulders and rubs her center against my hard length.

When I grab her hips to stop her, she mewls in protest.

I growl. "I don't want to come in my pants."

"Challenge accepted," she whispers before beginning to rub harder against me.

I bite her bottom lip as revenge. "Don't be a bad girl."

"Why?" She flutters her eyelashes. "Are you going to punish me?"

"Does orgasm denial count as punishment?"

She gasps. "You wouldn't dare. You promised to give me orgasms until I pass out."

"And you promised to behave."

She giggles and I moan at the feel of her body jiggling against mine. She is not helping the overeager cock in my pants.

The brown flecks in her green eyes flash. "I have never promised to behave in my life."

"My little stubborn princess rebel."

"I'm not a rebel."

I cock an eyebrow. "Then, please don't remove your pants. And you should definitely keep your shirt on."

She whips her shirt off and I have to duck before she elbows me in the face. A black eye is not the memory I want of this evening. She shoves the cups of her bra down and begins to massage her breasts.

"Are you trying to make me come in my pants?"

She winks. "Maybe."

"Jeans. Off. Now," I bark out.

She doesn't hesitate. She rips her jeans and panties down her legs until they meet the tops of her boots. While she's lifted up, I unbutton my jeans and take my cock out.

Cassie's gaze zeroes in on it. When she licks her lips, pre-cum leaks from the head.

"This is going to be fast," I say as I line my cock up at her entrance.

She sinks down and my eyes close as I moan at the feeling of having her wet heat surrounding me.

"Never again."

"Never again what?" She pants.

"Never again will I go for over a month without my cock buried in your pussy."

Her walls tighten at my words. "Okay."

She raises up and I look down at our joining. Oh crap. My hands on her hips squeeze. "Stop."

"What's wrong? Is someone out there?"

She scans the parking lot, but it's impossible to see outside as Winter Falls does not believe in streetlights. Streetlights cause light pollution and use too much energy.

"Fuck, princess. I'm sorry."

"Sorry for what? Is this the orgasm denial punishment? Because this is zero fun for me."

"I'm sorry I took you bare without your permission."

Her shoulders relax. "Phew. You scared me. It's fine. I get the shot. All the Dempsey sisters do. Beckett prefers to pretend all his little sisters are as pure as the snow, but he's not stupid. All of us have been getting the shot since we were teenagers."

"But I didn't ask your permission. I didn't reassure you I'm clean. I took what I wanted."

Her hands squish my cheeks together. "And I enjoyed every fucking second. No pun intended."

"I am clean. I get tested annually and I hadn't had sex in a long time before I met you."

"I'm clean, too." Her cheeks darken as she glances away.

I grasp her hands and squeeze. "What is it?"

"It's stupid."

"Princess, nothing you can tell me is stupid."

"I'veneverhadsexwithoutacondom." She speaks too fast for me to understand.

"What did you say?"

She sighs. "I've never had sex without a condom before."

I press my lips to hers. "Me either."

"Really?"

"Really," I assure her.

I place my hands on her hips. "You okay with this?"

"Okay with what? Having sex in the parking lot? You being fully dressed? Or you going bare inside of me?"

She's teasing but my answer is serious. "All of the above."

Her response is immediate and glorious. She sinks down on my cock until my balls slap her skin. And she doesn't stop. She lifts and lowers herself faster and faster while I hold on for the ride.

I release her hips to fondle her breasts. Each and every time I pinch her nipples, her walls squeeze my cock. I pinch them over and over again until she's chanting my name.

"Cedar. Cedar. Cedar. I'm going to—"

I cut her off with a nip of her lip. "No. You look at me when you come."

Her eyes fly open. She doesn't hesitate to stare into my eyes as she slams down on me one more time. I feel her walls flutter against me.

"Cedar!" she shouts.

I press my mouth to hers and swallow her moans as she climaxes. When I feel her relax, it's my turn. I lift her up and down my length until my balls pull up.

"Fuck. Cassie. Princess."

I cut myself off before I say I love you. With a start, I realize the words wouldn't be empty. I do love Cassandra. The stubborn woman plowed through all of my barriers and made a home for herself in my heart.

I better get ready for battle, because claiming Cassandra's heart is going to be the most difficult fight of my life.

Chapter 25

Digging in your heels is not the same as being stubborn ~ Cassie's rules for living her best life

I SMILE WHEN I find Cedar waiting at the entrance to the town hall. When he crosses his arms over his chest, his biceps bulge, and I consider skipping this meeting altogether to spend the evening exploring those muscles – preferably while naked – instead.

"What are you doing here?" I ask before kissing his cheek.

Tonight is the monthly meeting for business owners in Winter Falls. Since Cedar doesn't own a business in town, I didn't expect to see him here.

"I was summoned."

My eyes widen. "Summoned? Is something wrong? Are they suing you?" I lean close to whisper. "Do you need me to get you out of here?"

He barks out a laugh. Okay. A rescue is not needed. Duly noted.

He wraps his arms around my shoulders and pulls me near. I enjoy the feeling of his body moving against mine entirely too much. *Stop getting attached to this guy, Cassandra.* Unfortunately, the voice of reason was overruled last week when I decided to graduate from friends with benefits to 'something else'.

I refuse to give our relationship a name. Give it a name and it's real. I'm still living in a fairytale land where I get everything I want. Where I deserve things such as love. Unicorns are real here, too.

Cedar glances up and groans. "Uh oh."

"What? I've got a bug out bag. I can get you out of town in less than ten minutes."

And, no, I don't have a bug out bag because I'm some secret spy. How cool would that be? Unfortunately, the reason is boring. Much, more boring. Big protector brother Beckett insists we have them. Whenever I claim I forgot to prepare one, his head explodes. It's almost as fun as watching Elizabeth's head explode.

Cedar swivels us until I see what he does.

"Uh oh is right."

The gossip gals charge up the stairs wearing hot pink t-shirts with the words *Matchmaking: More than a dating service* printed on them. I guess the word 'subtle' isn't part of their vocabulary either. Time to get out of here.

"Yeah." Cayenne claps. "I'm glad Project Hermit is a success."

"Don't count your chickens before your eggs hatch. These two have issues to work out," Sage says.

I grasp Cedar's hand and try to drag him into the meeting room. I am not discussing my issues with the gossip gals. I'm not discussing my issues with anyone. They're mine and mine alone.

Unfortunately, he can't be dragged anywhere he doesn't want to go. He tugs on my hand and draws me near to him until he can wrap an arm around my shoulder.

"Ladies." He inclines his head in their direction. "How are you doing this evening?"

Feather looks us up and down. "Not as well as you two are doing."

"Are you sure you don't want some of my candles?" Petal asks. "You don't have to enjoy wax play. I also have massage oil ones."

Cedar's arm tightens around me. "No candles," he insists.

Eden stomps up the stairs. "Let's get this shit show started," she grumbles as she passes by. Someone is not happy about being selected mayor.

The gossip gals follow her inside, but when Cedar tries to guide me to the entrance, I stop him.

"How do you know?"

His brow wrinkles. "Know what?"

"About my fear of fire."

"Because I pay attention to every single thing about you." I frown. He can't possibly pay attention to everything.

"You won't go near the wood burning stove. You skirt so far away from it you have to climb over the sofa."

"I do not." I totally do, but I thought he hadn't noticed.

He tweaks my nose. "And you took the candles in my living room and hid them under the sofa."

"It was Diva."

"Wow. I didn't realize your dog could open cupboards and shuffle candles around without leaving behind bite marks."

"What can I say? She's a magical dog."

"She must be friends with your unicorn."

The door opens, and Elizabeth and Gabrielle walk in before I can think of a snarky reply.

"You have to sit with us," Elizabeth demands.

"Why?"

"We have drinking games."

"Drinking games? This is a business meeting."

She snorts. "You really don't understand Winter Falls yet." She snatches my hand. "Come on. Let's get popcorn and beer."

"Popcorn?"

I glance behind me and attempt to signal Cedar to rescue me but his only response is a wink. We need to work on our silent communication. Maybe come up with some hand signals.

Elizabeth drags me past the meeting room to the bathroom with Gabrielle following.

"What are we doing in the bathroom? Are you afraid to go alone?"

The door bangs open and Ashlyn rushes in. "I can't believe you forgot me."

Crap. If Ashlyn's involved, things are serious. I cross my arms over my chest and glare at my sisters. "What's going on? And why does Ashlyn know but I don't? Did you forget I'm your sister?"

"I'm your sister, too," Ashlyn claims.

I cock an eyebrow at her.

"Your brother is engaged to my sister. Sister connection number one. And you're dating the brother of my husband. Sister connection number two. Plus—"

I cut her off before she can go any further. "I'm not dating Cedar."

"Girl. I literally saw you all snuggled up to him."

"We were not snuggled together."

"I—"

Elizabeth pats Ashlyn's shoulder to stop her. "There's no use. Once Cassandra digs her feet in, she's stuck for-freaking-ever."

Gabrielle nods. "Ask me sometime about the year she insisted she loved Brussels sprouts. She ate them every single day. Gagging the entire time. She thought we were idiots and wouldn't figure it out."

Ha! They haven't figured out the clown thing yet, so there!

"Are you done now?" I check the non-existent watch on my wrist. "I want to get to the meeting on time since it's my first one."

Ashlyn giggles. "New residents are fun." I narrow my eyes on her and she shrugs. "What? It's the truth."

"But it doesn't explain why you think punctuality is a joke."

Although, this is Ashlyn. There's only one reason she arrives anywhere on time – because she wants the gossip first. I wouldn't be surprised if she's already submitted her application to become a gossip gal.

She waves away my concern. "They're not going to start without us."

"Besides, the line for beer and popcorn was out the door when I checked," Elizabeth adds.

"We should probably get in line then." If everyone's having beer and popcorn, who am I to say no?

Ashlyn's nose wrinkles. "She's not wrong."

"We'll continue this discussion later," Elizabeth says as she charges out of the bathroom with Gabrielle and Ashlyn on her heels.

"What discussion?" I still haven't figured out what the purpose of the bathroom visit was.

When I enter the hallway, Cedar is leaning against the wall waiting for me. He looks sexy as hell with his feet crossed at his ankles. Of course, the beer and popcorn in his hands helps.

"For me?"

I reach for one of the beers but he holds them above his head.

I stomp my foot. "What the hell?"

"Tell me you're okay first."

My stomach warms at his obvious concern for me, but I can't let him see any weakness. He can't know how much I'm coming to depend on him. It will give him too much power over me.

"Why wouldn't I be okay?" I sass to hide the barrage of feelings fighting for control in my stomach.

"Your sisters and Ashlyn just cornered you in the bathroom."

I don't need the reminder. I was there after all.

"Not all of my sisters," I hedge. "Olivia wasn't there."

"Neither was I," Lilac announces as she nears.

"You're not my sister."

"I am your soon-to-be sister-in-law and it's been pointed out to me how sister-in-law and sister are the same as far as familial obligations are concerned."

Cedar chuckles. "Ruby read you the riot act, huh?"

Lilac sighs. "Mom is determined to adopt all of the Dempsey sisters. Five girls are not enough for her?"

My eyes itch and I drop my gaze to the floor. Ruby wants to adopt us? I haven't had a mother since I was thirteen. I would love for Mrs. West to be my adoptive mom. But I don't deserve a mom any more than I deserve love.

Lyric pokes his head out of the meeting room. "They're starting."

"We'll chat later," Lilac says as she hurries off.

I'm not sure if I'm relieved she's gone or disappointed. I hate all these mushy feelings.

Cedar pinches my chin and forces me to meet his gaze.

"It's okay."

I feign ignorance. It's my go-to response. "What are you talking about?"

Of course, he doesn't drop it. "It's okay to show your feelings."

I frown. "What feelings?"

"It can't have been easy growing up without a mom."

"I had a mom," I growl.

"I know you did, princess. I know you did." He kisses my forehead. Thankfully, he drops the subject because if ever there was a sensitive subject it's my mom's death.

"Let's go inside before they start without us."

He hands me a beer before taking my hand and leading me toward the room. At the entrance, he slows to glance down at me.

"Take all the time you need, princess. But this conversation isn't over."

He doesn't give me a chance to sass back before dragging me into the room. Someone's a sneaky bastard. A trait I usually admire but not when it's directed my way.

Chapter 26

Holding a grudge is important so people understand how pissed you are ~ Cassandra's rules for living her best life

"What are the two of you doing here?" I ask when I step outside my apartment building to discover Gabrielle and Elizabeth waiting for me.

"We're riding with you to White Bridge," Gabrielle says as she opens the passenger door to my car.

"Whatever," I mutter as if I don't care, but I'm afraid I haven't had enough coffee for whatever this is yet.

"Well," Elizabeth says when we're on the road.

"Well what?" I feign confusion. It won't do me any good, but if it annoys Elizabeth, it's a win.

"How are things going with Cedar?"

"You two looked pretty cozy at the monthly business meeting," Gabrielle adds.

I don't know why they think I'm going to discuss my relationship with them. I never have before. Of course, I've never actually had a relationship, so I can see where there'd be a bit of confusion.

"Who's great idea was it for all three of us to drive together?" I complain.

"We all live in Winter Falls and are going to the same place," Gabrielle answers.

"And it's bad for the environment to use energy when it's unnecessary," Elizabeth adds.

I decide to drop it. Ever since my sister shacked up with River, she's become nearly as vigilant about saving the environment as our big brother. I don't need anyone to lecture me about what toothpaste I use, thank you very much.

The rest of the thirty-minute drive to White Bridge is blissfully quiet. When I park in front of the bridal boutique, Gabrielle and Elizabeth rush out of the car to the store.

I sigh. I'm not exactly excited about helping Lilac pick out a wedding dress. Don't get me wrong. I'm happy Beckett found her and they're getting married, but girly stuff like dress shopping is not my thing.

I force myself out of the car and into the boutique to find chaos. Who thought it was a good idea to merge the West and Dempsey families? There's now a total of eight women. I grew up with three sisters. The four of us never agreed on a thing. I don't know how five West daughters and three Dempsey sisters are going to manage to agree on a wedding dress or bridesmaids' dresses.

"How many bridesmaids is Lilac having anyway?"

"Eight," Lilac answers from behind me.

I spin around to confront her. "Eight? Have you lost your mind?"

"You do know you can't actually lose your mind."

Lilac the literal strikes again!

"Why are you having eight bridesmaids?"

"Ashlyn eloped, Aspen didn't have any bridesmaids, and Ellery's dragging her feet on setting a date."

"What about me?" Juniper asks.

"As I understand it, no one wants to be a bridesmaid when the entire ceremony will be live-streamed on Entertainment Tonight."

Juniper fists her hands on her hips. "It's a rumor. It's not true. My wedding will not be live-streamed."

Aspen pats her shoulder. "You're the one who fell in love with Maverick Langston, aka Hollywood's favorite romantic comedy hero."

"I'm still not having my wedding live-streamed. And I want all of you to be there as my bridesmaids."

Lilac nods. "Good."

Juniper narrows her eyes on her older sister. "You knew my wedding wasn't being live-streamed the entire time. You tricked me into asking you to be my bridesmaid."

I chuckle. Lilac may drive me nuts sometimes – most of the time actually – but she can be awesome when she wants to be.

"The bigger question I have is who's number eight?" Aspen asks. "There are four West sisters – me, Ellery, Juniper, and Ashlyn – and three Dempsey sisters – Gabrielle, Elizabeth, and Cassandra. If my math is correct—"

"Says the math hater who triggered the fire alarm anytime there was a test in high school," Ellery interrupts to say.

Aspen sticks her tongue out at her sister. "That makes seven bridesmaids and one bride. Who's the eighth bridesmaid?"

Ashlyn snorts. "It's not her best friend. Since we are her best friends."

Lilac isn't offended by Ashlyn's statement. "Correct."

"The suspense is literally killing me," Elizabeth mutters.

"Suspense can't actually kill you," Lilac claims.

"It can if I have a heart attack because my heart is going ba-bum ba-bum ba-bum."

I roll my eyes. Elizabeth and her drama. "It's probably one of her colleagues. Or a cousin."

"We don't have any cousins," Ashlyn says.

"We do, too," Aspen argues. "Mom has three step-brothers. They have four children between them."

"I meant female cousins. We don't have any female cousins."

The door bangs open. "I'm here!"

No. It can't be. I know that voice, but I haven't seen her since we moved to Colorado. I've barely spoken to her. Why would she be here? How did she get here?

"Olivia!" Elizabeth screams before rushing to our oldest sister and tackling her. They end up in a heap on the ground.

"Glad to see you haven't changed any," Olivia mutters as she pushes Elizabeth off of her and stands.

"I've changed!"

Olivia snorts. "Really?"

Elizabeth's face crumples at Olivia's response and I fist my hands before I slap my older sister. Violence is wrong, but damn I wish I could slap some sense into my sister once in a while.

"Ahem." Gabrielle clears her throat before approaching Olivia with her chin tucked in. I frown. Why is shy Gabrielle returning? "Hi, Olivia."

Ashlyn sidles up to me. "This is the long lost sister?" she whisper-shouts.

"Yep."

"You don't appear happy to see her."

Because I'm not. *Liar.* Fine. Maybe I'm a bit happy. But Olivia abandoned us. Does she think she can just sashay through the door and we'll welcome her back? Guessing by the hug Gabrielle's giving her, she does.

"Why are you here?" I demand.

"Why wouldn't I be here? Our brother is getting married."

"*Our* brother? I seem to remember someone screaming at Beckett about how he was dead to her."

Elizabeth rushes to stand in between us. "No fighting. Today is a joyous occasion. We're picking out Lilac's wedding dress."

"And the bridesmaids' dresses," Ashlyn adds. "This one's pretty." She twirls around in a canary yellow dress.

"How did you—"

Juniper cuts Lilac's question off. "I got this." She shackles Ashlyn's wrist and drags her away.

"How did you know where to find us?" I ask Olivia once Ashlyn and Juniper are gone.

Lilac clears her throat. "I invited her."

"Okay, but how did she actually get here? Why did she come?"

I have more questions, but I don't want to air our dirty laundry in front of the entire West clan who are all leaning close to ensure they don't miss a word. Rest assured. News of Olivia's arrival will spread through the Winter Falls' gossip chain before we leave this bridal boutique.

Olivia scratches her neck. A dead giveaway she's about to lie.

"I thought it was time to come see what all the fuss is about with this Winter Falls place."

I cross my arms over my chest and glare at her.

"Why don't you try telling the truth this time?"

She leans close to snarl in my face. "Why don't you mind your own business?"

I throw my arms in the air. "How is this not my business? You're literally standing in a room with all of your sisters and your soon-to-be sister-in-law. Why you showed up is definitely my business."

"Why don't we all calm down? Olivia is here. Nothing else matters."

I roll my eyes at Elizabeth. She's all puppies and rainbows when it comes to family. Family first is her motto. Gag.

"She's allowed to ignore us for two years and then show up as if nothing happened? What kind of bullshit is this?"

"I don't think you're supposed to say bullshit in a bridal boutique," Gabrielle whispers.

"Why not? Will Voldemort show up and Avada Kedra us?"

"It's Avada Kedavra," she corrects.

"I seriously don't give a flying fig."

Lilac steps next to me. "I brought her here."

I cock an eyebrow because I need more of an explanation than 'I brought her here'.

"I paid for her airline ticket."

This is getting weird. The Dempseys aren't exactly poor. Olivia could have paid for her own ticket. Unless…

"Did Beckett cut you off from your trust fund?"

The tips of her ears darken. "Maybe."

"And you thought you could show up here and Beckett would give you more money?"

While I've been working my ass off to not need my trust fund, she's been blowing through hers. Why did I ever think we were similar? She's a user. Plain and simple.

"Can we table this discussion for the moment?" Lilac asks, and I snarl at her. She holds her hands up in surrender. "I understand you're upset. I'm not trying to overlook it. But I do have a limited amount of time today to select my wedding gown." She pulls out her phone. "The dress should be selected this week. Next week—"

I cut her off before she can list her entire wedding planning schedule. "Of course, Lilac. We'll pick out your dress today."

"The bridesmaids' dresses need to be selected today, too."

"Naturally."

I whirl around to give Olivia my back. She turned her back on me and this family. She can experience how it feels for a change.

Chapter 27

Never tell a woman to calm down ~ Cedar's rules for living with his balls intact

C*EDAR*

"Freaking Olivia! Who does she think she is? Waltzing back into our lives without so much as an apology?"

Cassie stomps back and forth in front of the sofa as she rants. Diva chases after her but when her mommy doesn't notice her, she starts running in circles around Cassie's legs until Cassie's forced to stop or risk breaking her neck.

"Not now, Diva."

Diva yips at her.

"Just because your name is Diva doesn't mean you can be a diva all the time."

Another yip.

Cassie throws her arms in the air. "Who are you to say I'm self-centered? Have you met my sister? She's the definition of self-centered. She's arrogant, doesn't care for anyone besides herself, and doesn't think of anyone besides herself. Egocentric. Conceited. She's… she's…she's…UGH!" she screams. "Give me a dictionary. I need more synonyms for my self-centered sister."

A vein pulses on her forehead and her nostrils flare. Time to stop this before she gives herself a heart attack.

I grasp her shoulders and say the one thing guaranteed to push her off kilter. "She's me."

She rears back. "You are nothing like Olivia. Nothing!"

I cock my brow. "I'm not? I abandoned my family. I'm hiding out on this land and avoiding my hometown. I'm exactly like her."

"Really? Did you blow through your trust fund using all the money on alcohol and good times?"

She's got me there. "I didn't have a trust fund, but I've done some drinking in my day."

Her nose wrinkles. She's adorable and I can't resist leaning down to kiss the tip of her nose.

"You need to forgive her. If not for her, for yourself. This," I motion toward the living area she's been pacing up and down for the past hour, "is not healthy."

Her shoulders slump. "I need time. I'm not ready."

"Take all the time you need. There's no deadline here, princess."

"Okay," she gives in, but I know the battle isn't over.

In addition to being the most stubborn woman I've ever met, she avoids feelings and discussions of feelings as if they're contagious. She's hiding a bunch of hurt behind the wall she's erected. It's going to take a forklift and a metric ton of patience to dig it out of her. Good thing I'm a patient man.

"In the meantime, how about we watch a movie on my laptop?"

"Can we make out during it?"

I wiggle my eyebrows. "It wouldn't be a movie experience without a bit of making out."

"What about groping?"

I wink. "Guaranteed."

"Above or below the beltline?"

My cock twitches at her teasing. He's all for below the beltline. In fact, he's ready to skip the movie entirely. He's not as patient as I am.

"Do you want to watch a movie, or do you want me to tear your clothes off?"

She bites her lip as she pretends to consider my question. "Movie first."

My cock weeps in my jeans. "Tease."

She bats her eyelashes. "Me?"

I kiss her forehead before nudging her toward the sofa. I snag my laptop from the kitchen counter and hand it to her.

"Pick out a movie. I'll make us some popcorn."

She settles on the sofa with Diva on her lap. The dog immediately falls asleep and starts snoring.

I adjust my cock before gathering the ingredients to make popcorn. While the oil heats in the pan, I snag two beers from the refrigerator.

When I try to hand Cassie her beer, she doesn't look up from the computer she's scowling at.

"What's wrong? Can't find a movie you want to watch?"

She harrumphs. What she doesn't do is answer my question.

I set the beers on the coffee table and pick Diva up before sitting next to Cassie. My gaze lands on the screen of my laptop and I no longer need to ask what's wrong.

"It's not what you think."

"Oh really? It's not? I can see plain as day you've been offered a job in Boston."

"I have," I acknowledge since I promised myself to never lie to her again after the Archer-Cedar misunderstanding.

She slams the laptop shut. "Were you even going to tell me? Or were you going to sneak away like a thief in the night?"

"I wasn't going to tell you."

She jumps to her feet. "You were going to leave without saying a word!"

Her shriek wakes Diva who growls in response. I stand and set the furball in her doggy bed before approaching Cassie.

"No!" She sticks her arms out to prevent me from getting near. "I don't want to hear it!"

"You need to let me explain," I insist.

"Explain what? How you've been fooling around with me and it's all a joke to you?"

I growl. "Our relationship isn't a joke."

She leans close to snarl at me. "Our relationship is a lie!"

"It's not a lie! I'm not—"

She cuts me off before I can explain how I didn't apply for the job. How I didn't plan on telling her about it because I have no interest in leaving Winter Falls. How I'm not going anywhere without her because I love her.

"You admitted it yourself. You said, and I quote here, you didn't plan on telling me about the job offer."

Because I knew this would be the response and we'd get into a fight when I have no plans to accept the position.

"Can you calm down and we'll discuss this like two adults?"

"Calm down!"

Shit. Cassie made me forget every lesson I've ever learned about women. Never – and I do mean never – tell a woman to calm down. I'm a fucking idiot. There's no way she's calming down anytime soon now.

"I will calm down when I'm good and ready to calm down. You don't tell me when to calm down, mister."

Her eyes are bulging, and her teeth are clenched. Despite her prickly outside, I want to pull her into my arms and soothe her. I want to nibble on her ear until she melts into me.

She claps her hands. "Come on, Diva. We're out of here."

I'm not above begging when it comes to Cassie. "Please don't go, princess. Stay and we'll discuss this. I …"

I slam my mouth shut before I declare my love to her. She'll flee straight into the dark night if I say those three little words. I thought she was skittish before. I didn't realize how skittish she truly is if reading a letter with a job offer has her retreating behind her barbed wire walls.

"Diva!" she commands. "Get over here this instant."

Diva glances up from her bed and I swear she snorts.

"Fine!" Cassie stomps to the dog and picks her up. She cradles her to her chest as she rushes out the door.

"Cassie! Wait!"

"You're not the boss of me!"

"I know, but I thought you might want to put shoes on before you tramp through the woods to your car."

She whirls around, her hair flying behind her, before marching back to me. I place her shoes on my porch and retreat with my palms raised.

She shoves her feet into her shoes before stomping away again.

I grab her coat and purse and follow as she trudges through the woods. When she reaches her car, she glares at it as if it's the car's fault she forgot her keys.

I clear my throat.

She whirls around and shoots daggers at me from her eyes. "What?"

I hold up her purse and coat. "I thought you might want these."

She snatches the items from me. "I didn't forget them."

I hunch my shoulders to appear less intimidating. She doesn't need to know I'm finding this entire situation hilarious. I prefer my balls where they are.

"In case it's not clear, we're done."

My amusement evaporates. She's wrong. "Princess, we are not done."

"You can't unilaterally decide we're not done."

"And you can't unilaterally decide we are."

She lifts her nose in the air and sniffs. "Wrong. I just did."

"I don't accept."

"You don't have to accept. That's not how relationships work."

I lift my eyebrows. "Because you have so much experience with relationships?"

She pokes me in the stomach. "Don't you dare tell me what experience I do or do not have."

Obviously, anything I say now will be wrong. I keep my mouth shut as she climbs into her car and drives off.

"We are not over," I whisper when she's gone. "We will never be over."

I'm a patient man, I remind myself as I hike through the woods to my house. I'll break through to Cassie eventually.

Chapter 28

I SIGH WHEN I notice my sisters and Ashlyn enter *Electric Vibes* the next night. I knew they'd show up sooner or later. By now the whole town knows Cedar and I broke up. I've been catching people throwing me looks of sympathy all day. I may have snarled at a few of them.

I debate running away from them, but it's useless. The town residents would probably help them wrangle me. Better to do this in private before I end up handcuffed to a chair in the middle of my bar while the entire town lectures me. I shiver. Talk about the stuff nightmares are made of.

I motion toward my office.

"This was much easier than I expected," Elizabeth says as she closes the office door behind us.

She's cute. And naïve. I'm not making this easy for them. I'm making it easy for me.

"Where's Olivia?" I want to slap myself for letting the question slip from my mouth. She abandoned us. Why do I care where she is?

"She didn't want to interfere," Elizabeth answers.

Interfere? She didn't want to get involved with her own family is more like it.

Knock! Knock!

Now what? "Who is it?"

My question wasn't an invitation, but it doesn't stop Lilac from opening the door and peeking her head in. "I'm sorry I'm late. I had a meeting I couldn't get out of."

I cross my arms over my chest and glare at the group. "Can we get started or are we waiting for anyone else?"

Ashlyn bites her lip. "Well…"

I inhale a deep breath and straighten my back. I got this. I'll handle them before the rest of Ashlyn's sisters arrive. The happily married and happily engaged should stick to their own business. They don't know anything about this situation.

"I'm fine," I declare.

Elizabeth snorts. "Yeah, right."

Gabrielle nudges her. "You promised not to bicker with her today."

"I'm not bickering. I'm merely pointing out how she's a big, fat liar pants."

"I am not a liar pants. Are my pants currently on fire?"

Elizabeth opens her mouth to contradict me, but I hold up my hand to stop her.

"I'm serious. I'm fine. I'm not brokenhearted. Cedar and I aren't – weren't – a couple. We were friends with benefits. And now the benefits part of the equation has been eliminated."

Elizabeth's mouth gapes open. "I knew she was a liar, but I didn't realize she was also delusional."

Lilac purses her lips. "I prefer not to use the word delusional as it usually refers to a person with a mental illness, but I have to admit the word is used correctly in this instance."

I rub my temples as I chant to myself *it's not okay to smack your sister-in-law, it's not okay to smack your sister-in-law.*

Elizabeth claps. "Nailed it!"

I amend my earlier chant. *It's not okay to smack your sister or your sister-in-law. It's not okay to smack your sister or your sister-in-law.*

The chanting has no effect. My hands itch to kick everyone out of my office, lock the door behind them, and hide in here until my heart repairs itself.

Yeah, yeah, my heart. I'm not saying I'm in love with Cedar, but— Ah, crap. I'm in love with Cedar. When the hell did this happen? How did this happen? I've been protecting my heart from love since I was thirteen years old. This is a disaster.

"It's happening," Ashlyn says, and I glance her way to discover she has a phone aimed in my direction.

I slap the phone away. "What are you doing?"

"Duh. I'm recording this session since you don't want my sisters here."

"Do you not know what invasion of privacy means?"

She shrugs. "I prefer to ignore the existence of menial things such as privacy."

"You're worse than the gossip gals."

She bounces on her toes. "Thank you. Can I use you as a reference on my application?"

Forget smacking. I'm going to kill her. I'm going to wrap my hands around her neck and squeeze until it erupts like an ugly ass zit. *Pop!*

Lilac steps in front of me. "No."

I feign confusion. "No, what?"

"No, you will not kill my sister no matter how many times I may have wished to do the same thing in my life."

Ashlyn gasps and clutches her chest. "My own sister doesn't love me."

"E-freaking-nough!" Elizabeth screams loud enough the door rattles.

Although, the rattling door may have to do with the people in the hallway trying to get into the room. Too bad for them I have a remote locking mechanism for my office door. It was the first thing I installed when I took over the bar. Because, unlike the rest of this town, I treasure my privacy.

"Let us in!" Aspen shouts.

Elizabeth marches to the door, but when she twists the knob to open it, nothing happens. I raise the remote I'm holding in my hand, and she glares at me.

"Open it," she orders. "I won't let them in." When I don't respond, she sighs. "Pinky promise."

I click the button to unlock the door. As soon as the door opens, Aspen rushes forward, but Elizabeth holds her back.

"There's not enough room for everyone in here."

"Which is why I said we should wait and ambush her at her apartment after work," Juniper says from behind Aspen. Ambush me? She's off my Christmas card list.

"You don't know my sister. She probably already booked a hotel for a week to avoid us," Elizabeth says.

"Don't worry. I canceled her reservation," Lilac announces.

"You what?" Did I screech? I may have.

"It seemed the best course of action."

"You better teach me how to hack or I'll never forgive you."

Gabrielle nudges Lilac. "You should do it. Cassandra holds a mean grudge."

I can't deny it. I am the queen of holding a grudge. Or should I say princess? I rub my chest when an ache builds in it. No, I'm no one's princess. Not anymore.

"I'm not going anywhere as long as Ashlyn's allowed inside," Aspen declares.

"I thought there would be snacks and drinks," Ellery says.

"And a movie," Juniper adds.

"This is not a party!" I scream loud enough for the entire town to hear.

"It kind of is," Ashlyn disagrees. "It's a 'you're heartbroken and we're going to cheer you up'-party."

"The name's too long," Ellery says from where she's now standing inside my office with Aspen and Juniper.

I glare at Elizabeth. "Pinky promise, my ass."

Her eyes widen before she begins pushing the sisters out of the door. She's never going to kick them out now. I march toward them. I got this.

Lilac shackles my wrist to stop me. "I have a suggestion."

Ashlyn crosses her fingers. "Please involve cake. Please involve cake."

"I vote for booze," Juniper hollers.

"Not all of us can drink," Aspen pouts as she glances down at her baby bump.

"Can my sisters please be quiet for a moment?" Lilac asks but doesn't wait for their response before continuing. "All the West sisters will vacate the premises."

"But Cassie's my sister. I have two connections. First—"

Lilac doesn't wait for Ashlyn to finish her explanation before forcing her toward the door. Ashlyn fights her but Lilac's determined. She herds all of her sisters out of the doorway and down the hallway. There's a chance I'm crushing on my boyfriend's fiancée right now.

Elizabeth slams the door behind them. "Good. Now, we can get down to the nitty-gritty."

"Are you okay? What can we do to help?" Gabrielle asks.

"Okay?" I rear back. "Why wouldn't I be okay?"

She reaches for my hands but I stuff them in my pockets. "Because you broke up with the man you love."

"I don't love Cedar," I lie.

Elizabeth snorts. "Can we skip the lies? And jump straight to the healing portion of the evening?"

"I'm not lying. I don't love Cedar."

"I guess we can't." She pokes my stomach. "You, Cassandra Claire Dempsey, are in love with Cedar Archer Hansley. Do you deny the charges?"

"I—"

She holds up her palm to stop me and speaks to Gabrielle. "She's denying the charges."

I slap her hand away and lean into her face to hiss at her. "I'm not denying the charges. There are no charges. This is ridiculous. I don't love Cedar."

"Why are you lying about loving him?" Gabrielle asks.

At her quiet voice asking me about love, I lose it. All restraint is gone. Everything I've been hiding for twenty years pours out of me. The guilt. The fear. Every single bit.

"Because I don't deserve love!"

"Everyone deserves love."

I cross my arms over my chest and glare down at her. "Oh, yeah? Even people who killed their parents?"

"You didn't kill Mom and Dad. They died in an accident," Elizabeth says.

"I. Killed. Them." I slam my palm against my chest. "Me!"

She reaches for my hands, but I scoot backwards behind my desk where she can't touch me.

"And now you know why I don't deserve love."

"Bullshit, Cassie. Tell me you understand it's bullshit."

"It's not. It's all my fault Mom and Dad are dead."

"You're wrong."

My head hurts and my heart aches. My throat closes up and I can't breathe. Guilt and heartache choke me. They'll never forgive me for what I've done. I'm going to lose them. This is why I never intended to tell my sisters what I did.

"Please go."

"No, we need to—"

Gabrielle nudges Elizabeth toward the door. "Time to go."

"But she—"

"Isn't going to listen to you now."

"Fine. We're going. But this isn't over."

I'm about done with people telling me things aren't over. This is definitely over. I'm never discussing it again. In fact, it might be time to leave. The only reason I moved to Colorado was to be near my family, but I've lost them now. There's no reason to stay.

Chapter 29

Never tell your brother a secret ~ Cedar's rules for living in close proximity to his meddlesome family

CEDAR

I'm not surprised when I open my door to find Rowan standing on my porch. I motion him inside.

"Do you want a coffee or is this a beer conversation?"

"You tell me."

If we're talking about Cassie and what happened, the answer is clear. "Beer."

We settle on the sofa with our drinks. My bottle is half-empty before Rowan speaks.

"I'm surprised you broke up with Cassandra."

I snort. "Don't start with whatever reverse psychology crap this is. You know damn well and good Cassie broke up with me."

"Yeah. This town doesn't know how to keep a secret."

"Secret? This town doesn't understand privacy."

"Is the lack of privacy why you left? Because everyone's in everyone's business?"

Crap. Shit. Damn. And fuck. This is not the conversation I want to have today. Or ever.

I shrug. "I'm a wanderer."

"You're a fucking liar is what you are."

I never could fool my big brother. He's barely a year older than me, but Rowan will always be my big brother.

"I thought you came here to talk to me about how I'm ruining my life by letting Cassie go."

"I did come here to talk to you about how you're ruining your life. By letting Cassie go. By not settling down anywhere. By not allowing yourself to grow friendships. By not being around your family."

"I don't want to talk about this."

"I don't care. I've waited and waited and waited for you to come to me."

This is news to me. "You have?"

He rolls his eyes. "Of course, I have. I'm your big brother and I love you. You're hurting and I want to help."

I frown. "I'm not hurting."

"You're lying again."

"When did you get this smart?"

He smiles. "I'm not the dumb jock everyone thinks I am."

"I don't think you're a dumb jock." Why would I be jealous of him and his life if he was simply a dumb jock?

He cocks his eyebrow. "You don't?"

"Of course not."

"Okay, let's proceed to theory number two."

I chuckle. "Theory number two? Do you have a list of reasons why you think I'm hurting?"

"It's not written down or anything."

"Ashlyn's a good influence on you."

His smile stretches from ear to ear. "She is. She really is."

"I'm glad you finally got your head out of your ass and went for what you wanted."

"Me too." He clears his throat. "And now it's time for your head to get out of your ass so you can get what you want."

"My head's not up my ass. Cassie's the one who broke up with me."

"And you're going to just let her go."

I concentrate on peeling the label from my beer as I consider my answer. I don't want to let Cassie go. She's my princess and I love her.

But maybe she's better off without me. After all, someday a better job will come along and I'll leave. But Cassie's here to stay. Her business and her family are here. She won't want to go anywhere with me. Especially not after our last fight.

"What the hell, Cedar. You obviously love her. What's holding you back?"

A metric ton of baggage. The kind I've been dragging around with me for over a decade. It's heavy, but I've got this. I will always have this. Because I'm not discussing my baggage with him. I never want Rowan to know. I don't want this to come between us.

"What aren't you telling me?"

I bark out a laugh. "A lot."

He drops his gaze to his beer bottle. "You can tell me anything. I know how to keep a secret unlike the rest of the people in this town."

I frown. Keeping his infertility issues a secret was stupid. And wrong. But it can't be compared to the secrets I'm carrying.

"I'm staying until we iron this out."

"I think your wife and daughter won't be happy with your decision."

"Are you kidding? Ashlyn packed my tent and sleeping bag. She even filled a cooler with food, although how she thinks I can survive on chocolate caramel cake is beyond me. I don't even eat caramel. It's too sweet."

"Are you serious?" I don't wait for his answer before standing to peer out the window. Sure as shit, there's a backpack on my porch.

"Ashlyn doesn't mess around when it comes to what she wants."

"And yet it took you forever to admit you love her."

"I had issues." He clears his throat. "Thanks for circling back. Now, let's discuss yours."

"What are the chances I can kick you out?"

"You can try, but I don't think your dollhouse will survive the destruction when I kick your ass."

"Tiny house," I correct.

"Tiny house? Dollhouse? It's pretty much the same thing."

"This is what I get for opening the door," I mumble.

"My sparkling personality is free of charge."

"You've seriously been hanging around Ashlyn too much."

"That line is courtesy of Bryan."

"I can't believe he's been your assistant through the NFL until now with your bakery."

"Some people are loyal."

Shot to the heart. "I'm loyal."

"Which is why you're going to stick around this time."

"Being a wanderer doesn't mean I'm not loyal."

"And you're a wanderer because …"

I scratch my beard. "I was born this way."

"You're not a fucking pop song. Talk to me."

"I'm getting bored of this conversation."

"Welcome to the club. I was bored of this years ago and yet here we are." He opens his arms and gestures to the room around him.

I don't want to tell him, but he's backed me into a corner. Rowan's a laid back guy but when he focuses on an issue? He treats it like it's a football. And if there's one true thing about the former NFL quarterback, it's that he doesn't let go of the ball unless he's forced to.

"Are you certain you want to know this?"

He sits up and squeezes my shoulder. "I'm certain."

Crap. I guess it's time to come clean.

"I left because I was a burden to Mom and Dad. And once I was gone, I couldn't find my way back again."

He rears back. "Are you fucking kidding me?"

I shake my head.

He springs to his feet and paces the living area as he runs his hand through his hair. "Why would you think you were a burden?"

"Because I *was* a burden."

"You're going to have to explain this to me in short sentences with small words because I'm confused."

I down the rest of my beer as I try to figure out how to begin. As if there's an easy way to begin.

"Everything was about you when we were growing up."

He freezes. "What do you mean?"

I don't want to explain, but I'm in this now.

"You were this athletic prodigy. You trained with coaches all over the state. And you went to football camps all over the country. Me? I was the nerdy kid who was good in math."

"You were more than a nerdy kid."

"I wasn't and I've come to accept it."

He growls. "Which is why we're discussing this more than a decade after we graduated from high school."

I raise my hands. "This is why I don't want to talk about it. Whatever I say will offend you."

"I'm not offended," he's quick to say. "But you need to explain more. How does my being an athletic prodigy lead to you being a wanderer who's scared to step foot in Winter Falls?"

"I'm not scared to step foot in Winter Falls."

"Answer the question."

I blow out a breath and stare at the floor as I say the words I promised myself I'd never say to Rowan, "Mom and Dad didn't want me around, so I left."

"Now, you're making shit up. Mom and Dad love you."

Love and wanting someone around are two different things. "I heard them."

He motions for me to continue. "Go on. What did they say?"

I repeat the words that have haunted me for years. "It would be easier if we didn't have to drag Cedar with us."

"Those words sound damaging but you probably heard them out of context."

I scowl. "It's hard to imagine what context would make those words okay."

He marches toward the door. "I'm going to prove you wrong."

I squeeze his shoulder to stop him. "Let it be. I've processed it."

He snorts. "Processed it? You haven't even begun to process it." He brushes my hand from his shoulder and shoves his feet into his boots. "On the bright side, I won't be camping on the hard ground tonight."

He opens the door, grabs his backpack, and hurries down the stairs.

"You promised you can keep a secret," I shout after his retreating form.

"I got this!" he shouts back.

'I got this' is not a promise to keep his mouth shut. Crap. I rub a hand over my face. I shouldn't have told him. I should have hitched my house up to my truck when Cassie broke things off with me and left this town.

But, despite everything, I'm not ready to give up on my princess.

Chapter 30

Never stick around when you can run from a problem ~ Cassie's rules for surviving this thing called life

I HEAR A KNOCK on my apartment door and freeze. Damnit. I thought I was fast enough. I shove my suitcase under the bed before straightening my ponytail and strolling to the door as if nothing's wrong. Because nothing is wrong.

I open the door to discover Beckett standing there holding a key in his hand. I cock my eyebrow.

"I didn't think you were going to answer."

I cross my arms over my chest. "Where'd you get the key from?"

"I'm not at liberty to discuss it."

"I thought Lilac preferred to break in."

He shrugs. "Why break in when you have a key?"

I hold out my hand. "Gimme." He immediately places the key in my hand. Red flag! "And the other key you're hiding in your pocket."

"It's not in my pocket," he grumbles as he removes a key from his wallet.

"Nice doing business with you." I try to shut the door, but he plants his gigantic foot in the doorjamb to stop me.

"We haven't begun to do business yet."

"I don't have time for this."

He pushes his way inside. "You're making time."

"I'm serious. I have plans."

"Which are hereby cancelled."

"You can't cancel my plans," I growl.

"Already done."

He's bluffing. There's no way he cancelled my hotel reservations. "I sincerely doubt it."

"Lilac says if you want to reserve a hotel room anonymously you need to use a VPN to mask your IP address in addition to using a false name."

"Crap."

My brother just had to fall in love with a super smart woman, didn't he? He couldn't have settled for his blonde secretary. Although she was a bitch who did try to ruin his career, so avoiding her was probably a good choice.

I snag two beers out of the refrigerator and hand one to Beckett before collapsing on the sofa. "Let the lecture begin."

"What would I lecture you about?" he asks as he sits next to me.

"I don't know. About my running away. About my refusal to talk to the 'family' about Cedar. About Cedar. Pick a topic. Any topic."

Please don't. Please don't pick any topic. Please drink your beer and exit posthaste.

"How about none of the above?"

"Sounds good. We'll drink our beers in silence before you return to the lovely Lilac who is now at the top of my prank list."

I need to think of an epic prank for his fiancée. Something I've never done before. Something to make her realize messing with Cassandra was a mistake. Her worst mistake ever.

Beckett snorts. "Silence? You're funny."

"I'm hilarious," I mutter before downing my beer.

"You didn't kill our parents," he whispers.

"Yeah, I did."

"They died in a car accident."

Damnit. Why did I ever open my big, fat mouth and tell Gabrielle and Elizabeth the truth? I knew they wouldn't keep it to themselves. The Dempsey family is as bad at observing privacy boundaries as the people of Winter Falls. There's a reason my sisters feel at home here. Except for Olivia who is currently who the hell knows where.

"I don't want to talk about it." If it sounds like I'm pouting, it's because I am.

"Too bad. Mom and Dad died twenty years ago. You've been holding onto this guilt for all these years for no reason."

No reason? Wrong. There's a big reason. A ginormous reason. Because I'm guilty. Thus, the guilt.

"Still don't want to talk about it."

"You can't out stubborn me on this."

Oh yeah? Watch me.

"I'll sit here all night bugging you until you talk."

Did big bro throw down? It's on.

"Good thing I just bought groceries. You want another beer?" I stand.

"No. I don't want another beer. I want you to sit your ass down and talk to me."

"Sorry, big brother of mine. I don't take orders from you."

"No shit. You never listened to me when you were a teenager. This gray hair?" He motions to his temples where his brown hair is now gray. "It's all your fault."

"No way. Olivia's responsible for at least eighty percent of your gray hair."

I'll accept credit for twenty percent, but I won't go any higher.

"Thank the stars above the two of you fought like cats and dogs when you were teenagers. If the two of you ever teamed up?" He shivers. "I don't want to think about it."

I guess he's forgetting about the time Olivia signed me out of school and took me to her 'guy' to have a fake ID made before we went to the Anheuser-Busch brewery. We spent the afternoon drinking there before we decided riding the Gateway Arch while drunk would be the best experience of our lives.

I'm pretty sure the other three passengers in our barrel to the top didn't agree when I started throwing up all over the place. Heights and movement is not a good combination with drinking. Live and learn. At least the police gave us a warning that time.

Beckett grabs my wrist and pulls until I'm forced to sit down next to him.

"Enough with the jokes and distractions. I'm being serious. You didn't cause Mom and Dad's accident."

"And I'm being serious, too, when I say I did."

He squeezes my hand. "Can you explain why you think you caused the accident?"

"No, but I can explain how I did cause the accident."

He arches his brow and waits. Crap on a stick. Where did those words come from? I didn't plan on explaining shit to Beckett today.

"If I wanted to, I could."

"Don't be a brat. I'm trying to help you here."

"And I never asked for your help."

"Too bad. You're my sister. You're getting my help whenever you need it, whether you ask for it or not."

"And, apparently, whether I want it or not."

"Damn straight." He nods. "Now, go on. Tell me how you used your magical broom to push Mom and Dad's car into oncoming traffic."

"I'm not a witch. I don't have a magical broom."

"How else could you have caused the accident? Or did you forget you were at home with me when it happened?"

That's it. I'm done. I have had it with him and his bullshit. I'll tell him what I did and then he'll know. Of course, it will be the end of our relationship when he realizes the truth. I killed our parents.

I surge to my feet. "Because I'm the reason they were on the road late at night when it was raining and sleeting outside. Me!" I pound my chest as I shout.

"If it weren't for me, they would have never gone to the pharmacy to get cough medicine. If I hadn't been such a sickly child, they wouldn't have been out on those treacherous roads."

I can't breathe. Where's all the air? Did it disappear? I clutch my chest as I try to force oxygen into my lungs. But there's none to be had.

Beckett pushes me into a chair and presses on the back of my neck until I'm forced to bend over and place my head between my knees.

"Just breathe, Cassie. Just breathe."

"H-h-h-ow?"

"Breathe with me. Big inhale in. Big exhale out."

I follow his guidance until I remember how to inhale air into my lungs.

Beckett rubs my back. "You okay now?"

I keep my gaze fixed on the floor when I answer, "Yeah."

He pinches my chin and forces me to lift my head until our gazes meet. "You didn't kill Mom and Dad."

"But—"

"Nope. No buts about it. Mom and Dad drove to the pharmacy because their daughter was sick and they wanted her to feel better. Don't you know Mom and Dad would have done anything for you? They loved you more than anything in the world."

"Except you," I butt in to say.

"Yeah, but let's face it, you can't compete with me."

"But they wouldn't have been out in the storm if it weren't for me."

His hold on my chin tightens. "Did you cause the rain? Did you cause the sleet? Did you cause the man driving his truck to not have his brakes checked? Did you force him to speed through a red light?"

I bite my tongue.

"Well? Did you?"

"No."

"Then, I think it's safe to assume you didn't kill Mom and Dad. Do you understand me?"

I shrug. Maybe?

"I'm sorry."

I rear back and his hand drops from my face. "You? What are you sorry for?"

"I'm sorry you've been carrying this guilt around for years and I didn't know. I failed you."

I wag my finger at him. "Oh, no, you don't. You don't get to make this about you. This is my fucked up problem."

He smiles but it doesn't reach his eyes. "I should have paid more attention to you. I should have realized there was a reason you flirted from one-night stand to another. Always refusing to settle down."

"Okay, fine. Enough with the guilt trip. I should have talked to you about this sooner. Are we done now?"

He pulls me into his arms and squeezes.

"Can't breathe."

"Good. Now you understand how I feel when one of you girls is suffering."

His arms relax and I cuddle into his hold. "Thanks, big bro."

"Anytime, little sis. Anytime."

I don't know if I believe him when he says I didn't kill our parents, but at least he's not kicking me out of the family for what I did.

Chapter 31

CEDAR

I grunt when I hear banging on my door. Freaking Rowan. I knew he wouldn't leave this alone. But when I open the door, it's not my brother standing there.

"Mom. Dad. What are you doing here?"

I have a sneaking suspicion I know exactly what they're doing here. I'm going to kick my big brother's ass the next time I see him.

"Well, son, are you going to stand there staring at us all day or let us in?" Dad asks.

Mom doesn't wait for my reply before pushing her way inside. "Where's my hug?"

She throws her arms around me and pulls me close. I hesitate for a second before wrapping myself around her and laying my cheek on top of her head.

"It's a good thing we're staying with Rowan because there's no way the three of us would fit in here," Dad says, and I step away from Mom.

I feign not knowing why they're here. "Are you here to visit Patience?"

Mom fists her hands at her hip. "Are we here to visit Patience?"

I glance at Dad since I know better than to answer her. He shrugs. Apparently, he doesn't have a response either.

"Shall I make some coffee?"

"I'll make it," Mom says before she marches to the kitchen. She sets her purse down on the counter and purses her lips as she studies the area.

"At least it's better than the van you lived in when you were in Oregon," she mutters as she opens and shuts cupboards until she locates the coffee and some mugs.

"The van was only temporary," I say.

"Temporary?" She snorts. "What isn't temporary in your life?"

"This tiny house isn't temporary," I argue. "It's perfect for me, and it's completely off grid."

"And way too small for a family."

I rub a hand over my beard. "Aren't you supposed to give me a break since you already have one grandchild?"

"Nope. I want tons of the little critters running around the house."

"Critters?" I force a chuckle. "Are we discussing grandchildren or mice?"

"Enough!" Mom slams the kettle down on the stove and promptly bursts into tears.

Shit. I stand to go to her, but Dad stops me. "I got this."

Dad folds Mom into his arms. He whispers in her ear as he rocks her back and forth. Envy burns in my stomach and I have to look away. What they have is exactly what I want with Cassie. But I haven't heard from her since she stormed out of here over a week ago. I've phoned. I've messaged. No response.

Dad leads Mom to the sofa to sit down and I stand to finish making the coffee. While it brews, I try to think of how to get out of this situation. I don't want to hurt my parents by telling them what I overheard. What good could possibly come of it?

"Nuh-uh," Mom says when I hand her a mug of coffee.

"You don't want a coffee?"

She points to me. "Whatever you're thinking in that big old brain of yours is wrong."

I grab a chair from the kitchen table and drag it over to the sofa while I consider how much to tell them.

"Stop procrastinating."

I take a sip of coffee before answering, "I'm not procrastinating." I am, but apparently, I'm not very good at it.

Mom sets her coffee on the table. "Rowan told us."

"Told you what?" I hedge.

"We're the reason you abandoned Winter Falls and your family!" she shouts before bursting into tears again.

I fall to my knees in front of her. "It's not your fault, Mom."

"Yes, it is!" she wails.

I raise an eyebrow at Dad. He should know how to handle her. "She's been this way since Rowan called and told us to get our butts back to Colorado."

"What else did Rowan say?"

Mom drops her hands from her face to answer. "He said I'm a terrible mother!"

I squeeze her thighs. "I doubt Rowan said anything of the sort."

"But it's true. First, we know nothing about Rowan's infertility problems. We thought he got divorced because Sandra cheated on him."

He did get divorced because Sandra cheated on him but explaining Rowan's marital problems is not going to help me now.

"But we failed you even worse. We had no idea you left Winter Falls because of us."

"Having children is exhausting," Dad says, and my brow wrinkles.

"I don't—"

He raises a hand to stop me. "And having two gifted children is even more exhausting."

I frown. I wasn't gifted. "I—"

"Let me speak, son."

I nod for him to continue.

"We were always driving one of you to some special class or training session."

Special class? I don't remember any special classes.

"We were lucky you were in the same grade as Lilac West at school. We could trade off driving you to White Bridge for college classes with Ruby."

I forgot all about those college classes. But Dad is implying I'm some kind of genius. I wasn't. The simple truth is Winter

Falls High School didn't have math classes for someone like me or Lilac. Small towns don't have the resources for advanced classes in all subjects.

"I won't deny we made mistakes, but we did the best we could."

"We wanted to give you boys the world." Mom hiccups and Dad rubs her back. "I didn't realize how exhausting it would be."

"And when you're exhausted you sometimes say hurtful things. Hurtful things not meant for little ears."

I snort. My ears were hardly little when I overheard them.

Mom grasps my hands. "Why didn't you say anything?"

"You should have told us what you heard, and we could have handled it then instead of you letting it fester for over a decade," Dad adds.

"I haven't let it fester," I deny.

Dad snorts. "Which is why we're having this conversation now in a tiny home you have parked outside of Winter Falls instead of on your brother's property."

I spot the chance to change the subject and grab hold of it with both hands.

"On Rowan's property? Ashlyn would be on my doorstep every five minutes. And the gossip gals wouldn't let me rest until they matched me with some local."

Mom grins. "Speaking of matching, you have a girlfriend now?"

I groan. I don't know what's worse. Listening to Mom cry and berate herself for being a bad parent or dealing with her asking about my girlfriend.

"I don't have a girlfriend," I say as I return to my chair.

Mom ignores what I said. "I can't wait to meet her."

"I'm serious, Mom. I don't have a girlfriend. She broke up with me."

She purses her lips. "And what are you going to do about it? Are you going to let her run away?"

I scratch my beard. "Exactly how much gossip did you hear when you arrived in Winter Falls?"

Dad laughs. "As if we need to be in Winter Falls to learn the gossip."

I should have known. "How long are you staying in town?"

Mom widens her eyes, and Dad whistles as he looks away.

"How long?"

Mom's nose wrinkles. "Forever?"

"Forever? I thought you loved living in Florida."

After they retired, Rowan bought them a house in Florida. From everything they've said, they love it down there. Of course, there's a chance the homeowner's association is trying to kick them out since Mom thinks serving hash brownies at book club is perfectly normal.

Mom's lips purse. "The house is lovely, but the people are …"

Dad wraps an arm around Mom and draws her near. "What she's trying to say is no one will select her smutty books for the book club."

She slaps his chest. "As if you're any better trying to convince everyone to switch to solar power and electric cars."

"The house was already on the market when Rowan phoned us."

Mom beams at me. "And now we can be here when you make up with your girlfriend."

"You're going to join the gossip gals now, aren't you?"

"I don't need those ladies."

Interpretation. They turned her down.

Mom checks her watch. "We need to go. We promised to babysit Patience so Rowan and Ashlyn can have a date night."

She stands and kisses my cheek. "I love you to the moon and back. I'm sorry you ever doubted it."

Dad slaps my shoulder. "To the moon and back, son. To the moon and back."

I walk them to the parking area near my tiny home. As I'm returning, I happen upon Old Man Mercury.

"Mercury." I nod and continue on my way since the man doesn't usually waste time talking to me.

"Living as a hermit is no way to live," he says, and I stop in my tracks. I glance over my shoulder to find him frowning at me. "Life is meant to be lived. Hiding away doesn't help anything."

"I know, Mercury. I know."

"You won't run off again?"

I shake my head. "I'm here to stay."

He grunts and continues on his way without another word.

As I watch him leave, I realize I didn't lie. I am in Winter Falls to stay. My brother and his family are here and now my parents are too. I've missed too much of their lives because of one sentence I overheard and misinterpreted over a decade ago.

It's time to plant some roots. Now I just need to convince Cassie to stay here with me.

Chapter 32

When all else fails, try hiding in plain sight. Who knows? It might work ~ Cassie's rules for living her best life

I FINISH PLACING THE beer in the refrigerator under the bar and stand. The door opens and I glance over. When I see who it is, I debate dropping back down to my knees and crawling away.

"You can't hide when you manage a bar in Winter Falls," Cedar calls.

But I can try.

"I'm busy."

He motions to the empty bar. "No, you're not. The bar doesn't open for another hour."

How dare he point out I'm lying! I cross my arms over my chest and shoot daggers at him through my eyes. The daggers must not have any effect on him as he doesn't explode into a big ball of flames. Bummer.

"We need to talk."

Talking to him is at the top of my list of 'things I plan to do when hell freezes over'.

"There's no need to talk. I understand."

"What do you understand?"

"You're leaving," I grit out.

I'm such an idiot. I knew he was a wanderer when we met, but the knowledge didn't stop me from falling in love with the guy. I've kept my heart encased in the world's most thief-proof safe for decades but then Cedar comes along and – boom! – it flies open for him, and he didn't even need to learn the combination.

"I never considered taking the job."

Does he expect me to believe this bullshit?

"Sure, you didn't. Did you forget you're a drifter?"

The door bangs open and Lennon strolls in. "I'm here."

What is he doing here? It's the middle of the week. I don't need his help today. I didn't ask him to come in.

"I see you are. The question is why."

Cedar chuckles. "Princess."

I glare at him. "I'm not your princess. I'm not your any-thing."

My chest squeezes at the words, but they're true. Cedar and I are over.

He places his hands on the counter and hops over it to my side. My gaze drops to his arms, and he flexes his biceps. Holy shit. Cedar jumping over the bar was literally the sexiest thing I've ever seen. I debate crossing my legs to alleviate the ache growing in my center, but I don't want him to think he's won. Being sexually attracted to him doesn't change anything.

But you love him. Oh, shut up, little voice of reason. No one wants to hear your opinion.

"Do you want to talk about this out here in front of Lennon or in your office?"

"I vote not at all."

"Not an option."

I glance at Lennon across the bar. He smiles and winks at me. Crap. He won't hesitate to gather the gossip gals and the rest of the town together to listen if I stay out here to talk to Cedar.

"My office." I stomp my way through the bar down the hallway to my office with Cedar following.

"Princess, you need to let me explain," he begins once we're behind a closed door.

I rub my temples where I can feel a headache blossoming. I have no desire to have this conversation. On top of which, I'm tired as I haven't slept well since I found out Cedar's planning to leave before the dare is over. I wasn't prepared for him to leave early.

You weren't prepared for him to leave at all.

I'm going to strangle the voice of reason in my head before the day is over.

I collapse into the desk chair. "Whatever. Go ahead."

"Are you going to listen to me?"

"No. I'm planning to sit here and mentally go through my stock order."

"I got it!" Lennon shouts through the door.

Note to self: Buy a soundproof door.

Cedar sits in the chair across from my desk.

"Make yourself comfortable, why don't you?"

"Don't mind if I do. I'm sitting here until you stop being stubborn and listen to me."

I snort. "You can't out stubborn me."

He shrugs and settles back in his chair. "Maybe not. But I am sitting between you and the door."

I roll my eyes. "Big deal."

"The door leading to the restrooms."

I narrow my eyes at him. He knows my bladder is the size of a pea – a baby pea at that – and just mentioning a bathroom is enough to make me need to go.

"I'm not standing in your way." He motions to the door. "Go ahead. I'll be here when you return."

"Don't you need to work? Oh wait. You probably already gave notice at your old job," I snarl.

"I told you. I didn't accept the job."

"It doesn't matter. Sooner or later a job is going to come along and off you go."

"Wrong."

I narrow my eyes on him. "Why should I believe you?"

"I'm not leaving Winter Falls."

Liar. I wouldn't have had to dare him to stay if he wasn't planning on leaving sooner or later.

"Which is why you're hiding out on land outside of the town."

"I'm not hiding out anymore. In fact, my parents came by to see me yesterday."

"Your parents?" I'm confused. "I thought they lived in Flori-da."

"Apparently, they're moving back home."

"I'm not sure what this has to do with anything."

He rubs a hand over his beard. "There are reasons I became a wanderer."

Damnit! I'm curious. Intrigued actually. I want to know what those reasons are, but I feign nonchalance. "What does this have to do with me?"

"Everything, princess. Everything."

I hate how my belly warms at his nickname for me. I rub a hand over it. We're not falling for his bullshit, remember? *Speak for yourself!*

"I overheard my parents say they didn't want me when I was a teenager."

I gasp. "What? How dare they?"

My hands fist. I'll show them how they should treat their children.

"Calm down, trouble. It was a misunderstanding."

"How do you accidentally say you don't want one of your children?"

"They said it would be easier if they didn't have to drag me with them."

"No!" I jump to my feet and rush to him. "I'm sorry, Cedar."

He pulls me onto his lap until I'm straddling him. He tucks a strand of my hair behind my ear, and I shiver at the feel of his hands on my skin.

"They didn't mean it how it sounded."

I'm not ready to forgive them yet. "What did they mean?"

"They were exhausted. Between Rowan the football god and me, they were always driving one of us somewhere." He shrugs. "I kind of forgot about how they took me to White Bridge for college classes every day."

"Nerd."

"It always felt like Rowan was the golden child and I was the afterthought."

I run my hands through his hair. "I'm sorry."

"And, after I overheard them that one time, I decided to put Winter Falls in my rearview mirror as soon as I could."

"What about now?" The question slips out before I can stop it.

He pinches my chin until I'm forced to meet his gaze. "I'm not going anywhere."

"You're not accepting the job in Boston?"

"I'm not going anywhere," he repeats.

Excitement courses through me, but I find it hard to believe he would stay in one place after a decade of being a drifter.

"Won't you get bored?"

He chuckles. "Have you met the people of Winter Falls? There's no getting bored here."

He's not wrong.

Dare I believe him? Dare I take a chance on him staying here? If he leaves, he'll take my heart with him. Can I chance the heartbreak? I bite my lip as I contemplate my choices.

"I know you're scared."

I bristle. Cassandra Claire Dempsey isn't afraid of anything.

"I get it. I'm scared, too."

Cedar is not the type of man to be frightened of anything.

"What are you scared of?"

"Of you not giving us a chance."

He leans forward to nibble on my ear and I melt into him.

"Maybe I need a bit more convincing before I give us a chance."

I sound as if I'm teasing, but I'm not. Giving him a chance is a one-way street to heartbreak. I visited the location recently and it wasn't much fun.

He stands with me in his arms. "Challenge accepted."

He carries me toward the back door. "Where are you going? I need to work."

"I got it," Lennon says from the end of the hall. "You kids go enjoy yourselves."

Cedar gazes down at me. His eyes are on fire. "We will," he mutters. "We will."

Chapter 33

CEDAR

I spot Cassie's car in the parking lot and exhale a sigh of relief. I don't think I can walk the distance to her apartment with my cock hard and begging for me to take her. And there's no place in Winter Falls to have sex outside without someone happening upon you.

They wouldn't care. In fact, many residents would stop to watch and cheer you on. But I have no interest in sharing my most intimate moments with Cassie with anyone. They're mine and no one else's.

This time when I try to start her car, I need to input a pin code.

"What's the code?"

"One one two zero."

One one two zero, I repeat to myself as I punch in the number and the engine ignites. Is it a date? November twentieth. It's not her birthday. Could it be the date of her parents' death?

I would never ask her, but I do know one thing that happened on the date.

"November twentieth is the day we met."

"Don't make a big deal about it."

I glance to the left before she notices the smirk on my face. It's all the confirmation I need. She cares about me as much as I care about her. I was all in before, but now I won't let her push me away. Not anymore.

The drive to Cassie's apartment is fast. When we arrive, I hurry out of the car and rush to her door before dragging her out of the car and to her apartment.

She giggles. "In a hurry?"

Damn straight, I'm in a hurry. I've spent more than a week thinking I lost her. Wondering how to get her back. Worried she'd escape town before I had the chance to convince her we're perfect together.

I snatch the keys from her and open the apartment door. I'm immediately attacked by Diva. I pick her up and scratch behind her ear. Good thing I'm prepared for this.

"Here you go," I say as I offer her a piece of rawhide I stuck in my back pocket earlier.

She scurries off to her doggy bed without a second glance at Cassie who stands in the doorway staring at her dog with her mouth gaping open. I have better uses for her luscious mouth.

"Come on." I shackle her wrist and draw her into the apartment before slamming the door behind us. I throw her over my shoulder and march to the bedroom.

"I have legs. I can walk, you know."

"Too slow," I grunt.

"What does it say about me that this caveman routine is working for me?"

I reach the bedroom and fling her onto the bed.

"It says you know what you enjoy in the bedroom."

I put a knee on the mattress, but she wags a finger at me. "Nuh-uh. Clothes off first."

My princess wants a show? She gets a show.

I play with the hem of my Henley and she lifts up on her knees to watch. I tug it off to reveal my fitted t-shirt. Her eyes flare as she licks her lips.

"You approve of what you see?" I wink before I rid myself of the t-shirt.

Her hands reach out, but I step away. "No touching the talent."

She bats her eyelashes. "What if I pay extra?"

"I don't want payment in cash."

She immediately catches on and whips off her sweater. She's still wearing a long-sleeved t-shirt. I cock a brow.

She bats her eyelashes. "You show me yours and I'll show you mine."

I glide a hand down my naked chest toward my waist. "Princess, I'm already showing you mine."

Her gaze is fixated on where I'm toying with the button of my jeans.

"Princess," I warn. "You have some catching up to do."

She stares into my eyes as she grasps the hem of her t-shirt and draws it up over her body until she's left in her bra. She trails a finger over the edge of the satin material. "Am I caught up now?"

She pinches her nipples through the material, and I groan as my cock twitches. He wants to slide between her breasts as she pushes them together. Later, I promise.

I clear my throat. "Close enough."

I kick off my boots and unsnap my jeans before pushing the material down my legs until I'm standing completely naked before her.

I squeeze my cock to stop it from detonating before I can get inside Cassie.

She gasps. "Tug it again."

"What will you do if I agree?"

Her hand sneaks down her body and under the waistband of her jeans.

"Nope. I need to see what you're doing."

She flops down on the bed before unzipping her jeans and shoving the material along with her panties off.

I chuckle. "You in a hurry?"

"To watch you play with your cock? Hell yeah."

At her words, my cock juts toward her. He knows where the promised land is.

"Are you going to play with yourself at the same time?"

She lays down on the bed and spreads her legs for me. I groan and my hand reaches for my cock. As I pull on it, she sneaks her hand down her body and uses two fingers to enter herself. I want my fingers to be the ones inside of her, but it's hot as hell watching her pleasure herself.

My hand tightens until I'm gripping my cock for all its worth. Cassie arches her back, displaying her bra-covered tits for me.

"Remove your bra," I order.

She starts to withdraw her fingers from inside her, but I stop her. "Use your other hand."

She reaches behind her and flicks the bra open allowing the cups to fall and showcasing her magnificent breasts. I want to come all over them. I want to rub my semen into her petal soft skin.

At the idea, my cock swells, and my balls tighten. I kneel on the bed over Cassie as I work my cock.

"Gonna come."

"Come inside me."

"Can't. Not going to last." If I'm inside my princess, she's coming first.

Her breath hitches. "Me either."

Damn. I want inside her. I don't want to finish in my hand. "You sure?"

In response, she withdraws her fingers, wraps her legs around my waist, and draws me near until I have to let go of my cock or fall on her.

"I'm sure."

I'm not asking again. I line myself up at her opening and plunge inside.

"Yes," she hisses.

Despite my warning about coming too quickly, I stop once I'm fully seated to take a breath. I lean my forehead against hers.

"You ready for the ride of your life?"

I'm not referring to sex, but she'll learn soon enough what I'm talking about.

"Hell yeah."

I take my time pulling out and once only my tip remains inside her, I slam into her again. Her body slides forward with the force and I wrap an arm around her waist to stop her from hitting the headboard.

Her walls flutter around me before tightening. She wasn't lying. She's close.

I pound into her two more times before she's arching her back and rubbing her nipples against my chest.

"Yes. Yes. Yes."

"Wait for me," I grit out.

Her hands grip my hair and yank until I'm forced to look into her face. "If you want me to wait, you need to be quick."

"I'll be quick."

I don't want to rush, but the feeling of coming with Cassie is out of this world. Besides, we have the rest of our lives to explore each other. Today is only the beginning.

I plunge into her one, two, three more times before her eyes glaze over and her walls tighten.

"Cedar. Cedar. Cedar," she chants as she comes.

My climax isn't far behind hers. I continue to glide in and out of her until I've milked every last ounce of my orgasm.

I rest my forehead against hers as I catch my breath. "I love you, Cassandra."

Her eyes fly open before darting toward the door. I squeeze her neck. "There's no need to be frightened. There's no need to run away. Besides, I'd follow you."

Her panicked gaze returns to me. "Okay."

I'll take it. I didn't expect her to spout words of love. I know she needs time to come to grips with her feelings. As I said, I can be a patient man.

Chapter 34

Trust someone special with your secrets ~ Cassie's rules for living her best life

I sigh as I snuggle into the warmth surrounding me. I inhale and the smell of firewood wafts over me. *Cedar.* I wiggle my ass against him and he grunts in response, so I do it again.

"Good morning, princess," he mutters as he kisses my hair.

"Good…" My words trail off when the memory of what he said last night hits me. *He loves me?*

He rubs a hand down my back and squeezes my hip. "It's okay. There's no reason to panic."

"I'm not panicking," I immediately deny because when someone says there's no reason to panic, you deny panicking. Whether you're panicking or not is entirely immaterial.

He chuckles. "Liar."

Before I can deny it again, he rolls me over and climbs on top of me. His hazel eyes are full of warmth as he tucks a strand of hair behind my ear.

"I love you."

My chest tightens and inhaling a breath becomes impossible. Cedar shouldn't love me. I don't deserve love. *Yes, you do.* Beckett's words echo in my head.

Cedar shuffles us around until he's leaning against the headboard with me laying across his lap. He rubs his hand up and down my back as he rocks me from side to side.

"Everything's okay, princess," he whispers over and over again until I somehow manage to figure out how to breathe again.

I burrow into his shoulder. "I'm okay."

"Take your time. I'm happy to sit here all day with you."

I lean back to look at him. "Which has nothing to do with how we're naked."

He waggles his eyebrows. "Naked is just a bonus."

I jiggle my ass against him and feel him begin to harden. "Naughty girl."

"Everyone wins when I'm naughty." I wink.

"Let's hold off naughty for a few minutes."

I jut my bottom lip out and pout. "I hate waiting."

He barks out a laugh. "No shit."

I stick my tongue out.

"I'll make it worth your while," he whispers into my ear before nibbling on the lobe. Oh, he's cruel. He knows what it does to me when he bites my earlobe.

"Why are we waiting?" I sulk.

"We need to get some things straight about us."

I groan. "You've got a willing naked woman in your arms and you want to have the 'talk'?"

He tickles my ribs and I swat his hand away. "No fair. No tickling."

His hands cradle my face. "Are you ready to listen now?"

I roll my eyes. "Go on, then, Mr. Davis Downer."

He clears his throat. "I just want things to be clear. From here on out, we're together. No bets. No dares. Nothing is temporary anymore. When you're upset or read an email not meant for you—"

"It was an accident."

When he shakes his head, I know he doesn't believe me but he's smiling so obviously he isn't mad.

"We discuss things. You don't run off half-cocked."

I bat my eyelashes. "I'm always fully cocked."

He tweaks my nose. "Joke all you want, but I'm being serious. It's you and me against the world."

Him and me against the world? Crap. If we're really doing this thing, I need to tell him about my parents. I squirm.

"What's wrong? Am I going too fast for you?"

My nose wrinkles. "Yes, but there's something else."

He kisses the tip of my nose. "You want to discuss this naked or get dressed first?"

I'd rather be doing something else naked, but I'm going to lose my nerve if I don't say it all now.

"I thought I didn't deserve love because I killed my parents, but I didn't kill them. Or, at least, Beckett claims I didn't. I'm not convinced."

"I think you're going to have to slow down and explain."

I inhale a deep breath and let it out before beginning. "I was a sick child. Hard to believe now, I know."

He squeezes my hip. "Go on."

"The night my parents' died." I swallow the lump forming in my throat. "They were out on the roads because of me. Because they were fetching medicine for me."

"And you've convinced yourself it's your fault they were in a car accident."

I bite my lip as I stare at his chin. "Isn't it?"

"Baby. No." He cradles my face in his hands.

I glance up quickly before my gaze returns to his chin.

"Princess, look at me," he demands, and I force my gaze to meet his.

"You did not kill your parents."

"But—"

"No," he cuts me off. "You are not to blame for their deaths. They died in a car accident."

"But they wouldn't have been out on the roads in such bad weather if it weren't for me."

He sighs. "What would you do if Diva was sick? Really sick. She's throwing up and shitting everywhere."

"I'd take her to the vet."

"But she's going to make a mess on your leather seats."

I slap him. "I don't care about my stupid leather seats. They can be cleaned. I love Diva. If she's sick, I'm going to help her."

"Which is exactly how your parents felt."

I want to snap at him – he didn't know my mom and dad – but he's making a good point. The same one Beckett made in fact. Could it be true? Am I truly not to blame for my parents' death?

"Oh, baby," he says and wraps his arms around me and squishes me to his body. I feel his cock harden, but when I reach for it, he growls. "No. Stop trying to distract me."

Damnit. He's a man. He's supposed to be easily distracted by sex. Of course, I had to fall in love with a man who knows me to my core.

"It's okay. You don't have to say the words."

I lean back to look him in the eyes. "How do you know what I was thinking?"

"Princess, I know you."

I shoot daggers out of my eyes at him. They must be defective because he laughs.

"Do you understand now how you didn't kill your parents?"

"Maybe." I shrug.

"You're not alone. I abandoned my hometown and my family because I thought my parents didn't love me based on one thing they said when they were overwhelmed with raising two teenage prodigies."

"Prodigies? You're a prodigy now, are you?"

"Yep. And this prodigy will remind you how you didn't kill your parents and how you deserve love as many times as you need to hear it." He taps my forehead. "Until it sinks into your stubborn brain."

"I'm not stubborn," I say proving I am indeed stubborn.

"And I haven't been avoiding my brother Rowan for over a decade."

I blow out a puff of air. "Is this how it's going to be from now on? We're going to share feelings and talk about serious stuff."

"Don't look so disgusted." He chuckles. "Besides, maybe I'll reward you for sharing your feelings."

His gaze meets mine and his is full of anticipation. I know he's waiting for me to say I love him. I even open my mouth to speak the words, but nothing comes out.

He brushes the hair from my forehead. "Don't worry. When you're ready, I'll be here. I'm a patient man."

Good thing because he may be waiting a long time.

I'm done with this heavy conversation. It's time to move our morning on to more enjoyable activities.

"I'm ready for something else." I squirm on his lap to make my intentions clear.

"My little vixen," he murmurs before his mouth slams down on mine. This isn't a quick and tender kiss. No, Cedar is determined to devour me. I cling to his shoulders and my nails dig into his skin as I hold on for the ride.

He maneuvers me until I'm straddling him while his back is against the headboard. I rub my center against his cock but don't let him in just yet. Two can play at this teasing game.

He grunts before dragging his lips from mine. He wraps an arm around my waist before pressing on my shoulders until I'm forced to lean back. The position feels awkward, but I forget all about the awkwardness when his mouth latches onto my breast.

I grind against his cock as his teeth bite and nip at my breasts. I reach between us until I can grab his hard length. I'm done fooling around. But before I can sink down onto him, he jerks away.

"What the hell?" he grumbles.

"What the hell, what?"

I scan the room for whatever disturbed him, but I don't see anything out of order.

"Diva is trying to eat my toes."

What? I glance over my shoulder to discover my dog jumping all over Cedar's feet while snapping at his toes.

"Not now, Diva."

She ignores me. Naturally. There's a reason she failed discipline school after all. Hint – it's because she has zero discipline. Of course, me walking out on the first class when someone made fun of her missing an ear didn't help either.

"Diva," I growl. "It's not okay to interrupt sexy times."

Cedar lifts me up so he can get out from under me. He gives me a quick, hard kiss before getting to his feet.

"I think she's hungry."

"Hungry? Her bowl was full when we came home last night."

Diva – denied her toy – runs circles around the bed and I quickly cover myself with a blanket before she decides to bite at exposed parts of my body. Little cannibal. Wait. Is it still cannibalism if one party is a dog and the other a human?

Cedar picks her up and tucks her under his arm as he strolls for the door.

"Aren't you afraid she's going to bite you?" I nod toward his cock, which is still hard and jutting out.

He scowls at her. "Shit. Yeah."

He sets the furball down on the bed. While he searches for his jeans, she yips at him. Lucky for him, she's afraid to jump off of the bed by herself because I swear she's staring at his cock while licking her lips. It's not a hotdog, Diva.

He dons his jeans and t-shirt before picking my doggy up from the bed and strolling out of the room.

"Are you coming back?" I shout after him.

His response? He laughs.

Ugh! Stupid dog ruining sexy times. Note to self: Shut the door to keep Diva out whenever Cedar is sleeping over.

Chapter 35

Always be prepared for an ambush ~ Cedar's rules for living in close proximity to his family

CEDAR

I open the door when I hear the group trampling through the woods toward my house. I've been expecting Beckett, Rowan, Phoenix, and River for the past hour.

"I'm ready," I announce when they reach the clearing I consider my front yard.

"Ready for what?" Beckett asks.

"The male bonding ritual to indicate you accept me in Cassandra's life."

He crosses his arms over his chest. "How do you know the reason why we're here?"

I cock an eyebrow. "You're not here for the bonding ritual?"

"Maybe I don't accept you in Cassandra's life."

I chuckle. "You here to try and beat me up again?"

He growls. "There will be no trying."

"Didn't you promise Cassie you wouldn't return here to give me a lesson with your fists?"

Before Beckett can answer, Phoenix speaks up, "Can we get on with this? Some of us have busy lives to get back to."

River throws an arm around his brother's shoulders before rubbing his knuckles over his hair to give him a noogie. "Little brother's missing his goats."

Phoenix shoves him away. "I'll show you goats."

Rowan sighs before stepping between the brothers. "We agreed on no fighting today."

"Unless Cedar proves himself unworthy," Beckett adds.

"I seriously don't understand how Lilac puts up with you," I tell him.

He grins. "She loves me."

"Can we get on with this now?" Rowan asks the group before addressing me, "Are you ready?"

"I've been ready for the past hour."

"Let me guess. My wife messaged you."

"She's been blowing up my phone for the past hour." I wiggle my phone at him. "You really should give her the red velvet pancake recipe before she gets herself into trouble."

He smirks. "But it's fun to punish her when she's being bad."

I gag. "You're talking about my sister."

"But she's not my sister." He winks.

I shut and lock my door behind me. "Come on. Let's go."

Beckett frowns. "How do you know where we're going?"

I roll my eyes. "Just because I haven't lived in Winter Falls for the past decade doesn't mean I don't know all about the rituals."

We begin hiking through the woods toward the falls.

"You're lucky it's May. Some of us weren't this lucky," Phoenix grumbles. "The falls aren't very warm in November."

"The falls are never warm. There's a reason the town is named Winter Falls after all," I point out.

"We're not done interrogating Cedar, are we?" Beckett asks.

I throw my arms out wide. "Ask me anything."

He shoves my shoulder, and I pretend to stumble. "It's more fun if you fight it."

I bat my eyelashes and add a false vibrato to my voice. "Oh no, Beckett. Don't ask me questions about my feelings. I don't know if I can stand it."

Phoenix points to River. "This one was afraid to talk about his feelings until a few months ago."

River grunts. "I wasn't afraid."

Phoenix snorts. "Yeah, you were."

"Remember when he ran away when we were watching football because he was scared?" Rowan adds, and I frown.

I've missed way too much by staying away for the past decade. I should have spoken to my parents earlier. They've never acted in any way to indicate they didn't love me and yet I was quick to believe they didn't based on something I overheard when I was a teenager.

Rowan throws an arm around my shoulders. "Don't beat yourself up too hard. Everyone makes mistakes."

I narrow my eyes on him. "Why do you think I'm beating myself up?"

"I know you, little brother."

"You're barely a year older than me. I'm not your little anything."

He puffs out his chest and stands to his full height. "You sure?"

Rowan is six-foot-five to my six-foot and doesn't hesitate to rub his additional height in my face.

"Size isn't everything."

"That's what she said!" River says and Phoenix high-fives him.

We reach the falls, and everyone starts to strip. Rowan elbows me and gestures toward Beckett who's wearing a full bodysuit covering his arms and legs.

"Beckett's wearing a mankini," Phoenix teases.

"It's not a mankini. A mankini shows flesh. He's wearing the male equivalent of a burkini," River says.

"I'll have you know this is a wetsuit similar to what professional surfers wear," Beckett argues.

"Are you planning to surf in the falls?" Rowan asks.

"Not wanting to freeze my balls off, causing them to crawl back up my scrotum, makes me smart."

"Has Lilac seen you in this outfit?" I ask.

"My fiancée doesn't approve my clothing choices."

I lean close to whisper-shout to Rowan, "Which means she hasn't."

"The lot of you are supposed to help me question Cedar and his commitment to my sister, not make fun of me."

River raises his hand. "I can do both."

"So can I!" Phoenix adds.

"I'm a wonderful multi-tasker." Rowan wiggles his eyebrows. "Just ask my wife."

"Please don't ask his wife," I grumble.

River barks out a laugh. "There's no need to ask. Ashlyn volunteers information about their sex life each and every time I meet her."

"True story," Phoenix adds.

Beckett crosses his arms in front of his chest. "I'm not impressed with this so-called expertise in multi-tasking thus far."

Rowan clears his throat before placing his hands on my shoulders. "Are you going to hurt his sister, Cassandra?"

"Of course not. I love her."

He grins before pulling me into a hug. He slaps my back hard enough to give me bruises, but I know better than to complain. Complaining will cause him to slap me harder. It's his duty as my older brother.

"Glad you finally admitted it."

"Finally? I've never denied it."

"You love my sister?" Beckett asks.

"Cassandra, yes. The rest of them?" I shrug. Olivia is not my favorite person. She hurt Cassandra and anyone who hurts the woman I love is on my shit list.

"Hey!" River hip checks me. "Bessie's awesome."

"Don't forget Gabrielle," Phoenix adds. "She's the best of the sisters."

"The best of the Dempsey sisters," Rowan clarifies. "As for the West sisters, I think we all know who the best is of those five."

"Lilac," Beckett claims.

"Ashlyn," Rowan corrects.

River feigns gagging. "Can we stop discussing feelings now and go for a swim?"

"Sure!" Phoenix shouts before cannonballing into the water and splashing everyone.

"Asshole," River scolds.

Beckett smirks. "Unlike you heathens, I'm nice and dry."

"That's what she said!" River and Phoenix yell in unison.

River sprints toward the water and this time I'm smart enough to get out of the way. Rowan starts to rush after him but stops to nudge me before pointing at Beckett and mouthing, *talk to him.*

"You good?" I ask Beckett.

"I'd be better if everyone weren't running around with their junk out."

I never figured Lilac would marry a prude, but there's only one way to handle a prude. I open my arms wide. "Hey! If you've got it, flaunt it."

He growls. "You better not be flaunting it with anyone other than my sister. I'll gut you if you hurt her."

I lift my hands. "Message received."

"I'm serious. My dad taught me to fish. Gutting a person can't be much different than gutting a fish."

My hands hurry to cover my junk. "I'm not interested in anyone other than Cassie. She's my princess."

"And you'll treat her as such."

I bark out a laugh. "Have you met your sister? She'll cut my balls off herself if she thinks I'm not treating her the way she wants."

His smile is full of pride. "True."

"We good?" He nods. "Great. Let's get out of here and get some pancakes at the diner."

"You don't want to swim?"

"You're not the only one who enjoys his balls where they are."

After I dress, we walk toward town.

"You're not the man I envisioned with Cassie." I open my mouth to speak but he stops me with a raised hand. "But you're perfect for her."

"Thanks, but Cassie's opinion is the only one I care about."

"Right answer, hobo. Right answer."

"Reformed hobo."

Chapter 36

"I DON'T UNDERSTAND WHY you won't tell me what happened with my brother," I complain as we drive toward Beckett's house for family dinner night.

"Men stuff."

I roll my eyes. "Men stuff like you insisting you drive to White Bridge?"

He reaches over and places his hand on my thigh. "I know you hate to drive, princess."

I don't *hate* to drive, but I don't exactly enjoy it either. Which is why I don't put up a stink when Cedar drives. Otherwise, I would. No doubt.

I direct us to Beckett's house and Cedar parks in the drive. He gazes up at the house and whistles.

"Exactly how rich are you?"

"I'm not rich," I snap. "My parents had money."

Is he with me for my family's money? Are his declarations of love bullshit? Crap. I knew it. I don't deserve love. It's all a set up.

His hand on my thigh squeezes. "I'm sorry, princess. I shouldn't have asked you how rich you are. It's a rude question, but your brother's house surprised me."

His apology sounds sincere, but the truth of the matter is the Dempsey family does have money.

"Are you with me because of my money?" I blurt the question out before I can stop myself.

He rears back. "What? No!"

"Because I don't have access to most of it. In fact, I bought the bar with my own money." And the blurting out of information continues.

"And I'm proud of you for what you've accomplished. It couldn't have been easy." He cradles my face in his hands. "But why didn't you use your family money to buy *Electric Vibes?*"

I glance away but he pinches my chin forcing me to meet his gaze.

"You thought you didn't deserve the money because you killed your parents."

I narrow my eyes on him. "I never said anything of the sort."

"You didn't have to. I know you." He kisses the tip of my nose. "You didn't kill your parents."

Is he being genuine? Does he truly believe I didn't kill my parents? Do I – gulp – deserve love?

His thumbs glide over my cheeks. "I love you, princess. I'll repeat myself until I'm blue in the face and you believe me that you deserve love."

Bang! Bang! Bang!

"Are you two coming inside anytime this evening?" Elizabeth shouts through the window.

I've never been more glad to be interrupted in my life, but I can't let my sister know I'm happy to see her.

"Are you going to stop being nosy anytime this century?" I shout back.

I reach for the door handle. "We better get inside before the rest of the family comes out here to see what the hold up is."

He chuckles. "Nice try."

I feign confusion. "Try?"

"You didn't kill your parents."

"I know." I don't know, but I'm trying awful hard to believe it.

"You deserve love."

He's really pushing it now. I huff and cross my arms over my chest.

"And you have every right to the money your parents left you."

"Are you done now?"

Cedar crashing through my belief system is the last thing I need before I introduce him to my family. Granted, they've met him, but this is the first time I'm bringing a boyfriend to a family dinner.

He kisses the tip of my nose. "I love you."

Damn him. He knows ending a conversation with a declaration of love means he won. I want to tell him I love him back. But I'm too annoyed with him at the moment. How dare he declare I have the right to use my parents' money and then say I love you?

He opens my door and offers me a hand. "You ready, princess?"

When we enter the house, Elizabeth is waiting for us. "There's a surprise for you."

Cedar sighs. "My parents are here."

My eyes widen and my eyebrows fly off my forehead at his declaration. "You could have warned me your parents would be here today."

"What's the big deal?"

If it weren't a big deal, he would have warned me!

"Ha! Ha! Someone has to be on her best behavior today."

I lunge at Elizabeth but Cedar grabs me before I can reach her.

"You're lucky," I snarl at her.

She beams at me. "Damn straight I am." She glances over her shoulder at River standing at the end of the hallway.

I wasn't talking about her love life and she knows it.

Cedar squeezes my hand as I lead him toward the living room. The living room is full of my family, but my gaze immediately lands on the older couple standing near the window talking with Beckett. Cedar tugs me toward them.

"Mom, Dad, this is Cassandra."

I hold out my hand. "It's lovely to meet you."

His mom ignores my hand and engulfs me in a hug. "I've waited forever for you," she mumbles as she rocks me back and forth.

"Mom, can you stop squeezing my girlfriend to death?"

She grasps my shoulders as she studies me. Tears well in her eyes. "Thank you."

"Um…" I glance up at Cedar. "There's no reason to thank me?"

"I thought… We thought…" She promptly bursts into tears. Her husband draws her into his arms.

"There, there, dear. We discussed this."

Mr. Hansley smiles at me. "I'm sorry. She's a bit sensitive."

"Sensitive!" she shrieks as she shoves him away. "Don't you dare say I'm sensitive. I thought we'd lost our boy and now he's back and he's in love. And isn't she lovely?"

I place my hand over my mouth to cover my smile at her manic behavior.

"I'm Raven and this is Brooks." She pats her husband on his stomach. "Or, you can call us Mom and Dad if you prefer."

"Mom," Cedar grumbles.

She wags his finger at him. "No. You're not allowed to say anything." She grasps my hands. "I'm sorry about what happened to your parents. If you need anything, anything at all, I'm only a phone call away."

Now, I'm the one with tears welling in her eyes. I blink and force those traitorous emotions back inside. "Thank you, Mrs. Hansley."

"Raven."

"Thank you, Raven."

"Dinner is served," Lilac announces.

"You're not supposed to interrupt people when they're having emotional moments," Beckett scolds.

Her brow furrows. "Is this a rule? I've never heard of it before."

He sighs. "I'll explain later," he says as he leads her to the dining area.

I, for one, am glad she interrupted us. If she hadn't, I'd probably end up bawling my eyes out with Cedar's mom. Not exactly the kind of introduction to my boyfriend's parents I want.

I frown when I notice the extra spot at the table once everyone is seated.

"Are you expecting someone else?"

"Don't get mad," Beckett responds, which is a guarantee I'm going to lose my mind at whatever the answer is.

The door bangs shut. "I'm here. Sorry I'm late."

"What is she doing here?" I hiss at Beckett.

"She's your sister."

"I'm not the one who needs a reminder."

I'm not the one who abandoned this family for two years and only showed up when access to my trust fund was cut off.

Olivia skids to a halt in front of the dining room table. "What is everyone doing here?"

"It's a family dinner," I answer. "I think the correct question is what are *you* doing here."

Cedar wraps an arm around my shoulders and draws me near until I'm practically sitting in his lap. "Do you want to leave?" he whispers in my ear.

I shake my head. I'll be damned if I'll allow my long lost sister to force me away from a family gathering.

"I live here."

At Olivia's announcement, I pretend to clean out my ear. "I must be hearing things because there's no way you said you're living here now."

"She's staying with us while she figures out her next moves," Lilac explains. "Although I'm unsure what next moves means."

"It means she's milking you for your money until you get sick and tired of her."

Olivia cringes at my words. Don't tell me my big sister has grown a conscience.

Elizabeth taps the spot next to her. "Come sit next to me, big sis."

I clamp my jaw shut as Olivia sits down in between Elizabeth and Lilac.

Raven reaches over to squeeze my hand. "Are you okay, dear?"

I force a smile and nod. "I'm fine."

I'm not. I'm spitting mad at my big sister for abandoning us. For strolling back into our lives without an apology, let alone an explanation.

But I'm also sitting here with the arm of the man I love wrapped around me for support while his mother smiles at me and offers her support as well. Things could be worse. Much worse.

Chapter 37

If you want to tell your sister you're mad at her but you're not on speaking terms, a glitter bomb is the most effective method ~ Cassie's rules for living her best life

"ARE YOU READY?"

Cedar glances away and his forehead wrinkles.

"What's wrong?"

He blows out a puff of air. "Large crowds make me nervous."

Today is the Litha or Midsummer festival. All the pagan festivals Winter Falls puts on are tourist magnets. I can't blame the tourists since there's always plenty of fun to be had. But it does mean the town will be overcrowded.

I wrap my arms around his waist and cuddle into him. "We don't have to go if you don't want to."

"But you've been looking forward to the festival all week."

It's true, but I'm not going to force Cedar into a situation where he feels uncomfortable.

I waggle my eyebrows. "I'm certain we can come up with another activity to enjoy ourselves."

To help him make up his mind, my hands sneak down to squeeze his ass. The man has a magnificent ass. Muscular but not too hard to mold in my hands.

He punches his hips, and I feel his length against my stomach. "What did you have in mind?"

I lift up on my tiptoes. "This," I whisper before pressing my lips to his.

He immediately takes charge and pushes his tongue into my mouth. You won't hear me complaining about him assuming control. No, siree bob. I sit back and allow myself to enjoy how he devours my mouth as if it's the most delicious morsel he's ever eaten.

As our tongues duel, I circle his waist with my leg and rub myself against his now hard length. Before I have a chance to climb him, his phone dings with a message.

I rip my mouth from his. "Ignore it."

He doesn't, though. "It's my mom. She's wondering if we'll meet them for lunch."

At the mention of his parents, my libido takes a nose dive.

"Does this mean you want to go?" Since being reunited with his parents, he meets up with them as often as he can. "You sure?"

"I'm sure."

"Last chance."

He kisses my nose. "I'm fine now. Thanks to some excellent help from the woman I love."

I no longer panic when he says the l-word. Nope. I'm breathing just fine at the moment. Although the butterflies in my stomach are making it difficult to inhale a deep breath. I open my mouth, but as usual, no words come out.

Cedar doesn't comment or push me. He never does. Just one of the many things I love about him.

Instead, he asks, "You ready to go?"

I stretch my arms over my head before doing a few lunges. "Ready."

He chuckles. "We're going into town for a pagan festival. I'm not sure why stretching is required."

"Duh. I'm the reigning champion of the bonfire jumping competition. I need to be prepared."

And maybe I should be warmed up before Elizabeth finds me and I need to make a run for it.

Diva follows us as we walk to the door. "No. You're staying home."

She yips.

"You can show everyone your cute outfit when we go for a walk later."

She growls.

I wag my finger at her. "You can threaten to bark all you want. It doesn't matter. No one's going to be home to be annoyed by the noise."

She stares at me as she begins to squat. I snatch her from the floor before she can pee on the carpet.

"Fine. You can come with, but no complaining."

She yips before licking my face.

Cedar barks out a laugh. "She has you trained well."

"At least she doesn't try to eat my toes during sex."

Unfortunately, the toe-eating monster has struck on more than one occasion. Until Cedar decided he'd had enough and fixed the door latch so the fur monster couldn't sneak into the bedroom during our amorous activities.

He shudders. "Point taken."

We let Diva out on the grass in front of my apartment building before walking the three blocks to Main Street where the festival is taking place. The street is crowded with people and booths from vendors selling their wares.

"Who's holding down the fort at *Electric Vibes* today?"

Before I have a chance to answer, a woman shouts "Aha!" behind me. I whirl around to find the gossip gals standing there in their hot pink t-shirts. Today, the t-shirts say *Gossip Gals Do It Better In Summer.*

"Hi!" I wave.

"Congratulations! Project Hermit is a success."

I groan. The gossip gals' project to match me with Cedar is not my favorite topic of discussion.

Ruby and Raven force their way to the front of the group.

"You can't take credit for Project Hermit's success," Ruby declares.

"I should get all of the credit," Raven claims.

I lean close to whisper to Cedar. "I think your mother is auditioning to become a member of the gossip gals."

"And here I thought my parents returning to Winter Falls was a good thing," he mutters.

"Be careful what you wish for," I sing back.

"Oh good, you're here," Ashlyn says as she grasps my hand and starts hauling me away.

I yank my hand out of her grasp and dig in my heels. "What are you doing? Are you not going to at least say hi to your mom?"

"Hi, Mom!" She waves to Ruby.

"Where's Patience?" Ruby asks and Ashlyn indicates Rowan standing with the baby across the street. Without another word, Ruby dashes toward her granddaughter with Raven hot on her heels.

"There. Mom's all taken care of," Ashlyn says. "Now, come on."

"Come on where? What's going on? What are you doing?"

"Regaining my crown as champion of bonfire jumping."

To clarify, there's technically no bonfire. Apparently, a past fire got out of control and now flames of any kind are nixed. Thank goodness. Since me and fire, of any kind, do not go together. Instead, two poles are set up in the middle of the town square with hay in between them. The hay is the 'bonfire'. Whoever jumps highest over the 'bonfire' is the winner.

"I won last year," I remind Ashlyn.

"Only because I was pregnant."

I cock an eyebrow. "Oh yeah? It's on."

I hand Diva's leash to Cedar. "I'll be back."

He follows as we march toward the town square. "As if I'd miss this for the world."

"We're not done speaking to you," Sage calls after us.

"Later, Sage. We've got things to do. Bonfires to jump. Championships to regain." Ashlyn punches her first in the air.

"But what about the bets?" Petal asks.

"There's another month to go," Ashlyn responds.

Color me confused. I have no idea what they're talking about. And, frankly, I don't want to know.

Ashlyn grabs my hand as we hurry toward the town square. From the corner of my eye, I notice Elizabeth stomping toward me. Uh oh. I quicken our pace, but there's nowhere to hide.

"Cassandra Claire Dempsey, how dare you?" she yells.

The hubbub of conversation dies down as everyone focuses their attention on us.

I wrench my hand from Ashlyn's and cross my arms over my chest. "How dare I what?" Don't worry. I know exactly what she's talking about. It was epic.

She pokes my chest. "You know what you did."

I wipe the glitter from my shirt. "I'm sorry, but you'll have to explain."

"Explain!" She throws her arms in the air and glitter rains down onto the street.

"Did you glitter bomb her?" Ashlyn asks.

"Worse," Elizabeth snarls. "She put glitter in balloons and filled my house with them."

"You shouldn't have popped the balloons," Ashlyn says.

Elizabeth glares at her. "The house was packed to the rim with them. I had to pop them to reach the bathroom."

Ashlyn holds up her hand to me. "High five!"

I manage to smack her hand before Elizabeth shoves her way in between us. "What did I do to you?"

I cock an eyebrow. She must know what she did. Elizabeth is many things, but stupid is not one of them.

"Olivia's our sister." Yep. She knows.

I snort. Some sister.

Maa!

Pan the goat bleats before she headbutts me. I shriek and step back. This goat is possessed by the devil. Trust me. She can literally pee and shit on command. I shiver as I back away from the animal.

Phoenix rushes over with Gabrielle trailing behind him.

"Is it finally time to sacrifice a goat at the altar?" I tease.

Gabrielle gasps and throws her arms around Pan's neck. "Keep your grubby hands off her!"

"You do know Pan is a goat, right?"

She points to Diva who's currently dressed in a sundress with hearts on it and a matching bow in her hair. She's absolutely adorable in her summer solstice outfit.

"And you know Diva's a dog, right?"

I take Diva from Cedar's hold and cover her ears. "Shush. She'll hear you."

"Hello!" Elizabeth shouts. "I'm not done arguing with you."

Gabrielle glances over at Elizabeth and her eyes widen when she notices the glitter covering her hair and arms.

"What happened to you?"

"She got glitter bombed," Ashlyn answers.

Cedar circles my waist from behind and lays his forehead against my back. I can feel his body shaking as he laughs. "I don't know why I hesitated to come today."

Chapter 38

If you panic, keep your mouth shut and don't do anything stupid
~ advice Cassie has never taken

"ARE YOU WORKING NEXT Thursday?" Cedar asks as I walk into the kitchen.

I grunt in response. My brain isn't functioning yet since it's barely noon and I worked until three in the morning. He hands me a cup of coffee and I down half of it in one go. I sigh as the warm liquid travels through my body performing its magic.

"Better?"

I cradle the mug to my chest. "Much."

"Next Thursday?"

"Is the day before Friday."

He chuckles as he kisses my hair. "I asked if you're working next Thursday."

"You should know better than to ask me questions before I've had my first cup of coffee."

"My mistake."

I roll my eyes. "Obviously."

I'm not kidding. He should know better. He practically lives in my apartment now. He walks Diva while I'm working.

Makes me coffee in the morning. And keeps my bed warm so I don't have to slide in between cold sheets after a long night of working.

He squeezes my hip. "Are. You. Working. Next. Thursday?"

I shrug. "Probably. I'd have to check the schedule. Either way, I can always ask Lennon to fill in for me."

The former owner of *Electric Vibes* is a gem. Despite being ready to give up the responsibilities associated with owning a business, he still enjoys working at the bar a few nights a week. I don't know what I'd do without him.

"Why?"

"My parents want to take us out to dinner at the brewery with Rowan and Ashlyn."

"What about Patience?"

No matter how much Ashlyn claims she needs 'alone time' with her husband, her daughter is never far from her. Raven and Ruby actually keep track of when they're allowed to babysit. The grandmas are insistent they have equal rights to babysitting duties.

"I'm sure our niece will be joining us."

Our niece. I like the sound of that. Especially since I'm still waiting for Gabrielle or Elizabeth to give me a niece or nephew. They're both trying but no luck yet. Don't they know I'm ready to be Auntie Cassie already?

I search for my phone on the kitchen counter but it's not there.

"Looking for this?" Cedar dangles my phone in front of me.

I snag it from him. "Where was it?"

"On the floor by the front door with your jeans."

"Why do you sound grumpy? I climbed into bed naked last night. You should be happy."

He places his hands on the counter on either side of me to box me in. "I am happy."

He nips at my bottom lip before licking it and I grasp his t-shirt to draw him closer.

"Nuh-uh. No distracting me. Check your agenda before my mother barges in here. She's been blowing up my phone all morning asking about dinner next Thursday."

Weird. But not completely unusual. Ever since Raven and Brooks moved back to Winter Falls, they've made sure Cedar knows how much they love him. They're constantly inviting him to dinner or over to watch a movie or for a hike. And since I'm together with Cedar, I'm included in the invitations.

It's been a blissful two months since Cedar declared his love and we became a couple. Wait a second. Two months? I unlock my phone and open my agenda. July 15th. All day event. In all caps. *THE DARE ENDS.*

Panic seizes me. Hands squeeze my neck; strangling me. I scratch at them but I can't alleviate the fear choking me. He's leaving. The man I love is abandoning me. I knew life was too good to be true. *Stupid, stupid, Cassandra.* I should have never opened my heart to anyone.

The phone clatters to the ground as I shove Cedar away.

"Hey! What's wrong?"

I answer his question with one of my own. "When are you leaving?"

He scratches his beard. "Leaving for where? I need to pick up some clothes at my house sometime this weekend."

I growl. "I'm not talking about your fucking clothes."

His brow wrinkles. "What are you talking about? Are you feeling okay?"

He tries to lay his palm on my forehead, but I bat it away.

"Feeling okay?" I shout. "Am I feeling okay?"

He holds up his hands. "Obviously, something's wrong. Can you explain to me what it is?"

"Don't talk to me like I'm a baby. I'm an adult," I snarl at him.

"Then, explain to me what's wrong."

"What's wrong? What's wrong is you're leaving Winter Falls."

He rears back. "Where is this coming from? I'm not leaving Winter Falls."

"Yes, you are! Today marks the end of our dare."

"I don't give the first fuck about our dare. We discussed this. I'm not going anywhere."

I refuse to believe him. "Except you're still living in your mobile tiny house outside of town."

He cocks an eyebrow and lifts his chin toward the kitchen table where his laptop and work are laid out.

"You and I both know I spend more time in your apartment than in my house. Thus, the need for me to pick up more clothes."

I ignore him to continue my rant. "And you're still working online for some company who knows where."

"And? Big deal. Lots of people work online nowadays."

"Because they're digital nomads. A nomad is someone who doesn't stay in the same place for long."

He growls. "I know what the word nomad means. I'm no longer a nomad."

His reasonable responses are doing nothing to stop the panic. "There's nothing tying you to Winter Falls."

He cocks his brow. "Nothing? How about you?" Diva barks and he smiles down at her. "And you, too, Diva."

I glare at him. I will not be distracted by his concern for my dog. Distraction is the enemy.

"What if I wasn't here?"

He flinches. "I'm still connected with Winter Falls through my brother, my sister-in-law, my niece, and my parents. There's a lot tying me to this small town."

"I don't believe you. None of those people tied you to this town before. You left them easy enough for over a decade."

Hurt flashes in his eyes. "And it was a mistake. A mistake I'm rectifying now."

"You won the dare. You don't have to stay any longer."

He grasps my shoulders and his eyes bore into mine. "Hear me on this. I don't give the first fuck about the dare."

"Except you wouldn't be here if there hadn't been a dare."

"Are you listening to yourself?"

No, but the words are flowing out of my mouth anyway.

"I had no intention of leaving Winter Falls before we made the stupid dare."

I snort. "Which is why your movable house is sitting on land outside of town."

"Listen to my words. You, Cassandra Claire Dempsey, deserve love."

"I—"

"You did not kill your parents."

"I'm not talking about them now!"

"No? You're not panicking because you fear you don't deserve love?"

My hands fist and I scream at the top of my lungs, "I am not panicking!"

He blows out a breath of air. "You're obviously not willing to listen to reason now."

"Don't call me irrational!"

"I didn't say the word irrational. You did."

He backs away from me and strolls toward the kitchen table where he collects his laptop and papers.

"Aha! I told you you're leaving!"

"I'm not leaving for good. I'm leaving until you can ca—" He clears his throat. "I'm going to my house to work for the day. We'll talk later."

I follow him to the door and fling it open for him. I motion toward the hallway.

"No, we won't talk later."

"Yes, we will." He kisses my forehead before walking out of my apartment and straight out of my life.

"We're over!" I shout at his retreating form.

"I love you," he shouts back.

I slam the door in response. Diva scratches at my leg and I reach down to pick her up.

"It's okay, baby girl. We're better off without him."

She whimpers as she stares at the door.

"Come on. Let's get you a rawhide treat and me a bottle of wine."

She barks in response.

"I'm not going to work tonight but thanks for reminding me. I'll call Lennon to fill in now."

When she yips again, I ignore her. I'm not taking relationship advice from a dog.

"He was going to leave eventually anyway," I explain. "This way we cut him off before his leaving could hurt us."

Except it already hurts pretty freaking bad. In fact, I think I may be having a heart attack. My hands are trembling, I have no feeling in my limbs, and pain is bursting from my chest.

Should I call 911? Unfortunately, the only first responder in town is my brother-in-law, River. My break-up would be all over town before he arrived at my door to perform CPR.

"What are we going to do, Diva? What are we going to do?"

Chapter 39

Never give up on a skittish horse – Cedar's rules for capturing the woman he loves

CEDAR

I sigh when I hear people trampling through the woods toward my house. There's no sense worrying about who it is. No one hikes over on this side of Winter Falls unless they're on their way to visit me.

I expected them to be here sooner. I'm honestly surprised no one followed me home from Cassie's house after she threw me out.

Home. I study my tiny house. The tiny house has been with me for years. We've traveled around the country. Seen mountains and beaches. Highways and backroads. Poor spots and wealthy areas.

But this isn't home anymore. No, a home is not a place. Home is a person. And Cassie is my person. She just doesn't know it yet.

Correction. She does know it. But she's afraid to admit it. I know she loves me. It's in the way she looks at me. In the way she smiles at me. In the way she takes care of me.

But I understand her trepidation. She's spent two decades believing she wasn't worthy of love, thinking she was the cause of her parents' death. Her misconception can't be erased in a few short months. Although, I do have an idea of how to kickstart the process.

I only hope my idea won't end up with me on my way to the emergency room because Cassie kicked me in the balls with all her might. The woman's been working in bars for nearly a decade. She knows how to protect herself. She doesn't need to protect herself from me, but she hasn't figured that out yet. Thus, the whole throwing me out of her house and breaking up with me.

The door jiggles before it opens and my brother barges in with Cassie's brother hot on his heels.

"I should have locked the door," I grumble.

Rowan chuckles and holds up a key. "Except you gave my wife a key."

Mistake on my part. Obviously.

"We came here to talk you out of leaving." Beckett frowns as he scans the room. Boxes litter the area. "But we're too late."

"Who wants a beer?"

I don't wait for a reply before grabbing three beers from the refrigerator and handing them out. I gesture toward the door – my place isn't big enough for three men over six-foot tall on a normal day and today is not a normal day.

"What happened?" Rowan asks the second we're outside.

"I—"

My answer is cut off when I notice Mercury trudging toward me.

"What's wrong?"

The old man doesn't wander into this side of town unless he has a reason.

"You said you were here to stay," he accuses.

"I am."

He points to where my truck is backed up to my tiny house. The trailer hitch isn't connected yet, but it will be soon. "It looks otherwise."

"Appearances can be deceiving. You of all people should know better."

Mercury lives in a house outside of town. He's made sure people believe his house is haunted. Not because it is. But because he doesn't want visitors.

"Okay," he grunts before wandering off.

"Who is he?" Beckett asks as he watches the old man leave.

"Old Man Mercury," Rowan answers. "He founded this town with his wife, Adhara."

"I haven't met anyone named Adhara."

"Because she died along with their child. It was tragic." I don't explain further as I don't know any more details. The how and why of their deaths is a closely kept secret in Winter Falls. The only secret as far as I know.

"I'll ask Lilac." Unfortunately for him, this is one secret even his fiancée doesn't know.

"I don't care about Mercury," Rowan declares. "I what to know what happened with Cassie."

I don't want to talk about how the woman I love threw me out. I rub a hand over my chest. I know she panicked, but the knowledge doesn't alleviate the pain.

"She broke up with me."

Beckett growls. "What did you do to her?"

I want to lash out at him for assuming I did something wrong, but he's Cassie's brother. I need him as an ally. Especially over the next days as I push my princess further than she's willing to go.

"Besides love her?" I shrug.

"What brought it on? Did you accidentally say the wrong thing? You know you can't tell a woman what to do or to calm down." Rowan shivers.

I shake my head. "I know better than to try and tell a woman what to do."

"You must have some clue as to what you did wrong," Beckett says.

"I didn't do anything wrong."

"Are you sure?" Rowan asks. "Describe the last conversation you had with her."

I'm not going to stand here and dissect every single thing we said to each other.

"She panicked."

"Panicked? Why? What did you do?"

I clench my jaw before I lash out at Beckett. I know he's protecting his sister, but I'm about done with him assuming I was in the wrong.

"She saw the calendar and realized the date of our dare was over."

"Your dare? Didn't you explain to her earlier the dare was off?" Beckett asks.

"I told her I wasn't leaving no matter what. The dare be damned."

He sips on his beer as he considers my answer. "She obviously didn't believe you."

I waggle my eyebrows. "Don't worry. She believed me."

He pokes me. "Don't push it."

"Hey now." Rowan shoves between us. "The two of you fighting won't help the situation."

It would feel good, though. I'd love to get rid of some of this excess energy banging around in my body since Cassie kicked me out.

"You can't give up on her," Beckett insists.

I cock an eyebrow. "I can't? Aren't you the one who claimed I'm not good enough for her?"

His nostrils flare as he glares at me. "I raised her since she was thirteen years old. I'm protective of her. I have a right to make sure she's not being used."

Usually, I'd run with this admission and tease him about his overprotective ways. But not now. I've got bigger problems than Cassie's big brother.

I slap him on the back. "I know. Don't worry. I'm not giving up on her. I'm just giving you a hard time."

He gestures toward the tiny home. "But if you're not giving up on her, why are you packing to go away?"

"Who said I'm going away?"

Rowan smirks. "You have a plan."

"Of course, I have a plan."

"How can we help?"

Perfect. I knew they'd come on board when they realized I'm not leaving. And I do need help.

"Do you have Cole's phone number?" I ask Rowan.

"Cole? Ellery's baby daddy Cole?"

"I think he prefers to be referred to as Ellery's fiancé."

Beckett is already handing me his phone. "Here. I have no idea why you need Cole's phone number, but here it is."

"It's all part of my master plan."

I keep my response mysterious. The fewer people who know what I'm intending to do the better. This town doesn't keep secrets well and the last thing I need is Cassie knowing what I'm up to before I'm ready.

I want the entire scheme worked out into the tiniest details before I surprise my princess. She won't be able to say no when she finds out what I've got planned for her.

Chapter 40

Take what you want before someone else steals it away ~ Cassie's rules for life

DIVA YIPS WHILE RUNNING circles around my legs as I make my way to the front door.

"Yeah. Yeah. We're going for a walk."

The last thing I want to do is go for a walk with my dog – I'd rather spend my afternoon wallowing in my heartbreak the same as any normal heartbroken woman – but I want to clean her pee and poop out of my carpet even less.

I open my apartment door and she rushes out.

"Gee. I didn't realize you needed to go this badly. I'm sorry."

She wags her tail as I follow her down the stairs and out of the building. Once she's done her business, she continues down the street.

"Good afternoon," Petal greets with a wave but instead of continuing on her way, she makes a U-turn to follow us.

I sigh. Since Cedar and I broke up a few days ago, the townspeople have left me alone. I expected them to congregate en masse in the bar and lecture me about what a fool I am. But it's been crickets thus far.

It appears my peace and quiet is officially over. I glance over my shoulder and notice all of the gossip gals are now following me. Yep. No more peace and quiet for Cassie.

"What do you want?" I ask. You can call me all kinds of names but timid is not one of them.

"We're merely going for a hike," Sage answers.

I snort. She's a liar.

"It's a magnificent afternoon for a stroll," Cayenne adds.

It's gray and rain is on its way. There's nothing magnificent about this day.

"Oh look. Someone finally bought the empty lot," Clove says.

I keep walking. I have no interest in the local gossip about who's living where. If they want to talk about who's banging who, I'm interested. Although, maybe not today.

Diva tugs on her leash before escaping my hold. "Diva!" I shout as I chase after her. She flies across the empty lot and straight into the arms of Cedar.

Cedar? I come to a screeching halt when I realize he's standing in front of his tiny house. But we're not out in the forest. We're smack dab in the middle of town. A mere two blocks from Main Street.

"What are you doing here?"

"Yeah, Cedar, tell her," Ashlyn shouts.

I scan the yard to discover nearly every inhabitant of Winter Falls is here. My sisters, Gabrielle and Elizabeth, are standing with their men, Phoenix and River. I don't spot Olivia, but the

West sisters are here along with their partners as are Cedar's parents.

"Hi, Cassie," Raven waves.

"What is everyone doing here?" I ask the crowd.

"We're here to witness—"

I cut Elizabeth off. "I want to hear your answer," I tell Cedar.

He places Diva on the ground, and she rushes off to Juniper who picks her up and cradles her like a baby.

"This outfit is adorable on her!" Juniper isn't wrong. Diva's dress today is a pink tutu.

"Don't you dare think about dressing our pets in clothes," Maverick says. The movie star doesn't appear very Hollywood now as he strains to keep their dogs under control.

"It'd only be fair since she's the one sending me outfits for Diva," I tell him.

Juniper scowls at me. "You weren't supposed to tell."

Before I can answer, Aspen waddles over to us. "Please tell me your toilet is already hooked up to the sewage. You know what? I don't care."

She pushes past us and enters the tiny house.

"Sorry. Sorry," Lyric apologizes as he follows her. "She's seven months pregnant."

"Did you get rid of the compost toilet?" I ask just before Aspen squeals.

"What the hell is this?"

Cedar closes his eyes and his chin dips to his chest. "This is not how my grand gesture was supposed to go."

"I'm here!" Cole announces as he joins us.

Color me confused. I barely know Ellery's fiancé. Don't get me wrong. I'm sure he's a nice guy, but they have a baby and I manage a bar. We don't exactly have the same schedules.

"Why are you here?"

He hands Cedar a sheaf of papers and waves before walking off. I stare after him. "That was weird."

"This isn't working," Cedar grumbles before taking my hand and leading me to the path behind his house.

"You can't hide!" Sage hollers.

"Wanna bet?" I do love a challenge.

We stop a few feet into the forest.

I yank my hand from Cedar's and cross my arms over my chest. "No more procrastinating. What's going on?"

He waves the papers at me. "I've just been appointed the director of the community center."

My brow wrinkles. "The Winter Falls community center?" He nods. "But it's not open yet."

"It opens next month and I'm the new director."

"But you're a finance man."

"I can't help thinking if there had been a community center when I was a kid, my parents wouldn't have had such a hard time and I wouldn't have ended up hearing what they said and misinterpreting it."

"Do you need me to apologize again?" Raven calls.

Cedar grunts before grabbing my hand and dragging me further into the woods.

"This is to prove to you I'm not going anywhere."

I frown. I already know he's not going anywhere. I knew it the day I accused him of wanting to leave. Shit. I need to apologize.

"I may have overreacted."

He chuckles. "Ya think?"

I slap his shoulder. "You were right."

"I'm always—"

I slam my hand over his mouth. It's my turn to speak.

"I panicked when I saw the date on the calendar." I pause to gather my courage before continuing, "My head knows I didn't kill my parents but my heart is still working on it."

He nips at my hand and I yelp as I drop it.

"And I'll be here the entire time while you work through it."

"I guess that's why I love you."

"You love me?"

I blow out a puff of air. "Yeah."

He cradles my face. "Say the words." I huff and he kisses my forehead. "Say the words so I can say them back to you."

"I love you, Cedar pain-in-my-ass Hansley."

His eyes close and he leans his forehead against mine. "And I love you, Cassandra most-stubborn-woman-in-the-world Dempsey."

"Can we start the party now?" Ashlyn shouts and I jerk away from Cedar.

"I still need to ask her to move in with me," Cedar shouts back.

"Get on with it. I want to get my drink on!"

"You aren't drinking. You're still breastfeeding," Rowan grumbles.

"Ha! Joke's on you. I pumped today."

There's rustling in the trees as they leave us alone. Or, I assume alone, who knows who else is out here.

"Is there anyone else out here?" I ask to make sure.

"No," Raven answers.

"You weren't supposed to answer," Ruby scolds. "Now she knows we're here."

"Oh, I'll be quiet now."

Cedar sighs. "They're never going to leave us alone."

"You're going to ask me to move in with you?"

"I know the tiny house is small, but we can make it work. We can add on when we have kids. Or I'll build us a house. I'm flexible."

My eyes practically bug out of my head. "K-k-kids?"

"Or not have kids. Whatever you want."

I'm barely ready for the l-word. Kids is not a discussion I'm prepared to have. "We're tabling the kids talk."

"Not a problem."

"You want to live together?"

"Of course. I love you. You love me. I want to spend the rest of my days with you."

"This is awful quick."

"Princess, when you know, you know."

I stare into his eyes and all I see is sincerity and love. Crap. I'm going to do this, aren't I?

"Okay," I whisper.

"What did she say? I didn't hear her," Raven whisper-shouts.

"You're a sucky spy," Ruby mumbles before raising her voice. "We're going now. You have five minutes to have sexy times before the invasion begins."

"Five minutes? Who can have sexy times in five minutes?" I need way more than five minutes to enjoy Cedar's naked body.

"When you have five children, you figure it out."

Cedar is laughing as his lips find mine. I can practically feel the happiness radiating from him. Or maybe it's mine. My heart is about to burst from it.

All too soon he pulls away. "We better get back to our party before someone else comes out here searching for us."

I hate how he's not wrong. "Later?"

"Later I'm going to worship your body until you scream my name."

"Promises. Promises," I tease as we walk back to his yard.

He swats my ass. "I'll show you promises."

I glance over my shoulder and wink at him. "I know you will."

His – no, our – yard is even more crowded than ten minutes ago. Lennon set up a mobile bar in one corner and Gracious, from the diner, has a stand next to him. It's officially a party.

Feather, Petal, Cayenne, Clove, and Sage hurry toward us.

"One, two, three," Sage counts off.

"Ta da!" They yell in unison as they open their coats to display their hot pink t-shirts. *The Gossip Gals Did It Again.*

"You have got to be—"

My words are cut off when I hear someone shout in anger.

"What the hell are you doing here?"

I scan the area to figure out who it is and my gaze lands on Peace. One of the town's police officers. My eyes widen when I realize who he's yelling at. Olivia. I should have known. Olivia and the police do not get along.

"What am I doing here? Cassandra is my sister." Nice to hear she's claiming me as family at least. "What are *you* doing here?"

I start toward them since I have no desire to spend my money bailing Olivia out of jail but Cedar shackles my wrist to stop me.

"Let them be."

"But—"

He places a finger over my lips to hush me.

"This is our celebration. They can work their problems out by themselves."

I stare at where the two are now in a heated argument before blowing out a breath. He's right. Olivia has managed to not land in prison for the past two years without me. She can handle herself in Winter Falls just fine.

I bite my bottom lip and flutter my lashes. "How do you want to celebrate?"

"Princess, I have a list of ideas. We need a lifetime to work through it."

"A lifetime? I'm in."

He kisses the tip of my nose. "I love you, princess."

"And I love you, Cedar Archer Hansley."

Saying the words doesn't cause panic to course through my veins. Quite the opposite. Warmth and happiness spread through me. I'm certain I'll have moments of panic in the future, but for now, I'm celebrating that future with the man I love.

Chapter 41

Police are called pigs for a reason – Olivia's philosophy on life

OLIVIA

Please come.

As I stare at Elizabeth's message contemplating my response, another one pops up with the praying hands emoji.

I bite my lip. Cassandra is pissed at me. Rightfully so. I don't think she wants me attending her grand gesture party.

You have to start somewhere.

Damnit. Why did I tell Elizabeth about my desire for for-giveness from Cassie? I should have kept my mouth shut. I've had enough practice keeping my mouth shut over the years. Why did my mouth malfunction now?

Because you want a fresh start, my conscience reminds me.

You know what no one tells you? Fresh starts are freaking painful.

There's a knock on my bedroom door before Beckett sticks his head in the room. "You ready?"

"I don't know."

"You don't know?" He looks me up and down. "You're dressed. Your hair is brushed. Your make-up is done."

Behind him, Lilac rolls her eyes. "You look lovely, Olivia. And you're under no obligation to accompany us."

"Yes, she is," Beckett disagrees. "This is a family occasion. Family occasions are obligatory."

"I meant she can drive herself."

"Oh. I guess we'll see you there." He waves before leaving with Lilac following him.

Great. If I don't show up now, they'll think I chickened out. I may be a lot of things, but a chicken is definitely not one of them.

I wait until they're gone before putting on my shoes to follow. I stare at the fancy car Beckett bought me the second I agreed to stay with them while I get back on my feet. For all his bluster, my big brother didn't hesitate to help me out. He never does. Don't get me wrong. He bitches and complains, but in the end, he always gives in.

I can't even begin to thank him for all he's put up with regarding me. But I'm going to have to start figuring out a way soon.

I drive the thirty minutes to Winter Falls, but when I reach the small town, I realize I don't know where I'm going. I pull to a stop in front of *Earth Bliss* and get out.

I knock on the door, but when no one answers, I peer inside. It's a yoga studio. There's a yoga studio in Winter Falls? Maybe the small town isn't as backwards as I feared.

"Cayenne's at the party," someone calls, and I glance over to discover a man walking two small creatures on a leash.

"What are those?"

"This is Dale and Chip," he says as he comes closer. "Do you want to pet them? They're very friendly squirrels."

I back up until I'm plastered against the storefront. "Um, no. But thanks?"

He tips his non-existent hat to me. "I'm off. See you around."

"Wait!" I call after him. "Where's the party?"

His eyes narrow as he studies me. "What party?"

I don't remind him he mentioned a party a mere minute ago. I've had enough experience to recognize a suspicious older man when I encounter one.

"Cassandra's party?"

The suspicion doesn't fade from his eyes. "You know Cassandra?"

"She's my sister."

"You must be Olivia."

"Yes." I nod even though I want to ask how the hell he knows my name.

He points down the street. "Hang a left over there. Then, another left and the second right. You can't miss it."

"Thank you."

I rush to my car before he changes his mind and calls the police on me. No thanks. I've had enough clashes with police for a lifetime. Winter Falls is going to be different.

In the end, I don't need the squirrel owner's instructions. All I need to do is follow the crowd of people on their way to Cassandra's. I figure I'll end up parking a mile away, but there are hardly any cars in Winter Falls. The town is famous for being carbon neutral, whatever that means.

The nerves kick in again once I'm standing next to my car scanning the crowd for a familiar face. I don't know why I'm nervous. A crowd full of strangers never bothered me before.

Because it's Cassandra. My subconscious is ever so helpful. Not.

"Over here," Gabrielle shouts and waves me toward where she's standing with Phoenix and a goat.

"Is that a goat?"

Gabrielle scratches behind its ear. "This is Pan."

I shake my head. This town is weird.

"Where's Cassandra?"

She points to the forest behind the house. "They're 'talking'."

I spot a bar across the lawn. "I'm getting a drink."

"Grab me a ginger ale."

I nod before making my way through the crowd. I don't make it to the bar.

"What the hell are you doing here?" The police officer who pulled me over the first time I drove into Winter Falls asks.

I scowl at him. There's nothing illegal about attending this party. Trust me. I would know. I'm an expert in what's legal and what's not. I decide to feign confusion. Being blonde has its advantage.

"What am I doing here? Cassandra is my sister. What are you doing here?"

His answer isn't verbal. Instead, he grasps my arm and drags me away from the crowd.

I yank my arm from his grip. "You have no excuse to manhandle me. I'm not doing anything wrong."

He bends close and hisses at me, "I looked into you."

I clap. "Good job. You're a police officer and you know how to run a background check. Your mamma must be very proud."

"Your sarcasm is duly noted."

"Are you going to write down how sarcastic I am in your little notebook?" I make my eyes big. "I'm scared."

"You're going to ruin your sisters' lives."

I flinch. Shit. Talk about going for the jugular.

"It's none of your business."

It's not. He may be a police officer in Winter Falls, but being a cop doesn't give him the right to butt his nose into my private family situation.

"It is when you bring your troubles to town."

I open my arms wide. "What troubles? I've brought nothing to town."

Except for a super expensive electric car, but I have a feeling pointing that out will not help this situation. *Hey, Police Officer, not only am I trouble, but I have money.* Words no cop ever wants to hear. Been there. Done that.

"You don't need to bring anything. You're trouble all by yourself."

I am, but I'm trying to be better. He doesn't appear interested in listening to my woos, though.

"Olivia!" Elizabeth rushes across the yard to me. "I didn't realize you were here."

She wraps her arms around me. "Do you need help?" she whispers.

She doesn't wait for my reply before pushing me behind her. "Peace, good to see you."

Peace? Odd name for a peace officer. His eyes flash with pain. Huh. What's the story there?

"Hi, Elizabeth."

"Have you met my sister, Olivia?"

River chuckles as he saunters our way. "Obviously, they've met, Bessie."

Bessie? Elizabeth hates the nickname Bessie. But she's beaming up at her boyfriend as if he invented sliced cheese after he used it. Huh. Maybe Elizabeth has changed as well.

Elizabeth threads her arm through mine. "Shall we get a drink and go spy on Cassandra and Cedar?"

"Sounds good." I do love to spy on people, especially my sisters.

I wave to Peace as I walk off with Elizabeth.

"You should stay away from him," she says once we're out of earshot.

"Why? Is he your man on the side?"

River growls and I giggle.

Elizabeth pokes her boyfriend. "She's trying to rile you up. Don't fall for it."

He crosses his arms over his chest and grunts at me. Big talker this one.

"I meant stay away from him because he's a cop."

"Oh, I know he's a cop."

"You do? He's not in uniform today."

"Sister, I can smell a cop a mile away."

I'm lying. I know he's a cop because he pulled me over.

She sighs. "Please try to stay out of trouble."

"I make no promises," I sing as I head toward the bar.

Chapter 42

A diva knows how to ruin a party

NOVEMBER

Is everything set?

For the millionth time, we're ready. Get your butt over here.

I blow out a breath after reading Elizabeth's text. Everything's set for Cedar's surprise party. Now all I have to do is get the man there without him realizing something's up. It's a miracle I've managed to keep the party a secret until now. Secrets and Winter Falls do not get along.

"You ready?" I ask Cedar as I enter the living room. It's just another Friday night, Cassie. Nothing special. Act normal.

"No," he grunts.

Shit. How am I going to persuade him to go to the bar if he's not in the mood? Sometimes I forget Cedar was a loner when I met him.

"I thought we were going to the bar. It's Friday night." I don't sound too desperate, do I?

"We can't go."

Alert! Alert!

"Why not? Are you not feeling well?"

"I'm feeling fine, but someone else isn't." He points to where Diva is laying in her bed panting as if she just chased one of Forest's squirrels through the backyard.

I drop to my knees. "What's wrong, my precious girl?"

I pet her behind the ear and she whines in response. "Have you been eating cat poop again?"

Don't laugh. It's a thing dogs do. At least Juniper explained as much when I complained to her my dog was defective. After she finished laughing at me.

"I don't think it's cat poop," Cedar says as he kneels next to me.

"What do we do? Do we take her to the vet? The vet's over an hour away."

"Send a message to Juniper. She'll know what to do."

I don't send a message to Juniper. I send an SOS to the entire family who are waiting for us at *Electric Vibes.*

"What do we do in the meantime?" I ask as Diva goes to town on her genitals. I nudge her snout away, but she snaps at me before returning to the task at hand.

Cedar pulls me to my feet before hauling me into his arms. "She's going to be okay. Don't worry."

I shove him away. "Telling a woman not to worry is the equivalent of telling her to calm down."

He raises his palms up and backs away. "Message received. How about a cup of tea?"

"What am I? English now? I don't drink tea. Do we even have tea in the house?"

I start pacing our tiny living room. "What are we going to do? Diva's sick. What if she's dying?"

"Diva isn't sick or dying. She's having puppies."

I squeal at Lilac's explanation and whirl around on her.

"What are you doing here?"

"You sent out an SOS to the family. I was closest to your house."

"But you're not Juniper."

"I'm aware I'm not Juniper. Why do you want her?"

I motion toward my fur baby. "Because there's something wrong with Diva!"

She kneels next to the dog bed. "I told you. There's nothing wrong with Diva. She's having puppies. It's perfectly natural."

Cedar scratches his beard. "I thought you were getting Diva fixed."

"Fixed? She's not defective!"

"The last time she was in heat, she tried to hump my leg for three days straight."

"You're hot. You can't blame her for wanting a piece of you."

He ignores my thinly veiled innuendo. "And you didn't get her fixed because?"

"I couldn't do it. I took her to the vet, and she started crying and I thought she's lost enough in her life. Isn't losing a leg and an ear enough to sacrifice? She doesn't need to sacrifice her ovaries, too."

"And her uterus," Lilac adds.

I wring my hands. "What do we do? Do we heat blankets? Boil water?"

Juniper rushes into the house with Maverick following her. "I've got this. You go ahead and do your you-know-what."

Maverick picks Diva and her bed up and they leave as quick as they came. I stare after them.

"Shouldn't we go with them? Our baby's having babies."

"A dog has puppies, not babies."

I roll my eyes at Lilac. "I wasn't being literal."

"Is the party happening here now?" Ashlyn asks as she strolls inside our house. She's not alone. My sisters as well as Aspen and Ellery follow her inside.

I throw my arms in the air. "I give up. I'm never throwing a party again."

"What party?" Cedar asks.

I point to him. "A party to celebrate your one year anniversary in town."

"I thought we were celebrating Cassie's engagement," Olivia says.

I snort. "Joke's on you. I'm not engaged."

Cedar clears his throat and lowers to one knee. "I planned to do this while we were alone."

We're hardly alone now.

"Cassandra Claire Dempsey, will you marry me?"

As I look around our tiny house living room, I realize I've been had. Tonight's party wasn't kept a secret from Cedar. It was kept a secret from me.

"Was tonight a surprise engagement party?"

He smirks. "Maybe."

"But I thought I was surprising you."

He shrugs.

"We've known each other exactly one year today."

"I'm aware."

"It's too early to get engaged. People wait years after meeting each other to get engaged."

He clasps my hands in his. "When have we ever done things the way other people do them?"

"Good point."

I bite my bottom lip as I stare at the man I love down on his knees for me.

"I don't want a normal wedding."

"Whatever you want."

"I want a destination wedding."

"Where to?" Ashlyn asks.

"I'm not talking to you."

"I need to know if I should apply for a passport for Patience."

"Way to make this about you."

She beams at me and does a small bow. "Thank you."

Cedar surges to his feet and wraps an arm around my waist before throwing me over his shoulder.

"What are you doing?" I pound on his back.

"I'm getting us some privacy," he says as he shuts the bedroom door behind us.

"We can still hear you," Sage shouts.

"Where did she come from?" I whisper. She wasn't in the house.

There's a knock on the window and I look over to discover Sage and the rest of the gossip gals waving at us.

"I give up. Winter Falls has defeated me." Cedar sinks to his knees again. "Princess, say you'll marry me before I decide to let you pull off that prank against the gossip gals you've been talking about for months."

"Of course, I'll marry you." As if there was ever any doubt. I've learned my lesson. I may have thought I didn't deserve love when we first met, but I know better now. Most of the time. "I love you."

He shoves the ring on my finger and jumps to his feet. His lips meet mine and he dives in.

"Ha! I knew it! Clove, you owe me twenty bucks!"

I yank my lips away from his as I burst into laughter. "This town."

Cedar grins. "It's the best."

"And we've got our entire lives to enjoy living here."

About Author

D.E. Haggerty is an American who has spent the majority of her adult life abroad. She has lived in Istanbul, various places throughout Germany, and currently finds herself in The Hague. She has been a military policewoman, a lawyer, a B&B owner/operator and now a writer.